The Body Shop

ALSO BY DAVID BERLINSKI

A Clean Sweep
Less Than Meets the Eye
A Tour of the Calculus
Black Mischief

The Body Shop

An Aaron Asherfeld Mystery

DAVID BERLINSKI

ST. MARTIN'S PRESS
NEW YORK

PUBLISHED BY THOMAS DUNNE BOOKS.
An imprint of St. Martin's Press.

Library of Congress Cataloging-in-Publication Data

Berlinski, David.
The body shop / by David Berlinski.
p. cm.
ISBN 0-312-13935-7
1. Private investigators—California—San Francisco—Fiction.
2. San Francisco (Calif.)—Fiction I. Title.
PS3552.E72494B63 1996
813'.54—dc20 95-46783
CIP

First Edition: July 1996

10 9 8 7 6 5 4 3 2 1

for my Victoria

Behind every crime there is a beautiful woman,
and behind every beautiful woman, there is a crime. . . .

ANATOLE FRANCE

The Body Shop

That was the year the fog came in early, the foghorns on the bay sounding by two in the afternoon. The spring had a wet cold feeling. In the morning, the blackberry vines in the garden underneath my window were wet, glittering like gray necklaces. When the fog lifted late in the morning, the sky was filled with light but not warmth. I lived alone on the steep part of Greenwich Street in a yellow wooden house that rose with the rise in the hill; the second floor had a view of the Golden Gate. At first it was terrible coming back to the empty apartment, smelling the deep musty smell of the hallway and the clove cigarette smoke from the apartment of the two Dutch sisters who lived on the second floor; but then it wasn't terrible anymore, and after a while I didn't miss any of the people that I thought I'd miss and they didn't miss me. It wasn't the way that I expected things to work out, but it was the way they worked out anyway.

Pretty Funny

I SPENT MOST OF THE MORNING trying to figure out a good reason not to spend the afternoon doing my taxes. I hadn't done them in April and I hadn't filed for an extension either. It was just noon. I turned on the television and spent a few minutes standing in my stocking feet watching the news on CNN. A very pretty woman with Asian features was interviewing another very pretty woman. I turned the sound off with the remote and watched the two women waggling their sleek poodle heads. After a while I called Marvin Plumbeck and told him I needed an hour of his time.

"Do you this afternoon at four, Asher," he said companionably. Accountants are like gravediggers. They have nothing to do during the slow season.

I said that'd be great. I used up a couple of hours organizing my receipts and stapling my American Express chits together. I didn't have much to show Plumbeck and I didn't have much to file.

Marvin Plumbeck had started his practice with another CPA named Eddie Ergenweiler, the two of them conducting their business from a couple of shabby offices in the old Jack Tar Hotel on Van Ness. They worked hard and they didn't cut corners. Ergenweiler had a feel for precious metals and during the eighties he managed to put some very wealthy people into situations that made them even wealthier. By the time that Ronald Reagan went back to chopping wood, Plumbeck and Ergenweiler had left off being accountants and had become financial planners in a fancy suite on New Montgomery Street. Ergenweiler acquired an interest in a Sonoma winery; Plumbeck bought himself a black BMW coupe and had the French cuffs on his Custom Shop shirt monogrammed. We had all been friends once.

I got off on the fifteenth floor of the Spear Tower and opened the smoked-glass double door that led from the elevator landing to Plumbeck's office. Plumbeck had gone through a half-dozen glaziers before he found one who could etch *Plumbeck & Ergenweiler* into the doors in just the way he wished. "I keep telling them *discreet,* Asher," he had said to me. "They keep putting the thing in boldface, makes us look like a couple of hustling CPAs." The suite inside was supposed to look quiet and understated. It looked the way every high-priced accountant's office looks—like the sort of place you'd want to leave in a big hurry. There was a huge semicircular rosewood reception desk by the door and a teal carpet on the floor and a couple of low-slung chrome and leather chairs around a low glass table; the walls were covered with tan fabric.

The receptionist behind the rosewood desk gave me a cool, level, very amused glance. She was an absolute knockout. She knew it and I knew it and she had looked at me to make sure I knew it. She was wearing a fluffy angora sweater that was cut squarely in front to reveal the warm flush of her bosom. I didn't want to be caught staring, but I didn't want to miss anything either.

She smiled at me, her large shapely teeth glistening. It didn't look as if she did much more with her time than smile. She didn't have to.

"He's expecting me," I said.

She nodded and buzzed Plumbeck on the interoffice telephone, cradling the receiver on her shoulder so that her lovely neck was arched.

After a minute or so, Plumbeck came scuttling out from his office. I hadn't moved from the rosewood desk and I hadn't stopped looking at his receptionist from the corner of my eye.

"Yo, Asher," said Plumbeck cheerfully, thrusting out his hand. He was a compact, held-together man. His thick chestnut hair had not yet receded from his forehead and his dark eyes looked out from underneath heavy well-shaped eyebrows. He wasn't fat, but he wasn't trim either; he gave the impression of a man who had a hard time saying no to himself. He had done a good deal of coke in the eighties. It had given him a permanent kind of fretfulness. He walked me back to his office, which overlooked New Montgomery Street, and lowered himself into the black Naugehyde chair behind his desk.

"Good-looking woman," I said.

"You'd better believe it," Plumbeck said cheerfully. "We didn't hire her we figure she's going to be a whiz at operations."

I chuckled and after that we started talking about my taxes.

I looked forward to seeing the receptionist again after we had finished; but there was no one at the rosewood desk when I left the office and no one in the hall either.

I was disappointed. I wanted her to fill my eyes.

A couple of days later, Plumbeck called to tell me that my returns were in the mail. After that I didn't see him for almost two months. Then one day he called and asked me to meet him for lunch at a downtown bar and grill called Reptiles. He sounded tense and unhappy.

It was a bright clear day late in June. Except for the Asian schoolchildren straggling home for lunch, their raven hair glistening in the light, Greenwich Street was empty when I left the house. I walked over to Columbus and bought a salted pretzel at Luca's delicatessen and then hustled myself through the edge of Chinatown and over to the financial district.

Reptiles was located in the lobby of Plumbeck's building on New Montgomery; it was the sort of restaurant that took up a lot of space without filling it. Financial types went there to rest up from moving money and so did their short-waisted assistants, who figured they could do worse in life than marrying a broker.

Plumbeck was already there, sitting at a booth, a sweating Calistoga in front of him.

"So what's up, Plumbeck?" I said after we had shaken hands and volleyed a few hellos and how-you-doings back and forth. "You didn't ask me down here discuss revisions in the tax code."

"You got that right," he said, looking at me uneasily, his round face tight with tension. "Can I be honest with you, Asher? Lay it all out."

"Why not?"

Plumbeck told me what he needed to tell me. I didn't say anything. It wasn't that kind of a story.

"I mean it started out as a joke almost," he said, lifting his chin defiantly in the air. When he lowered his head I could see that his round brown eyes were sad and worried and unhappy.

I sipped at my whiskey sour and felt the sharp clean taste of lemon bite into the inside of my cheek.

I said: "A joke? You get a group of guys together, decide to rent a mistress? Pretty funny."

"You got it wrong, Asherfeld," said Plumbeck. "This wasn't some bimbo."

"Who was it, then?"

"Receptionist, the firm."

I was shocked. I shouldn't have been, but I was.

"Let me get this straight," I said, swizzling my drink with a swizzle stick. "You got this knockout working for you, you guys manage to talk her into quitting her job, sit home in some apartment, wait for one of you to show up for a little R and R? Not very nineties."

"Yeah, well," he said. "It didn't take much doing. Truth of the matter is, Alicia didn't actually have too much up here."

Plumbeck tapped his forehead significantly.

"What *did* she have?"

"Looks to die for."

"I guess. How many guys in on this?"

There was a beat in Plumbeck's delivery. He waved his hand from the wrist. Then he said: "Me, Eddie, young guy, Barry Finklestein, sort of an associate. We all thought she was terrific."

"So that's it? One minute you're watching this Alicia bend over pick up a piece of paper, the next minute you guys hit moisture?"

Plumbeck shifted in his seat. "It was pretty easy, actually," he said. "It was like in the cartoons, you know, when a bulb lights up over someone's head. We're sitting in the steam room over at the Bay Club, it hits us. None of us can afford a mistress, if we all go in together we make out. Next day, Eddie and me call Alicia into the conference room, lay it all out for her. We figure either she files for sexual harassment or she goes for the idea."

The waiter who had been waiting for us to order lunch swam suavely over to our table.

"You gentlemen ready to order yet?" he asked. He wasn't about to take no for an answer. I ordered a burger with fries. Plumbeck ordered the salad and a baked potato.

"Tell the chef, no butter on that potato, and the salad, only lemon juice, no oil?"

"Of course, sir," said the waiter pleasantly. "No butter, no oil." He had heard it all before.

"Pretty worried about your arteries?" I asked.

"Dad died of a heart attack I was ten."

"Think you can beat it by eating rabbit food?"

Plumbeck looked up at me with his thick melancholic look, his large brown eyes dense. He shrugged his shoulders.

"Doesn't matter," he said.

"What went wrong?"

"Didn't exercise," said Plumbeck, "didn't eat right."

"I'm not talking about your father."

"You mean Alicia?" Mentioning her name seemed to brighten him up. "It was terrific at first. We got this apartment nine-nine-

nine Green, you know the one on top of Russian Hill, big building, bay view. Me and Eddie sign the lease in the name of the firm. We set up a schedule. I see her Monday, Eddie, he sees her Wednesday, Finklestein, little dweeb, he gets Friday. Weekends she does what she wants."

"Only thing *we* ask is she doesn't see anyone else. We don't want to get one of those calls from the grief counselor some AIDS clinic. We put a thousand dollars in a bank account, set up a charge at Neiman Marcus. I'm telling you, she was thrilled. I mean she got into this mistress thing like you wouldn't believe. Go over at five-thirty, she'd be there in one of those sexy outfits from Victoria's Secret, you know, crotchless panties and all, she'd have drinks, line of coke ready, something on the stereo, lights be low, sun setting out over the bay. It was fantastic."

Plumbeck looked at me with his beaten sorrowful look.

"It was *more* than fantastic," he said.

"What happen to spoil all that happiness?"

"That's just it, Asherfeld," he said peevishly. "I don't know. None of us can figure it out. One day, Eddie, he goes over there, she's like not today, I don't feel like it. Eddie, he figures what the hey, she doesn't feel like it she doesn't feel like it. Next week, I go over there, she's standing in the door pair of sweatpants and a sweatshirt. I say nice outfit, she says you don't like it you can stuff it, slams the door in my face.

I didn't say anything, but I must have arched my eyebrows.

"Asherfeld," said Plumbeck, "woman doesn't want to sleep with me she doesn't want to sleep with me. But this is an apartment I'm paying the rent on. Slamming the door in my face, I mean that's not right."

"Regular outrage," I said.

Plumbeck caught the note in my voice, but he didn't say anything. Then after a while he said: "I wanted to fill you in on the background and all. The bad part is coming."

"What's the bad part?"

"Bad part is she's missing, gone, disappeared. One day, she's at the apartment, next day, Finklestein, he's over there, she's history.

Place is clean. No clothes, no perfume, no Victoria's Secret. Nothing."

I shrugged my shoulders.

"So? It's a free country. She decided she had enough of being a mistress."

"She didn't touch anything in the account we set up. Not a penny."

"Maybe she's honest."

"I went up to the apartment day after Finklestein. I don't think she just left."

"Why's that?"

"There were like these stains along the baseboard in the bathroom? When I looked close I could see that the tiles had been wiped down very carefully. Alicia wasn't like this terrific housekeeper. In fact, she was pretty much of a slob, if you want to know the truth. There was a kind of scum over the tiles. You could tell that someone had wiped down the walls because the sides of the tiles still like had this scum."

The waiter returned with our food. He placed Plumbeck's salad and baked potato ostentatiously in front of him.

"Salad, no oil, lemon," he sang out, so that diners in the next booth could hear. "Baked potato, no butter."

We ate in silence for the next few minutes.

Finally, I said: "What kind of stains?"

Plumbeck had forked the potato from its skin. He sat there mashing the lumps with his fork's tines.

"I don't want to know, Asherfeld," he said.

999 Green

SOMEONE HAD PUT 999 GREEN on top of Russian Hill in the fifties. The building was ugly in the way that only bad taste can make anything ugly. The exterior walls were faced in gray stucco.

The windows were small, almost slitted. They gave the building a prison look. Divorced dentists took out apartments at 999 Green and figured they were going to spend their time away from Muzak and bad teeth surrounded by pliant women. There were plenty of pliant women in the building—everyone from sadsack hookers specializing in bondage to expensive young entrepreneurs with cellular telephones and a smattering of Italian. But *they* never gave the dentists the time of day, and the sadsacks wanted their teeth capped before they would put out.

Plumbeck had given me the keys to Alicia's apartment. I crossed the little circular driveway in front of the building and stood for a moment on the marble square that led into the interior lobby. I wanted to figure out which way Alicia's apartment faced. The doorman in his green greatcoat edged out of his cabin and swaggered over to me.

"Looking for someone?" he asked.

"Looks like two-oh-one skipped," I said, holding up Alicia's keys. "Guys rented the apartment asked me to check on things."

The doorman nodded understandingly. He was about to turn away when he said: "You're talking about that good-looking blonde? Real statuesque like?" He described an hourglass in space with his hands.

I nodded.

"Nice girl," he said protectively. "Always had a smile." Then he said: "Can't say I thought much of her company."

"Why's that?"

"Forget I said anything," he said flatly.

I watched him walk stiffly back to his doorkeeper's cabin with that peculiarly dignified walk that doormen sometimes acquire, a kind of solemn strut.

Whatever it was that Plumbeck had offered Alicia, a terrific apartment wasn't high on the list; 201 was one of the building's efficiency jobs—two tiny rooms divided by a tiny kitchen, with the bathroom just off the bedroom. The ceilings were low and cottage-cheesed, the parquet floors badly scuffed. The furniture didn't put you in mind of Fred Astair and Ginger Rogers either. There was a dark green sofa in the living room, a pair of square-cut easy chairs covered in some coarse fabric, a Formica table. The living room window looked out over the bay, all right, but from the second floor, all that I could see was a thin edge of gray water in the distance.

There was nothing in the place to suggest a knockout blonde and the knockout blonde that had lived there had stripped the apartment of everything but a couple of hangers.

I went into the bathroom to check the stains on the tile. The tiny little room had no window and no one had turned the overhead fan on: the place was still damp from whoever had taken the last bath or shower. Plumbeck had been right. The sides of the bathtub *had* been partially wiped down by someone who had run a cloth through the soap scum a couple of times. I bent down to take a look at the baseboard on the wall. The trim might have been discolored by a stain, but it could have been a discoloration in the wood itself. It was hard to tell.

I got up from the floor with a grunt and took a last look around the apartment and got myself downstairs to the lobby. A small pile of mail had accumulated for Alicia on the chipped marble stand that faced the lobby's mirror. I scooped it up, put it in the breast pocket of my sports coat. No one had asked me to take it, and no one had told me not to.

It was just after noon when I left 999 Green. There were heavy clouds in the sky and the bay at the bottom of Russian Hill looked cold and turbid, the color of smoked glass. The doorman was standing stiffly in front of the building. He recognized me as I came out onto his platform and for a moment his face broke just slightly, as if he wanted to say something. Whatever it was that he wanted to say, he didn't say it.

I got back to my apartment in mid-afternoon, the sky still lowering, still gray; I opened up the windows and let the smell of the sea into the living room. Marvin Plumbeck wasn't in his office. His new receptionist told me he wasn't expected back. She had the smoke-raspened voice of a woman well into middle age.

"I'll make sure he returns your call," she said decisively.

"You do that," I started to say, but she cut me off before I could finish the sentence.

An enormous cargo ship was making its way sedately toward the Golden Gate. For a moment, it seemed to fill the entire bay, a slowly moving monster, and then quite suddenly it regained its normal size. I thought of how San Francisco must look to the Filipino or Taiwanese sailors manning the ship—a small city of hills covered with white and pink houses. I remembered seeing it all for the first time. I had driven across country with my first wife. We had run out of money somewhere along the northern California coast and slept under picnic benches in the state parks. When we got to San Francisco, I found a Greek grocer willing to cash an out-of-state check. We ate calamari steaks and salmon at a restaurant on Fisherman's Wharf and afterward we walked up the street I had walked down earlier that afternoon, stopping to catch our breath at one of the mossy little alleyways straggling off mysteriously into the flank of Russian Hill. My wife turned to look at the bay. She squeezed my hand and said: "Tell me it will always be like this, Asher."

Some people don't have much trouble leaving places. Me? I don't have much trouble leaving people. It's the places that get to me.

Marvin Plumbeck had given me a copy of Alicia's original job application, together with her personnel file. Later that afternoon, I propped my stocking feet onto my desk and looked through the yellow file folder. She may have been Alicia to the boys in the back room, but she was plain Alice Tamaroff on her job application. She was born in 1971 in La Roya, Arizona; she had graduated from Scottsdale High School. I imagined all that golden childish beauty gathering itself. She had been a cheerleader, a Boosterette, a member of the Spanish Club. After that, she had spent a year studying marketing at Scottsdale Community College. Alicia's handwriting on the personnel forms was sweet and pat and dopey; it didn't much put me in mind of the woman whose deep thrilling beauty had turned an office upside down.

I called information at Scottsdale and got the number for Scottsdale Community College. I wanted to make sure that Alicia's story made sense. Someone with a student's uncertain voice answered the telephone. I told her I needed to verify information I had been given about Alice Tamaroff. I spelled the name slowly.

"And when did you say this person was at Scottsdale?"

"Nineteen eighty-nine, nineteen ninety."

"Could you like hold for a minute?"

I like held for a minute. Then someone came on the line and said brusquely: "Leander Malveaux here. Who's this?"

"It's Aaron Asherfeld."

"That supposed to mean anything to me?"

"About as much as Leander Malveaux means to me."

"Are you calling from budget? Is that what this is all about?"

"Don't get yourself into an uproar, Leander," I said. "I'm calling from San Francisco. I'm just trying to verify an employment application."

Leander Malveaux needed a long moment to master his indignation; it must have been like taming wild horses.

"Let me get this straight," he finally said. "You telling me you got someone there claims they went to *this* institution in nineteen eighty-nine?"

"That's what I'm telling you."

"Either they're lying or you're lying."

"Why's that, Leander?"

"For your information, it's *Dr.* Malveaux. And Scottsdale Community College opened a year ago this fall."

I hung up with the doctor pretty much convinced that Alicia had simply tacked an imaginary year of college onto her job application —a lot of kids do it; but when I called Scottsdale High School, I got the same answer.

"Tamaroff, Tamaroff, Tamaroff," said the woman in the personnel office who had taken my call. "Hold on a sec, hon."

I held on to the dead telephone and kept looking at the bay, calm and clear in the late afternoon.

"You sure you have the name right, hon? No Alice Tamaroff, class of nineteen eighty-nine. I know what you're going to ask. No Alice Tamaroff, class of nineteen eighty-eight either. Only thing that even *sounds* like Tamaroff is Taminsky, class of nineteen eighty-five. And she's not going to be of much use to you."

"Why's that?"

"Died a year later, it says here. Greyhound, it crashed into a feed truck on the interstate. You probably read about it."

"Sure," I said, "it was front-page news in San Francisco."

"Whatever."

I gave up on Alice Tamaroff for the rest of the afternoon; Plumbeck called me early the next morning.

"Asherfeld," he said urgently, "what's up?"

"I don't know, Plumbeck," I said, my voice still hoarse from sleep. "I can't tell anything from the place on Green, looks to me like those stains you're so worried about are just discolorations in the wood."

"You think?"

"Thing that *is* curious though is that your little cupcake lied on her job application. You guys were so busy appreciating her cleavage you didn't bother checking anything she said."

"Lied like how?"

"She never attended Scottsdale High School *or* Scottsdale Community College. Far as I can tell, she never even lived in Arizona."

"What's it mean, Asherfeld?" Plumbeck asked fretfully.

"I don't know," I said. "You tell me."

Due Diligence

IF MARVIN PLUMBECK had any ideas about paying me to track down his mistress, he kept them to himself. I spent the next few days doing things I needed to do. I took my shirts to the dry cleaners on Columbus and told the woman behind the counter that the shirts needed medium starch. She fingered the collars of my white shirts absently and said: "You bring these in sooner, Mr. Asherfeld, they gonna last longer." Then she tapped the crease of the collar meaningfully. "This here's ground-in dirt. You understand what I'm saying?" She enjoyed giving lessons in life. She had been a handsome and vividly colored woman when I first began bringing my shirts to the store; now she had begun to shrink in on herself. Small lines had appeared on her upper lip.

That afternoon I cleaned out the glove compartment of my car, discovering somewhere among the maps and old parking tickets an elegant cigarette lighter that I had long thought lost. One of my wives had intended to give it to me as a birthday gift. She had wrapped the lighter in silvery gift paper and placed it in her dresser drawer; but our marriage ended before my birthday, my wife calling from Santa Barbara to tell me that she needed space. "Do you understand, Aaron?" she had asked. "I need a healing space." It was what women said in the eighties when they wanted to justify having an affair.

The next morning, the downstairs buzzer rang.

"Asher, this is Irene," said someone who figured I would know right away who she was.

"That's terrific," I said.

"Irene *Ergenweiler,* Asher."

Irene Ergenweiler and one of my wives had been good friends.

I listened to her ascend the stairs with sharp staccato steps. When I opened the door, we both of us paused inquisitively.

She was a tall, rangy athletic woman, who had spent years smoking cigarettes and baking in the sun when she wasn't playing tennis. She had looked used up the last time I had seen her. Someone had since done her eyes and then her entire face. I could see that her brown leathery skin had been stretched over her facial bones. She wore her lustrous black hair pulled severely back into a ponytail. She looked fierce and predatory and vaguely Indian.

"You look pudgy, Asher," she said.

I flattened my pudgy self against the door. Irene Ergenweiler came into my apartment and stood in the foyer defiantly.

"This," she said, indicting my apartment with a sweeping brown arm, "is how you live? I mean, really."

I lifted up my hands. "It doesn't matter anymore, I'm out of it, Irene."

"God, are you happy? Tell me that at least you're happy."

"I get by."

"What does *that* mean, Asher?" she asked as she walked decisively into my living room.

I followed her into the living room and sat down at my desk, easing my feet up. "It means I come home evenings, I get to sit in my own chair, knock back a few of my own beers, watch the container ships move across the bay."

"That's it? That's how you've decided to spend the rest of your life? *Watching?*"

"It was swell of you to come here remind me what I'm missing not being married, Irene."

"That's not why I'm here, Asher," she said.

"Why, then?"

She stood there, her arms wrapped around her torso. I could see the blood rising in her face, suffusing her brown skin.

"Asher, I *know* all about Marvin's little bimbo. It's going to ruin Marvin and it will absolutely destroy Miriam."

Miriam was Marvin Plumbeck's ex-wife; she had left him theatrically in the eighties to live in the east bay. I didn't think she had much ruin left in her.

"Not my problem."

All of a sudden, Irene Ergenweiler's small dark eyes filled with tears, the light from the window winking from the wet sheen. I remembered what she had been like when I had first met her.

"What is it you think I can do for you, Irene?"

Irene Ergenweiler took a moment to collect herself, holding her head obliquely and snuffling. The color came flooding back into her face.

"Help me protect Eddie," she said. "He's not the one who fell for that fat-titted little tramp. He just went along with the whole thing because he's Eddie and he wanted to have a good time and he doesn't think. It was Marvin's idea, Asher, and now Eddie's going to be punished for it."

The speech seemed to tap into a well of bitterness. She cupped her elbow with her hand, holding her arms tight against her body, and pressed her other hand to her mouth, pushing up her taut cheeks.

"I'm not sure I know what you're talking about, Irene. Setting up a mistress may have been stupid. It isn't much of a crime."

Irene Ergenweiler gave me a sharp stare through her tear-filled eyes. "You really don't understand anything," she said. "Why am I surprised?"

"Tell me what I'm missing, Irene. You're going to do it sooner or later. You might as well do it now."

"You mind if I smoke in here, Asher?" she asked. "Or are you going to give me that look they give you now if you want to have a cigarette?"

She had taken a long packet of cigarettes in a gold lamé holder from her purse and was busy tapping a thin cigarette against the face of her elegant watch.

I waved my hand. "Go ahead."

She lit her cigarette with a tiny gold lighter and exhaled with the voluptuous satisfaction of someone born to smoke.

"They're going to be indicted, the two of them, Marvin and Eddie. There'll be an announcement sometime next week."

I was shocked. "Indicted? You're not serious, Irene. For stashing a bimbo in an apartment?" I felt guilty referring to Alicia as a bimbo.

"For criminal conspiracy," she said bitterly. "It's a federal indictment. Maison Jarr is the principal. Marvin and Eddie are being named as co-conspirators."

Maison Jarr was a cutesy English pharmaceutical house that put out a line of cosmetics. They boasted that they never tested the goop on animals. Their stock was very very hot.

"Still doesn't make much sense to me, Irene," I said. "Marvin and Eddie? Your boys aren't bent."

"I *know* that, Asher," said Irene Ergenweiler explosively. "Don't you think I know that?"

"What's the indictment claim?"

"Failure of due diligence."

"Isn't that Maison Jarr's problem? Marvin and Eddie, they're not selling stocks, peddling limited partnerships, anything like that."

"That's *not* how it looks on the books, Asher," said Irene, weary all of a sudden. She sat herself primly on the wooden chair in front of my living room window and stubbed out her cigarette against the bottom of an ashtray she had taken from my desk. I could smell the sharp acrid odor of her cigarette stub from where I was sitting. "On the books it looks as if Marvin and Eddie provided Maison Jarr with false financials. It *looks* terrible."

Irene Ergenweiler seemed hard and cold and vulnerable all at once, her burnt sienna face taut. She lifted her chin and opened her eyes to look at me directly. "Eddie's not a bad person," she said.

"I know that." For the first time I thought of Eddie Ergenweiler, calling him to mind. He was goofy and rambunctious without actually being charming; he had liked to punch my shoulder and say *Asherfeld* in a loud voice.

"You call Knesterman?" I asked.

Irene Ergenweiler nodded, her face twisting itself ever so slightly. "He's representing the two of them, Marvin and Eddie."

"Nothing but the best," I said.

"Tell me about it," she said bitterly. "Eddie needed to empty his 401K just to make Knesterman's retainer."

I let out a slight wheeze of astonishment.

"You never had the nerve to ask for those sorts of fees, Asher. I'll say that for you."

"I never had any chance of getting them. What's he say, Knesterman? Tell Marvin and Eddie to plead it out?"

Irene Ergenweiler looked at me in surprise. "How'd you know?"

I shrugged my shoulders aimlessly. "It's the simple thing to do. It's clean."

"Clean? Asher, Marvin and Eddie didn't *do* anything wrong. They're not going to plead guilty to criminal charges if they haven't done anything wrong. It would be the end of them."

"It's going to be the end of them anyway," I said.

Irene Ergenweiler looked at me full in the face for a long heavy moment.

"It's so unfair," she said with a deep terrible bitterness.

"It happens."

"Is that all you have to say? These are your *friends* we're talking about and they are about to be *destroyed.*"

"My friends? I don't have any friends, Irene, just people I once knew."

Irene Ergenweiler withdrew another cigarette from her case. She sat there in my living room, tamping the filtered end against her watch crystal. The sun had aged her skin but it had given her face a certain savage nobility. She tucked her top lip underneath her teeth for a long moment. "Will you talk to Eddie?" she finally asked.

"What for?" I asked.

"Just see if you can talk some sense into him."

"For old time's sake?"

"We were all friends once, Asher," Irene Ergenweiler said. "Doesn't that count for something?"

I thought for a long moment. "Wouldn't it be nice to think so," I said.

Call for the Mick

"ASHER," MICK SHAUGNESSY SAID companionably when I entered the front office; he was sitting at his oak desk. He had his shirt sleeves cuffed high on his thin forearms. "Something for the chill?" he asked, inclining his head toward a half-full bottle of Jim Beam.

"Sure."

I pulled up a chair and put my feet up on his desk. Shaugnessy withdrew two paper cups from his bottom drawer and poured us both a finger.

"Cheers," he said morosely. I sipped at the evil-tasting liquor and felt it warm my throat and chest.

Shaugnessy let me use the back of his office when I needed a place to go. It wasn't much, just an old oak desk and an old oak filing cabinet, but I liked going there when I couldn't stand looking at the walls of my apartment, and I liked the rundown, sawdust smell of the place and the way the yellow electrical light spilled out onto the fog-covered avenue.

We sat together sipping the liquor. It may have been high summer in Ohio, but out here in the Sunset it was late June and the fog had already swept up Irving and was slithering into Golden Gate Park. It felt good to be sitting with my feet propped up on Shaugnessy's desk and it felt good to be sipping Jim Beam at three in the afternoon.

"Let me ask you something, Mick?" I said, when the liquor had thrown a warm glow across my chest.

"Can't hurt to ask."

"You know this building top of Russian Hill, nine-nine-nine Green?"

"Certainly, I know it," said Mick, "place is full of hookers. Italian Embassy wants to celebrate the discovery of pasta, they put in a call over nine-nine-nine Green."

I sipped at my drink; Shaugnessy leaned over to fill my cup.

"Know someone over there I could call, Mick?"

"You looking to drain the weasel, Asher, or this something else?"

"Something else."

"Doorman's waste of time. Management pays him time and a half keep his mouth shut. There's a big TV on five, pretty much knows what's going on in the building."

"You know its name?"

"Something like Finsternagel, Rupert Finsternagel, does business out of *The Spectator* under the name of Chloé. Supposed to be showstopper, docs put in enough silicone float a barge. I hear he sits on a can tuna fish get the smell just right."

"Thanks, Mick," I said, taking a long swallow of Jim Beam.

"Don't mention it, Asher. You lose something up there?"

"Hard to tell, Mick," I said. "Couple guys I know had a good-looking blonde in an apartment. One day she's there, next day, *poof.*"

"Happens," said Mick philosophically. "Sooner or later happens to all of us. *Poof.*"

Later that afternoon, I got a copy of *The Spectator* from a rack on Ninth Avenue; it's the place where all the hookers and mistresses and HIV-negative ball boys and sad TVs advertise. I found Chloé under Adult Entertainment. I called her from a pay phone and got a pager. I punched in the pay phone's number and decided to give it five minutes. I got a call back right away.

"Hi, handsome," said someone who was using a resonant baritone to sound like a tremulous soprano.

"Hi, yourself," I said. "Mick Shaugnessy gave me your name, said you might have some time."

"Mick? Oh, he's such a dear. When were you thinking of coming?" she tittered.

"How about now?"

"Now would be delicious."

Chloé paused delicately.

"Now did Mick tell you all about the donation? He's so so discreet, I'm sure he didn't mention it. It's two hundred for the hour. Will that be all right, sweetie?"

I told Chloé that would be fine; I told her I'd be over in half an hour.

I walked across the park in the late afternoon, the lowering fog making the day seem darker than it really was, the cars crossing on Nineteenth Avenue all of them with their headlights on; I got as far as Geary and caught a cab that had been idling in front of a Korean grocer. Its driver was a short muscular Korean in a splashy iridescent shirt. He was placidly finishing up an early dinner of spring rolls. The interior of the taxi reeked of fish and soy sauce.

"You want to take me up to the top of Russian Hill?" I said.

"Sure," said the Korean, pulling out onto Geary without checking traffic. "You mind I eat?" He had placed his spring rolls on the seat beside him.

"You figure you can eat and drive?" I asked dubiously.

"We find out," said the Korean, pounding his steering wheel and laughing uproariously.

I got to 999 Green a little after six. Larry, the day doorman, must have knocked off at five. His replacement was a tiny Filipino named Manuel; he was dressed in a greatcoat that almost buried him. He held the door open for me. "Can I announce you, sir?" he asked in that beaten way Filipinos have.

"Chloé? I think she's on the fifth floor. Tell her it's Aaron Asherfeld."

"Very well, sir," he said. He rang up to Chloé's apartment; her deep improbable voice came booming down: "Send him right up, sweetie," she said.

The elevator with its art deco metal paneling swished silently up to the fifth floor. Chloé was standing by her half-opened door; she had the same apartment Alicia had had three floors up. Shaugnessy had been right about one thing: Chloé looked a lot like a woman. She was at least five eleven or so, with broad shoulders; and she had a man's square-cut head and broad forehead and well-developed chin; but she had let her hair grow long and somehow arranged it in a chignon so that it actually looked feminine, and her face was artfully made up so that it might have been a woman's face on the far margins of the biologically possible. She had an enormous jutting bosom and flaring hips and powerful well-shaped legs; she was dressed in a tight cashmere sweater and a tight black skirt. She wore low-cut high heels. She stood there at the doorway to her apartment and surveyed me critically.

"Well," she finally said. "Aren't you a big one?"

I edged past her trying not to press against her chest: I figured the recoil might knock me down.

The mean little apartment was set off with red lights; there was a smoky smell of incense in the air; someone was playing a jazz set on the stereo. The furniture was strictly Cost-Plus: a fabric-covered couch on wooden legs, a couple of nondescript easy chairs, and a print above the couch showing a sad-eyed señorita holding a guitar. The view was a little better than the view from Alicia's apartment. I could see the fog streaming across the bay.

I stood there in that mean little living room facing someone I figured could probably hoist me over her shoulders. "Why don't you just make yourself comfortable," Chloé said. "Can I get you something? An apéritif? That's a drink, you know."

I smiled: "I know what an apéritif is, but I'll take something cold if you have it?"

"Coming right up," Chloé sang out, tripping off into the kitchen with little mincing steps. It was odd to see that large powerful body contorting itself to appear feminine.

I settled myself into one of the easy chairs; Chloé reappeared moments later carrying a tray, which she put down delicately on the Lucite stand next to my chair. There was a bowl of mixed nuts on the tray and a tall glass of some reddish-looking stuff.

"It's from Brazil, silly," she said, catching my look. "Drink it, you'll love it."

I took a sip; the stuff tasted vaguely like mangoes. Chloé perched herself on the arm of the easy chair opposite mine.

"Mick sends his best regards," I said.

"Michael is such a dear," she said. "Is he still like sip, sip, sip?" She pantomimed someone taking delicate sips from a highball glass, her pinkie held stiff.

"The usual."

"I like a man who's not afraid to drink. These days it's all don't eat this and don't take that and don't *do* anything at all. It's like more than a girl can bear."

"First thing you know they'll be telling you to be careful about sexually transmitted diseases."

"That is *not* a funny remark, Aaron. I am positively fanatical about safe sex."

"It's a big relief. Thing is, though, I'm not really here for pleasure."

Chloé looked at me levelly; her eyes were cool and gray and no matter how expertly they had been made up, they still looked like a man's eyes. "Don't tell me. You're collecting for the Ancient

Order of the Hibernians. You're going to say that the proceeds go to supporting all those priests, you know, the ones who get caught with choirboys. Not that I have anything against choirboys, mind you."

She had a fast bitchy line of chatter.

"I'm here because Mick said you were intelligent enough to know what was going on in the building."

"Michael said that? Really? He is such a dear. A girl needs to keep her eyes and ears open. It's still two hundred, though, whether you have my brain or my body."

I nodded agreeably. "Did you know someone lived in two-oh-one, Alicia? Very pretty blonde."

"Alicia?" Pronouncing Alicia's name made the hard brittle edge disappear completely from Chloé's voice. "She was such a dear thing. Like a yummy little teddy bear. Give her my love when you see her. *All* my love."

"I'll do that. You know anything about her friends, people who came to see her?"

There was a flat dead pause in the conversation. Finally, Chloé said: "Are you with the police, sweetie, is that what this is all about? Because if you're with the police I have only three little words for you. *Speak to my attorney.*"

"That's four words, Chloé, and I'm not with the police."

"You're positive? Cross your heart and hope to die? You know, it's a crime to say you're not with the police when you really are."

"I know it is."

"A girl can't be too careful, Aaron."

"Sure."

"Everyone was a little bit in love with her. She was so darling. And that skin!"

I looked at Chloé's face; a blue shadow had already formed over her chin and throat.

"I can't say I thought much of her friends, though."

"Why is that?"

"They were very mean to her," she said simply. "I used to see her crying in the laundry room. She had this great big black eye and she would sit there and cry and cry."

I was stupefied. "You're telling me the people came to see her beat up on her?"

Chloé looked at me in surprise. "Hello, Aaron, do we have a communication problem here?"

"We're talking about someone five six or so, sort of a tired-looking businessman type, thick chestnut hair, good dresser?" I was trying my best to describe Marvin Plumbeck. I could imagine Plumbeck doing a lot of things; I couldn't imagine him hitting a woman like Alicia.

Chloé shook her square head. "Nothing like that at all. Honey, let me tell you, I *know* rough trade when I see it."

"You're sure about this?"

"Hello, Aaron. Is Paris a city?"

"I suppose," I said dubiously.

"These were people positively talking another language. Persian, I think, or something like that. You know the sound you make when you try to talk with a mouthful of Gummi Bears? That's how they were talking."

I got up heavily. "She's in trouble, isn't she?" Chloé asked suddenly. "That's why you're here, because she's in some sort of trouble."

"I don't know," I said. It was the truth. I didn't know.

Vapor Charge

THE GREAT MAN'S SECRETARY called me the very next morning. I was sitting at my desk, my feet up, watching the last of the night's heavy fog breaking up over the bay. It didn't seem to me that I had anything better to do and I had lots of time in which to do it. "Mr. Asherfeld," she said in her very cold voice, "this is Frieda, Seybold Knesterman's secretary."

"*Shalom,* Frieda."

"Yes, I'm sure. Please hold for Mr. Knesterman."

Seybold Knesterman's rich plummy baritone came on the line. It was like hearing maple syrup flow. "Irene Ergenweiler just rang me up, Asherfeld," he said without bothering to say anything else. "She asked that I call you."

"You're the best friend a boy ever had, Knesterman."

"I can't imagine what Irene was thinking when she suggested bringing you into this. We have paralegals for your kind of work."

"Think of it as a social statement, Knesterman. She never liked blacks and doesn't trust women."

"That's really a very insensitive remark, Asherfeld."

"Insensitive? Knesterman, you voted *against* universal suffrage."

"At least," he said suavely, "I have the good sense not to remind people of it."

"So tell me, Knesterman, what's with Eddie and Marvin?"

"I don't know, Asherfeld," Knesterman said slowly, choosing his words with even more care than usual. "It certainly is an odd business." For a moment, I thought Knesterman might wish to unburden himself of a meditation. Then abruptly he said: "Perhaps you might come down after lunch. The Pullets can fill you in on the details."

"The Pullets? As in chickens?"

"They handle tax law and accounting for us. Share an appointment. That sort of thing."

"Share an appointment? Knesterman, how the mighty have fallen. Next you'll be telling me you've converted the executive lunchroom into a child-care center. Probably be a diaper pail right outside your office."

Knesterman chuckled his rich plummy mirthless chuckle and hung up.

I spent an hour or so getting myself showered and shaved. I clipped my toenails and polished my teeth and rubbed hair gel into my hair and patted my stinging cheeks with Old Spice. The fog had finally dissipated over the bay, a gentle golden morning light filling my apartment, warming the stark white walls and scattering pink and violet into the air. One of my wives had been dismayed at the thought of doing ordinary things alone. "Asher," she had said, "wouldn't it be terrible to get up and take a shower and brush your teeth and not have anybody *know?"* She worked her pretty rosebud mouth into a moue and looked at me full in the face, her large brown eyes wide and staring. Now we were both brushing our teeth alone. It didn't seem so terrible after all.

I thought briefly of putting on a suit to see the spunky appointment-sharing Pullets, but in the end I figured they were probably too spunky and up-to-date and unisex to notice. I wore what I generally wear: a pair of double-pleated gray slacks that I had made for me years ago by an Italian tailor on Market Street and a plain white shirt. I checked myself in the bathroom mirror, still steamy from my shower. Some men lose their face entirely in middle age. Their bones spread apart and their face becomes bigger and fatter and coarser. I had the face I had always had. Only it was older.

The great clock at St. Mary's Cathedral by the park was tolling eleven as I walked down Greenwich toward Columbus, feeling the brilliant sunshine bathe my back. There was no wind in the air and no clouds in the sky anymore. The street was empty and the calm neat two- and three-story houses looked as if they had been bathed in just this brilliant sunlight since time began.

Knesterman had ostentatiously omitted lunch in his plans for me, so I hiked up Columbus, past the Fior D'Italia, which wouldn't be open until lunchtime, and past Luca's delicatessen, with its heavy hanging sausages in the window and its coiled loaves of old-fashioned Italian bread, and then I cut over to Broadway and took a bus through the tunnel and over to Swan's Oyster Bar on Polk.

The place was strictly shellfish. It was run by a group of muscular brothers who gave the impression that nothing in life beat working with cold shrimp. Each order was taken with an explosion of pleasure. "You want lox? You got it," a brother would sing out. The elderly party who had wanted lox would sit there, dazzled, no doubt, by the radiance his order had prompted. Every morning the brothers had a load of enormous prawns flown in from Mexico. They reposed in the window on a bed of chipped ice. "Prawns to go," one brother would shout joyously from the telephone at the rear of the restaurant. "Prawns coming up," another brother would shout in response. Dipping his hands in the chipped ice, he worked with a gusto suggesting that it really doesn't get any better than this.

They may have been right, those brothers.

I settled my haunches onto one of the metal chairs.

"What'll it be, Mr. A?" said one of the brothers, smiling broadly.

I ordered prawns and Anchor Steam. Except for the brothers volleying orders to one another and talking of family matters, the place was quiet in the way almost nothing is quiet anymore. No acned teenager thrashing a guitar and sending a hormonal drone over the soundtrack; no rap artists demanding service from their women. I chowed down the shrimp and scooped up the rich Louis dressing with a heel of sourdough bread and drank down my beer in two long swallows.

Afterward, it was a straight shot down California on the cable car to the Bank of America building, where Knesterman, Woodger, Schutzenberger and Rota had a suite of offices somewhere in the stratosphere. I was on the escalators leading to the elevators on the second floor by one o'clock.

The receptionist at the firm's front desk didn't give me the impression that the Pullets were in great demand. She was a grandmotherly woman with piercing blue eyes.

"The Pullets? Are you sure you have that right?" she asked dubiously.

"They're a unisex couple," I said. "Two heads on one body."

Grandmother let those piercing blue eyes look me over; then she rifled slowly through the firm's address book. "Panterhouse, Penrose, Ackerman, Penrose, Roger, Penrose, Winfield, Pluvet—it's not Amy *Pluvet* you want, is it? She's in Wills and Trusts."

"No."

After another rifle rifled itself she burst out triumphantly: "Here we are, Frank and Robin Pullet. They're all the way in the back. I'll just call and have them bring you back."

"Travel together, do they?"

Blue Eyes looked up at me without blinking. Strong blue eyes are almost a force of nature.

As it turned out, Frank Pullet came to fetch me alone. He was an unobtrusive man dressed in brown from his tortoiseshell glasses to his brown Mephisto walking shoes. He wore his brown thinning hair parted low on the side of his head.

"Aaron?" he asked diffidently. "Robin's on a call." He pantomimed holding a receiver to his ear with his shoulder and twirled a dial in space. "She asked me to come get you."

"And here I am. What a lucky break."

We walked back through the long corridors. Law offices are all alike. As soon as you leave the reception area or the partner's offices, things get shabby in a hurry. At Knesterman, Woodger, Schutzenberger, and Rota, the reception area put you in mind of Versailles, with a lot of glitzy chandeliers and chrome and leather chairs; but the long corridors were faced with cheap stucco and the ceilings were all soundproofing particle board.

By the time we got to the back of the suite, Robin Pullet had finished up with whomever she was finishing up. She stood at her desk to shake hands with me. "Aaron," she said, giving my hand a single tight shake, as if she were snapping a leash. She was at least a head taller than her husband, with a mop of tightly corkscrewed hair and the kind of rough sandy skin that some women have from the day of their birth. She wasn't someone you'd see on a garage calender, but she wasn't unattractive either. Her high coloring made her sandy cheeks blaze; it gave her a kind of raffishness.

There were two high-backed leather chairs behind the wide black mahogany desk. Frank stood behind the vacant one. Then the Pullets sat down together.

"So," said Frank Pullet brightly.

"So," I said right back.

"Really," said Robin Pullet.

I sat myself down on the low little leather couch by the side of the office and wiggled my back to take the pressure off my spine. "So how come a couple of upstanding citizens are looking at a criminal indictment?" I asked when I had gotten comfortable.

Frank and Robin Pullet turned their palms up, almost at the same time, as if to suggest that the whole thing was mystifying beyond belief.

Then Frank Pullet said diffidently: "The indictment is going to allege failure of due diligence."

"I know that, guys," I said. "Tell me what they *did* that wasn't so diligent."

"You mean specifically?" asked Robin Pullet.

"Sure. That's what I mean." I wasn't too surprised the two of them shared an appointment; I got the impression that the tax code was more than either of them could have handled separately.

"Specifically," Frank Pullet said, "the indictment alleges a failure to use generally accepted accounting procedures."

"I know this is asking a lot," I said, "but can you be even more specific than that?"

Frank Pullet seemed to take a beat of a second to check his wife's eyes. Then he said: "It's the 10Q that Ergwenweiler and Plumbeck prepared for Maison Jarr. That's a quarterly report that accountants—"

I cut him off. "I know what a 10Q is, Pullet. What's wrong with the one they prepared?"

"It's a little odd," said Robin Pullet.

"What they do, type the thing on vermilion paper? Odd *how?*"

"There's the way in which they handled the receivables," said Frank Pullet. "That's odd."

Listening to Pullet was like listening to a stalling motor; I rolled my hand in my lap to keep him going.

Pullet checked his wife's eyes and then went on: "Well, in the 10Q they prepared in March, they list Maison Jarr as having twenty-five million dollars in receivables."

"So?"

"No, no. That's okay. The odd part is that when you like *look* at the way they handle money coming in, there's this category called *unbilled* receivables. It's more than ten million dollars."

"Aaron," Robin Pullet cut in. "We can't figure out what that is."

"It *looks* like an improper way of blowing up a company's receivables," Frank Pullet said. "That's what it looks like."

"So? Eddie and Marvin are accountants. Isn't that what accountants do?"

"Financial documents are supposed to be transparent," Robin Pullet said. She said it as if she remembered saying it in law school.

"And you guys are supposed to be lawyers," I said, "not moral philosophers. Putting a blurry 10Q into circulation doesn't sound like much of a crime to me."

"That's true, Aaron," she said. "The statute doesn't really *define* accepted accounting procedures."

"What the courts say?"

"There haven't been all that many cases in California," said Frank Pullet. "You'd think there'd be a lot, but there really haven't been that many." He was happy to retreat to a world of facts and cases.

"What am I missing here? You got a couple of hardworking accountants and a vapor charge. Why are our boys facing the firing squad?"

The Pullets looked at me in their embarrassed way. "That's just it, Aaron," said Frank Pullet. "We don't know. The federal attorney as much as *said* that he would be willing to forget the whole thing for a slap on the wrist, maybe a fine."

"What's the problem, then?"

"The problem lies with Mr. Ergenweiler and Mr. Plumbeck," said Robin Pullet with a frown of distaste. "They categorically refuse to consider confessing to any wrongdoing."

"Maybe they figure they didn't *do* anything wrong. Don't want to confess to something they didn't do. A lot of innocent people are fussy like that."

"That would make sense, Aaron," Robin Pullet said sternly, *"if* they hadn't done anything wrong."

I was mystified. "You're telling me Marvin and Eddie screwed up a 10Q and are simply too proud to admit it?"

The Pullets solemnly shook their heads sideways. Frank Pullet tapped his index finger on the desk as if he were touching the offending 10Q. "Aaron," he said, "this isn't the sort of thing trained accountants do."

"Why would Marvin and Eddie *deliberately* put out a phony 10Q? It doesn't make any sense."

"No, it doesn't, Aaron," said Robin Pullet.

* * *

The rest of the week knocked politely on my door and left without staying. On Saturday morning, I pulled on my blue windbreaker and hiked over the top of Russian Hill. I had coffee and a cruller at Ahrens on Van Ness. It's one of these sad old pastry shops that you find in San Francisco. Years ago the place was always packed. There were no tables—just a horseshoed counter edged with red swivel stools. The menu was strictly tuna sandwiches on white bread with mayonnaise, bacon, lettuce, and tomato sandwiches, donuts and crullers and coffee. Nothing ever tasted good, but everything was clean. The waitresses all had bunions and red elbows and called everyone hon. The men wore gray suits and sharp hats with snappy brims; the women, flowing flowery dresses. Everyone smoked, tapping their cigarettes in the glass ashtrays that faced every seat. San Francisco was still a secret kept by those who lived there.

The men in gray suits and sharp hats had long since died; the women in the flowing flowery dresses were old now and arthritic or bent over by osteoporosis. They came hobbling into the shop to stand at the counter and peer at the pastries. The horseshoe was closed. Now all you could get was waxy pastry and coffee; you got to drink the coffee standing up. The rich vibrant life had leaked out of the place.

I walked up Pacific and through Pacific Heights over to Presidio Heights; I carried my coffee container and sipped at the hot bitter stuff every now and then. The beautiful streets were empty. They always are. Going out toward the Presidio, the houses get grander by degrees. Before you hit Fillmore Street, there are still apartment houses lining the silent blocks, and two-story houses that look as if you didn't really have to be the Aga Khan to live there; past Fillmore, the apartment houses disappear. The blocks are consumed by great looming mansions. There isn't much greenery in front of them, but what there is is arranged elaborately. The hedges are clipped to within an inch of their lives, and the evergreens are carefully manicured so that they look like poodles. Most of the mansions sit there, silent and inscrutable as the sun, but every now and then you can sort of look into one and see through the front windows to the polished parquetry floor, and the huge flower-filled living rooms, and beyond that to the spectacular water-filled view of the bay. It may be that money doesn't buy happiness: it definitely buys beauty, though.

I didn't have much of a plan in mind, beyond taking a look at some of the most gorgeous real estate in the world; when I came to the top of Presidio Heights I stood for a few moments looking out at the tremendous expanse of the bay below me, glistening in the harsh morning sunlight. I figured I might as well hike down to the basketball courts at the Julius Kahn playground and see if Eddie Ergenweiler was shooting hoops. He generally did on Saturday morning.

I walked down the old cobblestone part of Pacific, with the dark trees of the Presidio to my right, and the beautiful pink and yellow houses on my left. The playground was part of an enormous tract of land that rolled up and down a couple of spectacular hills and spilled itself onto the bay. The southern flank faced Presidio Heights and gave all the people rich enough to live there another reason to congratulate themselves for being rich enough to live there.

The basketball courts were tucked into a little playground on the western side of a great lawn. The artifacts were strictly WPA style from the thirties—well-maintained wooden benches on well-maintained asphalt walkways, neat domed little restrooms, and basketball courts with basketball hoops without nets.

Eddie Ergenweiler was playing by himself on one of the side baskets. He was a stretched six feet or so, and although he was lean, there was nothing chiseled about his body. He stood there on the court dribbling furiously, feinting out a platoon of imaginary opponents; after a while he broke free of the pack and took a lilting but unsuccessful jump shot from beyond the key.

The sky was a deep thrilling blue above the court, and the evergreens at the edge of the great lawn were shockingly vivid. I stood there with my shoulders hunched into my windbreaker.

"Yo, Eddie."

Eddie Ergenweiler stopped dribbling for a moment and peered over toward me. "Asher?" he asked.

"In person."

"Hey, man, what're you doing out here?" He resumed dribbling and stood rooted there; he didn't seem in a big hurry to walk over to me.

"Auditioning for the Harlem Globetrotters. They think I'm a natural."

"Go for it," said Ergenweiler, endeavoring to bounce the ball through his legs.

"Irene came to see me," I said. That was enough to get Ergenweiler's attention. He stopped dribbling and walked over to me with the ball tucked underneath his elbow.

"Irene came to see you, Asher?"

"She's pretty worried about things."

Ergenweiler smoothed his thinning hair back over his scalp; perspiration had made it matted. He had that trick some men have of entering middle age without ever quite losing the imprint of his adolescence. Everything about his long narrow face and floppy body suggested somehow that nineteen sixty-five or so—*that* was the great year, the time to be alive. He had grown up in Bel Vista, a suburb of Los Angeles. He kept a photograph on his desk of himself in a red convertible, with a bright bubbly blonde by his side.

We walked up the asphalt walkway to the round-domed restrooms; Ergenweiler took a long thirsty drink from the steel water fountain set in a concrete basin, slurping a good deal because the fountain didn't send up anything more than a little button of frothy water.

"It's nothing I can't handle, Asher," he said, wiping his lips.

We resumed walking up the path; after a while, the asphalt gave out onto a dirt path that circumnavigated the great lawn of the park.

"Eddie, I need to be straight with you. Knesterman had me speak to the Pullets."

"The Pullets? Jesus, aren't they a pair of light bulbs? Little twerp probably needs a roadmap find his own pecker."

Ergenweiler stopped at a bench to tie his shoelaces; he stood there like that, poised on one foot like a heron. Then he asked: "So bottom line, Asher. What they tell you?"

"Bottom line, Eddie, is that they can't figure out why you and Plumbeck screwed around breaking out the receivables on Maison Jarr's 10Q."

"Screwed around? Asher, we're accountants. This is what we do for a living. These guys come to us, they're like we want receivables broken out this way, conform to English accounting practices, we're going to say hey wait a minute guys we can't take your quarter-million-dollar retainer handle all your work because maybe, *maybe* some rinky-dink federal attorney with his head up his butt has never heard of breaking out receivables this way?"

"Eddie, you guys are too shrewd just to screw up a 10Q. Maybe they don't believe in generally accepted accounting procedures in Britain. They don't believe in orthodonture either. Over here, Tammy's teeth come in crooked, you see a dentist."

Ergenweiler paused, stood there for a moment, his right leg still on the bench, the basketball still tucked under his elbow. He looked directly at me, the brilliant sun streaming over his deeply tanned but hopelessly frail shoulders.

"Asher, I'm teaching freshman accounting over Diabolo College I tell all the little pumpkins there's no such thing as an unbilled receivable. A receivable is a receivable. You start dicking around with unbilled receivables you can list the lottery on a 10Q. Thing is, I'm *not* teaching freshman accounting over Diabolo or any other place. I'm running a business. We start telling the client that this that the other thing is generally accepted accounting this that the other thing we're out of business. Finished. *Finito.* We're a service, Asher. Plenty other people out there providing exactly the same service."

We resumed walking up the path, past mothers wheeling prams, and past Filipino maids exercising great stupid dogs. The lawn was almost empty.

"I hear what you're saying, Eddie. You may be right. Why not just take a slap on the wrist, pay a fine, make Irene happy?"

Ergenweiler stopped again and clutched the basketball to his chest. I could see that he wanted to be angry. He had a big sloppy temperament, but he had never been able to focus his irritation.

"Asher," he said, bouncing the basketball furiously. Then he stopped walking and clutched the ball to his chest. "We didn't do anything anyone in the business doesn't do. *You* don't do anything some federal attorney comes over to *your* house sticks out his hand and says *hey* guess what, guy, you didn't do anything but I'm going to ruin your reputation *and* I want you to pay some upfront fine just so I know whatever it is you didn't do you're not going to do it anymore, I mean give me a break. What would you do?"

I looked at Ergenweiler standing there, his hair still sweat-matted, the small vein at the base of his neck pounding.

"Me, Eddie?" I finally said. "Me, I'd pay the fine."

The Doctor Is In

IT HADN'T BEEN MUCH of a day. An old client had called me from Los Angeles and asked that I drive down to the Peninsula to check out a warehouse full of oriental rugs that had been seized by customs. The appraiser was someone named Fawzi. He was supposed to tell if the merchandise was legitimate and I was supposed to enter a bid for auction. I picked him up at one of those fly-by-night places peddling rugs over on Folsom. He was a tiny man, with a thick full beard; he was dressed severely in black. He didn't speak much English; he muttered a good deal. We were halfway down the Peninsula when he said: "Now you stop."

I looked over at him. He seemed all right to me, but I thought that he might need a bathroom.

"Next exit, I'll pull off."

"Now you stop now or otherwise I depart, my blood being on your head by the will of Allah, the All-Seeing One."

It was a pretty passionate speech. He had his hand on the door handle and he seemed serious. I swung over three lanes and pulled the car onto the shoulder of the road.

Fawzi hopped out, looked quickly at the sun, and withdrew a small silk shawl from his inside pocket and spread it on the ground in front of him. Then he fell to his knees and began praying to

Mecca as the traffic thundered by on 101. He had a lot of special requests on line; he must have prayed for five or more minutes.

I figured that he was due to have his pious backside upholstered by a semi, but the Big Guy evidently kept a hand in freeway management. When he had finished explaining his affairs to the All-Seeing One, Dr. Fawzi got back into my car without another word.

At the warehouse in Los Gatos, he looked quickly at half a dozen rugs, turning them over and poking his none-too-clean index finger into their backing. He made a clucking noise with his tongue and said, "Pakistani." Then he made a spitting sound.

I pointed to the label, which said State of Iraq. Fawzi shrugged his shoulders as if to indicate that my ignorance of the world's ways defied explanation.

I hustled Fawzi back up to San Francisco before he received another call to prayer and called my contact in Los Angeles. "What Fawzi say, Asher?"

"You trust this guy?" I asked.

"Best in the business."

"He said the stuff is cheap Pakistani junk."

"Towel-head," my client said sadly. "Probably wants to make a bid on it himself."

I had lunch at a pizzeria on Broadway, just to clear all that blessedness from my system. Afterward I walked down Columbus from Broadway and up Greenwich. The fog was just starting to roll in off the bay. The light over the avenue was already nacreous. It was only two o'clock, but by the time I was halfway up Greenwich I could see that it had already spread over the low-lying areas of the city. Only the top of Telegraph Hill remained sheathed in the sunshine.

I let myself in my apartment and opened the windows so that I could smell the fog and the salt. It's a smell as old as water.

Then I remembered Alicia's mail.

The letters were still in the breast pocket of the jacket I had worn. There wasn't much there. A couple of advertising flyers addressed to Occupant; a postcard from Ireland addressed to someone named Bootsie that had clearly wound up with Alicia's mail by mistake; a notice from a health club, and the telephone bill.

I eased myself out of my shoes and eased myself onto my living room couch and eased my head onto the armrest and eased open Alicia Tamaroff's telephone bill. She hadn't made more than her minimum in local service; but she had rung up almost thirty dollars in toll calls to Marin. She had called the same Mill Valley number every day for almost a month.

I reached over to grab the Princess on my desk and dialed the number. I got a machine.

"This is Dr. Maxine Stuntvesal, providing a centered environment in which to discuss rootedness, eating disorders, and relationships. Our community of care is limited to women. Please respect our limits. Peace and love."

The voice had the low, sensuous, well-modulated quality that so many dippy women have these days. Thirty years ago it would, that voice, have been saying things like "Why don't you slip out of that jacket and make yourself comfortable?" Now it was talking about women-centered environments.

I waited until the beep and left my name and telephone number. I didn't think I'd get a call back.

I was wrong. The telephone rang just after I clicked the obliging Princess off.

"This is Maxine Stunvesal," said the voice I had just heard.

"Aaron Asherfeld."

Maxine Stuntvesal allowed herself a cautious "Yes?"

"I'm having a problem with a relationship."

"Mr. Asherfeld, my practice is restricted to women. I thought my message said that very clearly? I'm sure there are therapists who feel comfortable dealing with a heteropatriarchal environment. I do not."

"That's pretty terrific, Doctor. You and ten thousand other women. The problem I'm having doesn't require therapy."

"Then why for heaven's sake are you calling me?"

"The relationship I'm having trouble with is on account of the fact that one of the relations is missing."

The doctor breathed sharply again; she was not a woman with a gift for disguising her emotions. She said: "And who might that be?" She meant it to sound flip and insouciant; it sounded leaden instead.

"Alicia Tamaroff. Big beautiful blonde. Sort of a mascot for a couple of guys in the city."

"Mr. Asherfeld, I'm not interested in bimbos and their problems. My practice is limited to women who are serious about self-discovery and renewal."

"Sure it is. You probably spend so much time dealing with bulimics you wouldn't be able to spot a beautiful blonde if she showed up on your doorstep. Only thing is, *this* beautiful blonde called your office thirty times in thirty days. She may have been dippy but it sounds to me as if she were pretty serious about self-discovery."

Stuntvesal took in her next breath sharply. "I have a duty to protect the privacy of my patients," she said.

"Sure you do," I said. "Seeing how you want to keep confidences to yourself, I'll just turn over what I have to the police. They're pretty big on respecting limits. You shouldn't have any problem explaining things to them."

"Listen you—" Stuntvesal suddenly snapped; then she recaptured herself and said very slowly through what seemed to be clenched teeth: "I am not going to lose my temper."

"Attagirl."

"All right, Mr. Asherfeld. I can see you are going to be something of a nuisance. If you want to talk to me I'm going to ask that you to come to my office. Can you do that? I'm not going to discuss anything with you over the telephone."

I didn't much want to drive out to Mill Valley and face the traffic on the way back; but I didn't want to leave Stuntvesal with a lot of time to think about seeing me either. "I'm on my way," I said.

Getting in and out of other cities is like crawling through an intestinal tract, but the Golden Gate Bridge is a hinge of paradise—the bay to one side, the Pacific to the other. The fog had come straight over the bridge, leaving just the orange towers exposed. I could see it slinking over the water like a fluffy expansive tube. The sky above the bridge was shot through with a lot of oranges and deep purples. And then I was into the deep fog itself, cold all of a sudden, gray and wet. The universe seemed to shrink. And then I was on the other side just as quickly, the brilliant Marin sunshine spilling over the wet car, lighting up the landscape.

Mill Valley is a cute little town in a cute little valley at the foot of a cute little mountain just across the Golden Gate. It's tucked into a weather pocket so that the place is always sunny. Drug dealers go there to retire. There's a little square in the center of town in back of an old railway depot and a lot of expensive food stores and a hugely upscale food market featuring enough low-fat food to power a gas turbine reactor and a movie theater still playing Antonioni movies and at least three places to get double decaf espresso.

Stuntvesal had her office in a cute little red house on Greene Street, one block from the main thoroughfare leading into town.

I lifted the heavy brass door knocker and let it fall. The door latch opened silently. I walked into a tiny parlor that had been furnished like a waiting room—a couple of plastic chairs, a tiny couch, a table with a pile of magazines.

"Be right with you," someone said through the intercom. I sat down and looked through the coffee-table literature. The magazines had titles like *Common Ground* or *Psychic Reader*. They were pretty upbeat, those magazines. There was a lot of good news they needed to share. It seems this business about cancer had a lot more to do with a positive centered attitude than anyone might have thought. Then there were the advertisements. The New Foundation offered FST—Female Sexuality Training. The place offered practical consultation for sexual self-mastery. Two weeks of hard work and bang! you go off like a firecracker. Norman Waldburger offered therapy for body, mind, and spirit; he used a lot of breath work in his practice and offered his patients the chance to shake hands with the inner core of being. Suszanne Foispot offered a breakthrough in healing. Her technique was called EMDR, short for eye-movement desensitivizing and reprocessing. It seems that bad eye movements were this terrific problem and . . .

"Mr. Asherfeld?" asked Maxine Stuntvesal, standing by the door. She was a fleshy woman of sixty or so, with a well-sculpted face and dark hair streaked with gray, and dark accusing eyes. She might have been Italian. She gave off a slightly sour smell.

I stood up and shook hands with her. Shaking her hand was like grasping a steak.

"Come this way, please," she said, leading me from the reception room to the back of the house. The walls of the hall were close and the ceiling low. Everything seemed just a little too small, as if the house had been designed for Koreans.

The parlor at the rear of the house was a small, very intense room, furnished in what seemed to be large-scale children's furniture. The walls were bright pink and the plastic table and chairs were all painted in vivid primary reds and greens and blues. Stuntvesal must have caught my look. She sat down in a bright blue chair. Then she said: "We do past lives work here. My patients find this a supportive environment."

"I'll bet," I said, seating myself on one of the outrageously yellow yellow chairs. "Sit in one of these, your past life is liable to pop right out. Next thing you know you're shaking hands with the king of France."

Stuntvesal looked at me with distaste.

There was a brush-soft knock on the door. "See," I said brightly. "Here comes His Majesty now."

"Capo," murmured Maxine Burnett Stuntvesal warmly at someone pink and Presbyterian. And then: "Mr. Asherfeld, this is Capo N. Titus. He is a dear dear friend. He is also my attorney. I took the liberty of asking him to meet with us. I was sure you wouldn't mind."

It was all supposed to be suave and vaguely threatening, but Stuntvesal didn't have it right, though.

"Counselor," I said.

Titus settled himself in a red chair and crossed his bony legs at the knee. He was one of these terrifically spry old parties who feel the world owes them congratulations for being terrifically spry and terrifically old. I had a feeling that he had a high regard for his own legal talent. He was itching to get something out right away. "Look here, Asherman, Asherfeld, whatever your name is. Maxine tells me that you've been harassing her. I won't stand for it. I want you to know that." He leaned over to stab at my knee with a bony forefinger. "This woman is a *therapist,*" he said.

"You all through, Counselor, or should I hold on for a while in case you catch a second wind?"

Capo Titus withdrew his finger from my knee and straightened himself out. He was dying to say something sharp but he had nothing sharp to say. "As long as we understand one another, yes I'm all through," he finally grumped.

Stuntvesal got up from her chair and smoothed the front of her plaid skirt with her palms; she was nicely dressed but you had the feeling that underneath it all something rotten had been progressing for a long time. She turned to stare out the window at her little garden. "What is it you want from me?" she asked, her back still toward me. Her voice had lost its modulation.

"I appreciate the fact that you've got your attorney here, Doctor," I said. "It's really the sort of thing make me watch my step, but what I want from you is the same thing I wanted when I spoke to you on the telephone."

Maxine Stuntvesal turned toward me; she was livid with fury. "I would die before I betrayed that child into your hands," she said.

"We talking about the child you said you didn't know? I'm just asking to be sure."

"You know very well who we're talking about."

"In that case, it couldn't be a child. *I'm* talking about a full-grown woman. Last thing anyone on this planet would call Alicia Tamaroff is a child."

"She is a child lost in a world of men," said Stuntvesal decisively. "She needs a healing space and I am going to give it to her."

"Doctor, she can have a healing space as large as the Belgian Congo as far as I'm concerned. The guys who paid her rent and bought her food and worried about her charge accounts would kind of like to know what happened to her. That doesn't seem like such an unreasonable request."

"What happened to her?" Stuntvesal exploded. *"What happened to her?"*

"Now, Maxine," said Titus pacifyingly.

"Don't Maxine me, Capo."

"I'm just asking you to consider what's at stake."

"I understand what's at stake. Just don't Maxine me," she said.

Then she turned toward me. "You have a group of men keep this child, yes, this *child* in conditions of white slavery and you have the unmitigated gall to tell me that *they* would like to know what happened to *her?* Didn't they accomplish enough, keeping her in that *seraglio* like some sort of erotic pet? Is there something else they would like to do to her?"

"Look, Doctor," I said, "it's swell to see how indignant you can get. You probably stopped just before you had a hemorrhage. But let me tell you something. Out *here* it's always seventy degrees and sunny and the big problem is making sure the deli stocks low-fat brie. Back *there* it rains a lot and a mean wet fog blows in from the ocean."

"Meaning what?" Stuntvesal sneered.

"Meaning that the real world is full of men who like big beautiful blondes and full of big beautiful blondes who like men who like them. It's not what goes down well in therapy, but it's the truth anyway. Now you can tell me from now until David Letterman goes into reruns that Alicia was broken by the world of men. *I'm* telling you she seemed about as helpless as Niagara Falls."

"Mr. Asherfeld," said Maxine Stuntvesal gravely, "I'm going to ask you to leave now."

I got up heavily, pressing up from the yellow yellow chair with my thighs. "I'll do that," I said. Then I angled myself so that I was facing Titus as well as Stuntvesal. "I'm not going to tell you I think it was a great idea to stash Alicia Tamaroff in an apartment, have her available for recreation. It's not a moral judgment. Woman wants to entertain a *platoon* of men, that's her call. I *am* going to tell you that the guys who set her up were crazy about her and now she's missing. You know where she is you've got an obligation to reveal it." I paused for a beat. "If not to me, then to someone else."

"Is that a threat?" asked Maxine Stuntvesal incredulously.

"Sure. That's just what it is."

"That's all your type can do, isn't it?" Capo Titus said with a snort. "Threaten and bluster."

"Counselor," I said, "that's all my type *has* to do."

"Mr. Asherfeld," said Maxine Stuntvesal, "you are free to follow your own conscience—*if* you can find it. I promise you one thing, though. You are going to look very very foolish if you go to the police or anyone else. Alicia Tamaroff is in a warm and caring environment, a healing place. For the first time in her life she is being protected."

I walked across the little room and over to the little door that led back to the reception room. "I hope so," I said dubiously.

They both caught my tone. Maxine Burnett Stuntvesal's cheeks immediately began to flame; Titus turned his bony body in his seat so that I could see how indignant he was. He had a lot of faith in his gestures.

"You are absolutely outrageous," he said, winding himself up for a long speech. Stuntvesal held up her hand and said: "Capo, please."

"You think *I'm* outrageous? Wait till your reception room is filled with big beefy guys look like if they breathed twice this place would fall down, telling you that lady you're an accessory after the fact."

Both Titus and Stuntvesal looked at me uncertainly.

"Accessory after the fact, Counselor," I said. "It's kind of a legal term."

Feeling No Pain

MARVIN PLUMBECK CAME UP to Telegraph Hill from his office that night looking rumpled and sweaty; he was carrying his expensive dark suit jacket over his shoulder. He had turned the French cuffs of his shirt back so that the world could see the gleam of his gold watchband against the dark skin of his wrist. We met at the Maudit at the base of the hill and then wandered over to Chinatown. It was one of those surprisingly warm pink June nights. The fog had stayed where the fog sometimes stays, twenty miles or so out to sea, and the wind had come in from the countryside, carrying with it the smell of orchards in bloom. The western sky over the Golden Gate was shot through with a lot of ruby reds and pinks, but overhead, the sky was that incredible deep purple that you don't get any other place in the world besides California. It's the kind of light that holds the streetlights and the neon signs together and gives them a thrilling edge, as if they were communicating secret messages.

"Nice night," I said, as we walked up Columbus.

Plumbeck turned to look. He seemed genuinely surprised to see that it was a nice night. "It *is* a nice night," he said warmly. For a moment, he stopped and stood there on the sidewalk, letting the colored air wash around him.

At Broadway we hiked up the little hill to the throat of Grant. The Chinese in San Francisco are the last ethnic group sincerely to believe in neon. The street was blazing. We wound up after a while at one of those hole-in-the-wall Chinese restaurants that are popular for a couple of weeks. The *Chronicle* had given it a great write-up, and every night the line in front of the place snaked up the block. We happened by just as the owner was pulling back the metal screen in front of the restaurant.

"We get in now?" Plumbeck asked.

The owner answered with a gabble of Cantonese. "What he say?" said Plumbeck.

"He said go on in."

We seated ourselves at the cold Formica table nearest the window; we both ordered the special.

"That's pretty cool, Asher," said Plumbeck. "You pick up enough Chinese make sense of what he said?"

"Not a word. I just figured the man wasn't going to open the gate in order to keep paying customers out."

Plumbeck nodded happily. "What I love about you, Asher," he said. "Always thinking."

The specials came almost before we finished up our T'sing Taos. Wok cooking is pretty fast if it's done right. The food was fine. The chef had figured out that people in San Francisco will eat anything. His stuff was full of braised sweet potatoes and charred eggplant.

After we had eaten for a few minutes, I said: "Good news and bad news, Plumbeck, which you want first?"

"Bad news," Plumbeck said; he was trying to cut some of his

vegetables with his chopsticks; I thought he might have paled under his tan. It was hard to tell.

I told Plumbeck about Maxine Stuntvesal. He listened alertly, chewing his food with exaggerated care. "So what's the good news?" he asked when I had finished.

"Bad news *is* the good news, Plumbeck. It's kind of a Zen thing. If your little cupcake is busy being worried about her self-esteem, nothing bad's happened to her."

"You're right," he said, brightening immediately, as if he had solved a difficult problem. "You actually see her out there with this Stuntvesal?" he asked. "She say anything about me?"

I took a long swallow of beer. "They seemed pretty determined to keep her under wraps, Plumbeck."

"You think it's just what they're telling you because she doesn't want to see me?"

"Hard to imagine," I said.

Plumbeck put his chopsticks across his plate and placed his forearms beside his dish. "So let me get this straight," he said. "You've got this therapist out in Mill Valley telling you she's got Alicia doing big-time self-analysis?" He shook his head as if the novelty of it all defied belief.

"You think that part doesn't compute, Plumbeck?"

"Asher, we're talking *major* airhead here, I mean zeppelin class. Self-analysis! I can just see it, I mean it'd be like 'Doctor, tell me the truth, you think I'm too big to wear a Wonderbra?' "

I thought for a moment of Alicia, and her deep thrilling beauty, the way the light caught the fine golden hairs at her temples.

"She didn't give me that impression," I said slowly.

"Asher, *you* didn't have to sit and listen to her. I mean this was not a woman to keep Susan Sontag up nights worrying about the competition."

"I guess," I said.

"It's going to be *years* before anyone makes a feminist out of her."

"Could be she's just lonely," I said. "It doesn't sound like too much fun sitting in some little apartment waiting for you or Eddie or anyone else to show up."

Plumbeck reddened just slightly. "Asher, no one ever *forced* her up there. I mean, no one was holding a gun to her head."

"Maybe she figured that out."

The fortune cookies arrived, together with a quartered orange. By the time we had finished, the little place was full of kids in leather jackets and nose rings and yuppie couples up from the financial district. Plumbeck withdrew an enormous cigar from a leather cigar case and sniffed the thing reverently.

"You want one, Asher?" he asked. "We smoke these outside, maybe catch a little late-night action at Centerfolds?"

I shook my head. "Not me, Plumbeck. I'm going home, watch the last of the color go out of the sky."

We both stood up heavily, surprised by how much we had eaten and how fast we had eaten it. I reached for my wallet, but Plumbeck shook his head. "My treat," he said. He had always been a man of instinctive generosity. Spending money was as natural to him as breathing and he was happy to spend it on others.

When we reached the street, Plumbeck sliced the base of his enormous cigar with his thumbnail and tried to light it by burying his head in the shelter formed by his back and rounded shoulders. He looked like an anteater. Finally he got the thing lit to his satisfaction. We walked sedately down Grant for a while, looking into the sad shops selling Chinese screens and name stamps and cheap painted furniture.

After a while I said: "You worried about the thing with Maison Jarr, Plumbeck?"

Plumbeck rolled his cigar in his mouth with his fingertips and finally sucked on it. The tip glowed cherry red for a moment through the gray ash that he had been careful to cultivate.

"I'm feeling no pain, Asher."

"Why's that?"

Plumbeck paused on the street and clenched his expensive cigar between his teeth and stretched out his hands.

"Maison Jarr's Eddie's client, Asher," he said, wrapping his words around his cigar. "He's the spearchucker on that one."

"You guys are a partnership, though."

Plumbeck withdrew his cigar from his mouth. "What you're saying is what?"

"What I'm saying is you've got joint liability. It's something I figure you know."

"You're right, Asher. Push comes to shove, we could both go down together on this. But let me tell you something. Couple years ago, this surgeon comes in, he's pulling down more than a mil a year, does nothing but look up people's behinds, it's a terrific line of work, I'm telling you. Anyway, his buddy tells him about some tax shelter buying oil rigs or something in Houston. I take one look, I know this is strictly for high rollers, even though he *thinks* he's rich he shouldn't even be looking at this kind of exposure. Anyway, what goes around comes around. I put him in this shelter, next thing *he* knows, he's still looking up people's behinds, only now he doesn't have a million dollars to show for it. Next thing *I* know, his lawyer is on the telephone."

I said: "Terrific story, Plumbeck. What's the point?"

Plumbeck looked at me as if he couldn't understand my slowness.

"Asher, the point is the ship goes down while I'm on the bridge, *I* go down with the ship. Simple as that. We got this tush-hunting yo-yo to settle for ten cents on the dollar, *I* picked up the bill. Eddie, he screws around with a 10Q, he's going to do the right thing."

"You think Eddie screwed around or screwed up?"

Plumbeck hunched his shoulders up and rolled his cigar around his lips.

"What I think, Asher, is that it doesn't make much difference, but just between you me and the lamppost, I think that Eddie knows the difference between unbilled and billable receivables."

After that we walked in silence until we had come back to the corner of Broadway and Columbus. The night had deepened, but the sky above Telegraph Hill was still purple.

I said goodbye to Plumbeck and watched him trudge off down Broadway. He was still carrying his suit jacket over his shoulder.

The fog came back much later that night; I had been asleep, but

I could feel it slither up the hill and cross the little yard behind my window and coat the blackberry vines with the bitter salt of the sea. When I awoke, the dawn was gray.

All the Brave Little Bunnies

I DIDN'T KNOW MUCH about Maison Jarr except that they sold cosmetics and had a lock on young women who were vegetarians and wore leather boots. They had stores all over San Francisco and a corporate office somewhere south of Market. I didn't think anyone there would talk to me, but I was wrong.

"This is Ray Chandler." The accent was fuzzy London, the kind of sloughy careless accent the English acquire after about a week in California.

I told Ray Chandler who I was and what I wanted. To my surprise he said: "Pop right on by, be glad to talk to you. It's number nine Mint Street. South of Market, Heart of Darkness, actually."

I got myself ready to do some popping and then I popped on by, driving from my house through the financial district and across Market.

I had thought at first that Maison Jarr's corporate office would be in one of the glitzy high rises just off New Montgomery; but Mint Street was in the Mission badlands in a little alley behind the old San Francisco mint. The neighborhood was seedy and unreconstructed—cheap bodegas selling Sterno and refried beans, cheap pawn shops with dented trumpets and a lot of little pistols in the window, cheap taverns that looked as if they dated from the Mesolithic. Years ago, the neighborhood was strictly Skid Row; but now there were raddled druggies sleeping on the sidewalks, and lunatics walking up and down the streets, singing to themselves or listening intently to voices. The welfare hotels were full of sad sacks from El Salvador. They sat on the stoops or looked out from the windows, glaring at a world that didn't speak enough Spanish to explain their welfare rights properly. I had nothing against Skid Row and nothing against drunks. Years ago I used to walk down here and figure if worse came to worst and I went to the dogs I'd go where the dogs went. It didn't seem so bad then. The streets were full of sunshine and the bars were cool and dark. Now even the dogs don't wander the neighborhood. Some immigrant is likely to take a look at their haunches and think chops.

I parked in a lot over on Mission. For ten dollars you were supposed to get security. That meant the big moose sitting in the lot's wooden shack was supposed to protect your car. I handed him his ten dollars and my keys after I parked my car myself.

"Somebody comes over urinates on my fender, what is it you're going to do?" I asked. "I'm just curious."

Big Moose looked at me through eyes that had been narrowed by pockets of fat. The radio was clattering away in Spanish.

"I see heem do a bad theeng," he finally said, "maybe I call the police."

It was a reassuring conversation.

I walked down Mission half a block and over to Mint. It wasn't much of a street, just an alley really that dead-ended abruptly into a brick retaining wall.

Chandler's building was protected by a heavy mesh gate, which someone had forgotten to lock. The vestibule inside was dark and smelled vaguely of pizza. There were only two offices in the place —Maison Jarr and an outfit called Systems International. Maison Jarr was on the second floor. I trudged up two flights of stairs and knocked heavily on the locked steel door.

The bolt slid back noiselessly.

The waiting room inside had a black Naugahyde couch and a coffee table with a lot of promotional material. There were huge pictures on the wall of a tall ugly woman with thick furry eyebrows. From in the back, a voice shouted: "Be with you in a jiffy."

I sat myself down on the couch and looked through some of the promo material. The stuff had a lot of italics in it. Maison Jarr had been founded by someone named Elizabeth Kneeblebone. She had *determined* to create a *new* kind of company, one that never, *ever* abused animals. A company that would *love* the earth, our *Mother.*

There was a picture in the brochure of Kneeblebone looking solemnly over an Alpine vista, an expression of concern on her big wide ugly face. The vista didn't look as if it needed loving and Kneeblebone didn't much look as if she were prepared to love it.

The door to the back opened, and a youngish man of perhaps thirty-five walked in, his hand extended.

"Reading about our sainted founder, I see," he said pleasantly.

Ray Chandler shook hands expeditiously, as if he weren't all that crazy about body contact. He had a lined face, very blue eyes and blond eyebrows. His long blond hair fell over his forehead. Every now and then, he would sweep it back with his hand.

"Love the earth, our Mother?" I asked.

"Yes, well it was that or ritual Satanism," said Chandler. "Have the stores painted black, shampoo the Druids used, that sort of thing."

"It must have been a tough choice."

"Elizabeth, bless her heart, was very fine about it. She simply didn't want to be associated with anything tacky."

"Like cheap environmentalism."

"Exactly. I say, it's not too early for a drink, is it?"

"It's nine-thirty in the morning, Chandler."

"There you go," said Chandler happily. "Not too early at all. I'll just be a minute. He darted off to the back and redarted a moment later, wearing a sober sports coat over his open-throated yellow shirt. He was carrying a small cardboard tube.

"Latest of the latest," he said.

I looked at the tube. It was called Lilac Blush. "What's it do?"

"It's an exfoliant, silly," said Chandler, turning off the office lights and fumbling with the lock. "Takes the top layer of your skin off."

I followed Chandler out the door and down the worn linoleum-covered steps toward the street.

"Why would I want to do that?"

Chandler shrugged. "It's the thing to do if you have sad, ratty-looking old skin, although I don't suppose that if you *did* have sad, ratty-looking old skin there's any reason to think there's going to be anything besides sad, ratty-looking old skin underneath it all.

Don't let any in your eyes, though. I'm not sure, but I think it might make you blind."

I chuckled as we exited the building. "That's what happens when you don't test on animals."

"Oh, but of course we test on animals," said Chandler sprightly. "Our *un*tested material is like nerve gas. One drop and off you go. We'd never hear the end of it from the FDA. All those spotty adolescents complaining about their comas and whatnot."

I was astonished. I stopped in the street and said: "Chandler, your whole pitch is you never use animals to test your products."

"Abuse," said Chandler imperturbably, "we never *abuse* animals to test our products. There's a difference, you know."

I held up the tube and said: "You rub this stuff in some rabbit's eye you don't call that abuse?"

"Not at all, Asherfeld," said Chandler. "Our rabbits are *volunteers*. Brave little bunnies, actually. It would be abuse if we *forced* them to participate in the experiment, but they have a choice. They can do the right thing or stay back with the slackers."

"Just how do you figure a rabbit's going to let you know he's a slacker, Chandler?"

"Elizabeth is very intuitive about nature, you know. I'm sure the Goddess would whisper something to her."

"She ever spot a slacker, bunny says I'm out of here?"

"We've been very lucky, actually. Our bunnies are splendid little rodents. Not a slacker among them. That *is* what they are, isn't it, rodents? Or is that wolves? I'm afraid I was asleep at the switch when they were nattering on about flora and fauna."

We had reached a tavern named Thruggs at the foot of Mint and Mission. Chandler pushed open the door and sang out a cheery "Hullo, mates" to the dilapidated barflies already mounted on their stools. There was a murmur of assent, a kind of susurrus in the cool brown room, although no one bothered actually to say anything.

We seated ourselves at a table in the back. The place smelled overpoweringly of beer.

Chandler ordered a double gin, straight up; I ordered a beer, although it was the last thing I felt like that early in the morning.

The drinks were carried over to our table by an immensely stout young Mexican woman who made the floorboards shake as she walked heavily from the bar.

Chandler lifted his glass. I could see it hadn't been completely washed. "To the brave little bunnies," he said. "Did I tell you they're all rotated back to England when their tour of duty is up?"

"You forgot that, Chandler."

"How careless of me," he said, taking another hit of gin. "Now that I've unburdened myself of all that whimsy, why don't you tell me what you wish to know. Perhaps I can help you."

It was an odd touch, his suggesting that he might help me. I was sure that he knew as much as I did, but I told him what I knew anyway. He sat there, listening intently. He hadn't quite finished his gin and he didn't seem about to order another shot. He wasn't the least inebriated. The alcohol had only served to restore him to himself.

I wound up: "Guys you hired do your American accounts are facing some serious heat, Chandler. Are you going to back them up or move to the other side, get in on the kill?"

"Back them up on *what* precisely, Asherfeld?"

"On their story."

"Which is?"

"I just told you."

"Remind me, then."

"Eddie Ergenweiler's claiming you told him to blow up your receivables."

"Blow up our receivables? I don't know if I'd put it quite that way."

"Which way would you put it? I'll make allowances for your special English sensibility."

"We had a legitimate interest in presenting ourselves in the best light, Asherfeld. Every company does. These 10Q reports are quite volatile. We asked Mr. Ergenweiler to make sure nothing was overlooked. That's how I'd put it."

"Chandler, federal attorney is claiming that you took a fifteen-million-dollar company and made it *seem* like it was a twenty-five-million-dollar company. That's making sure a lot of nothing wasn't overlooked."

Chandler looked at me steadily. Then he said: "It may have been an error in judgment. Under English law a chartered accountant has a good deal of latitude in breaking out receivables."

"You're not in England, Chandler. Ocean out there is the Pacific, not the Atlantic. Ergenweiler and Plumbeck aren't chartered accountants."

"That's quite true," Chandler said flatly. "They should have known better."

"Is that what you're going to tell the federal attorney? *They* should have known better?"

Chandler didn't say anything; he was pretty unflappable. Then he stretched his hand across the table, pulling at the sleeves of his sports jacket, and made a fist.

"Do you see my fist?" he asked quietly. I had no idea what he meant to do.

"You've got it under my nose, Chandler."

Of a sudden, he opened his hand, splaying his fingers.

"Now it's gone, Asherfeld. My fist *was* here and *now* it is gone."

"That's pretty deep," I said.

"It is, actually." He pulled at the last of the gin in his tumbler and clenched his fist again and splayed his fingers again. "Elizabeth is a very wise woman. You may not think so, but she is. A wise woman isn't interested in *solving* problems, you know. Anyone can solve problems. The world is full of dismal little people who go about *solving* problems. Elizabeth is interested in converting problems into opportunities. There is a difference, you know. A *considerable* difference."

"Just how do you figure on converting *this* problem into an opportunity?"

Chandler waved his open hand airily above the tabletop. "Elizabeth will find a way," he said. "She always does."

Panties in an Uproar

THE NEXT WEEK, Seybold Knesterman proved that he was worth his retainer by getting the federal attorney handling Ergenweiler and Plumbeck's case to agree to a sixty-day continuance. "Armstrong is a sweet boy, actually," Knesterman told me as he bit daintily into a Stanley Steamer. "Perhaps a trifle unforthcoming, but a sweet boy."

I had come down from Telegraph Hill in order to grab a frank and a Coke with the great man.

"This Armstrong Hrska, you're talking about?"

Knesterman nodded, beaming with snobbish pleasure. "His father and I served on the mayor's waterfront commission together. I was able to remind him of that."

"Good thing you didn't remind him what the commission did, Knesterman."

The mayor's waterfront commission had managed in the space of no more than five years to divert almost all of San Francisco's shipping business to Oakland. The port now lay empty and deserted.

"Blood is thicker than water, you know," said Knesterman, waving his Steamer in the air. The noontime crowds had begun to wash over Giannini Plaza. There were pretty girls everywhere: cute little button blondes and big leggy Amazons wearing flats and great open-eyed brunettes with light-toast skin showing through sleeveless dresses. "I do hope Mr. Ergenweiler sees reason on this, Asherfeld. The last time we spoke, he seemed bound and determined to fight to the bitter end."

"He hasn't seen your bill for trial work, Knesterman. Probably take a compromise with a sob of gratitude."

"Let's hope. Somehow I have the feeling that Mr. *Plum*beck isn't likely to turn up his nose at a settlement." Knesterman chewed delicately for a moment; he had the gift of being able to eat a large Stanley Steamer, one covered with mustard and sauerkraut, without dribbling on himself or seeming to wolf the thing down. "Speaking of the devil, Asherfeld," he said, dabbing at his lips with a paper napkin, "Plumbeck left a message for you with Frieda."

"What he say?"

"He didn't. You're to call him."

I finished the last of my frank and cleared the franky taste from my mouth with a pull of diet Coke. Nothing beats a sidewalk frank. Every now and then the police discover that someone selling Polish sausages on the street corner is stuffing the skin with pigeon meat. It doesn't make a difference. You catch that smell in the air and the things could be stuffed with dirt.

I left Knesterman standing there sipping chastely from his can of soda and cut over to Post Street and called Plumbeck from the pay phone outside Vidal Sasson's salon. His new receptionist put me through right away.

"Asher," he said explosively. "Am I glad you called."

"What's up?"

"It's Miriam. She's got her panties in an uproar."

"Plumbeck, she *always* has her panties in an uproar."

"Listen, you in the neighborhood or something? I'll buy you lunch."

"I just had lunch with Knesterman," I said. "My stomach can't take too much happiness. I'll meet you in front of your building five minutes."

I walked down Post Street, past the expensive stores selling Vuitton luggage and Chanel perfumes, and cut across Market on the diagonal, jaywalking through four lanes of traffic. Plumbeck was already in front of his building, pacing with his hands behind his back. He was wearing one of his two-thousand-dollar suits. Sometime in the eighties a group of English tailors discovered that if they came to San Francisco for a week each fall, there would be guys like Plumbeck prepared to spend a fortune just to wear a jacket that said Huntsman on the label. The suits didn't actually fit all that well, but the fabrics were beautiful and the jacket sleeves could be buttoned and unbuttoned. "Nothing like it, Asher," Plumbeck had said when he had taken possession of his first suit. "See, buttons on the sleeve actually work." He unbuttoned the four buttons on his sleeve to show me. "It's a miracle, Plumbeck," I said. "Hang the jacket up somewhere in Mexico, whole lot of peasants'll worship it as the living God."

Plumbeck spotted me coming up New Montgomery and left off pacing to hurry on over. He had a kind of urgent short man's walk. He shook hands with me, taking care to give my hand a lingering squeeze and palpated my biceps. "You're a bud," he said, motioning with his head to the side of the building, where there were benches arranged around a fountain with an abstract metal sculpture in its center.

"So what she do, Plumbeck, decide to go live in a yurt?"

"I wish," said Plumbeck. "She won't tell me what it's about, only thing she tells me is she needs fifty-thousand dollars, she needs it like yesterday, she doesn't get it her blood will be on my hands."

"So?"

Plumbeck looked at me with a pained expression. "I think this time she's in some kind of trouble." Plumbeck turned his palms upward. I plunged my hands into my pockets, pulling at my pants.

"You want me to go out there, speak to her. That your idea?"

"Pretty much."

"And the reason you're not scooting over the Bay Bridge is you don't want to get a shine on your suit pants from doing all that driving. Am I right?"

"Asher, reason I don't want to go out there is I'm facing a federal indictment in the city last thing I need is to get involved in one of Miriam's *stories*. I mean she could be peddling hashish off the Oakland docks for all I know. You don't want to do it as a friend, do it as a business deal. You straighten this out for me, I'll pay your regular retainer, whatever."

"You're right about one thing, Plumbeck."

"What's that?"

"I don't want to do it as a friend."

Miriam Polniakowsky had been a radiant young woman when she became Mrs. Marvin Plumbeck. They had exchanged vows, the two of them, at a Unitarian church on Union Street. Afterward, they had had a reception at the San Francisco yacht club. A local combo played an assortment of rock songs adapted for the accordion and the electric guitar. Miriam draped both her arms around Plumbeck's tuxedoed shoulders; there were yellow flowers in her thick, very dark hair. The sun sank beneath the Pacific, leaving the sky above the bay gashed with pink and gold. "Isn't it romantic," my wife said to me, pinching my arm, "it is *so* romantic."

Miriam Plumbeck left off being Mrs. Marvin Plumbeck eight years later; I went to see her just before she moved out.

"It's over, Asher," she said. She shook her dark curly hair; she had fine flashing eyes.

I didn't say anything: I didn't have anything to say.

"I want to live in the real world," she said.

"What world you figure you've *been* living in?" I asked.

"I want to know people who aren't white. I want neighbors who don't wear bras. I want to walk to demonstrations at Sproul Hall and go see mime troop plays in the park. Does that make any sense to you?"

"Sure. It's called slumming."

She turned to face me, her hands on her hips. "I guess if I have to explain it to you it's not something I can explain."

"I guess, Miriam."

She moved that spring to a house in the Berkeley flats. Plumbeck paid the mortgage. For a time, she lived with a registered nurse named Bertha. She wore tough matey clothes and cut her lovely dark hair short. Then the nurse moved out to marry a pharmacist and Miriam let her hair grow back. She couldn't understand how her lover could have left her for a man. "I never thought she was a breeder," she said sadly.

"It just goes to show you," I had said.

"Shows you *what,* Asherfeld?"

"I don't know, actually. Whatever you want."

She was a passionate frivolous woman; I had always liked her. I called her the afternoon that Plumbeck told me she was in trouble.

"Asher," she said explosively. "Marvin told you to call, didn't he? He told you to come out here?"

"It's not what you think, Miriam. He's just afraid to see for himself how swell multicultural living can be."

"That pathetic little prick."

"I wouldn't be too hard on him."

She snorted demurely into the telephone.

I drove out to Berkeley an hour or so later. Miriam lived in the flats, just below Martin Luther King Way. The houses aren't bad—cheap California bungalows set on pink or white stucco, or two-story redwood numbers, or ramshackle brick jobs, with green shutters; but the flat pockmarked streets look unkempt and the fig trees droop over the carports, leaving stains from squashed fruit everywhere, and the cyclone fences around the vacant yards are torn. No one keeps up their property much and no one takes care of their shrubbery or lawns. It's the sort of neighborhood that makes you remember that the big trouble with the classless society is that it's classless.

Miriam's house was in the middle of a block in the middle of the flats. She had been thrilled with the poor raddled thing when she moved in, saying "It's so funky" as she surveyed the low beamed ceilings and the redwood paneling on the living room walls. It was old when she moved in and smelled of damp wallpaper.

I knocked on the unpainted wooden door. It had never been locked in the old days, but now I could hear Miriam unlatching the master lock and then toggling a police lock. She stood there finally, peeping out at me through the chained crack in the door. "Asher," she said, unfastening the chain and opening the door slightly to let me in.

"You were expecting the lesbian avenger? What's with the security, Miriam?"

"Out here you need it."

I arched my eyebrow. "You worried some person of color's about to make a social statement on your VCR?"

She stood there, her arms wrapped around herself. "Very funny," she said.

We walked back into the little house. Most of the furniture had been acquired from thrift shops over on Shattuck, but Miriam had discovered her horribly ugly living room couch standing on a Berkeley side street. "I mean it's an antique," she had said at her housewarming. "Someone was just going to throw it out."

"Hard to believe," I had said.

Her expectations had given the house a certain vibrancy; now it seemed to hold an unclean feeling.

"You want coffee, Asher?" she asked.

"Sure, coffee be great."

We walked back into the large round kitchen together. It was the best room in the house.

"Don't ask for cookies. I don't have any."

"I won't ask for them, Miriam. Fantasizing about a plate of chocolate-chip cookies be all right with you? You know, the kind with chips *and* nuts in them?"

"You can fantasize about whatever you want, Asher," she said, busying herself by the counter, loading coffee into one of those Italian coffee machines—the kind you turn over when the water has boiled. She placed the elegant little machine on the electric stove and stood with her back toward me, her shoulder blades raised underneath her thin cotton shirt, the mass of her disorganized dark hair tumbling over her shoulders.

"He give you the money?"

"Marvin?"

"Yes, Marvin."

I shook my head. She must have felt the gesture with her back.

"For heaven's sake, why not?"

"I think he figures it's not his problem, Miriam."

She turned from the stove to face me, her hands on her hips, her cheeks blazing.

"Not his problem? Asher, *I am his wife.* Don't you think that makes it his problem?"

"Wife? Seems to me I remember a divorce somewhere along the line."

"What difference does that make? A divorce is just a piece of paper."

"Let me see if I get this straight," I said tentatively.

"Don't see if you get anything straight, Asher," Miriam shouted at me with a dangerously rising tide of hysteria in her voice. "I'm telling you what I *feel.*" She sat herself down on one of the white wooden bar stools that faced the rear counter of the kitchen and placed her hands on her knees. "He has enough money to support a *mistress,* for God's sake. I mean it is absolutely pathetic. He puts some twenty-year-old *bimbo* in a penthouse and I have to live here in this absolute slum. Don't tell me you don't think it's pathetic, Asher."

"It's awfully pathetic, Miriam."

"Don't make fun of me."

"All right. It's not awfully pathetic."

"I hope he drops dead," she said. "I hope he has a heart attack and he's just lying there in that penthouse and moaning and she's like oh Marvin, you say the cutest things when you're excited. I hope he's impotent. Did you know he was impotent a lot? It's probably not the sort of thing he likes to tell his buddies. You *didn't* know, did you, Asher? I could tell you things about Marvin Plumbeck that would make your hair stand on end."

I thought for a moment that she would just keep it up, but all at once the anger leaked out of her. She got up from the stool and turned the coffeepot over. Then she poured the hot black liquid into two tiny cups. I could see she was sniffling from the way her frail shoulders jerked. She set the cups on the table and retreated to her stool.

"I owe these people money, Asher," she said, wiping at her eye with the back of her hand.

"How much?"

"A lot. Fifty thousand dollars. You're not going to give me a lecture, are you? That's all I get these days. Everyone wants to give me a lecture. I couldn't bear a lecture."

"I won't give you a lecture. What the money go for?"

"You know very well what it went for."

"Fifty thousand dollars? Buys a lot of drugs."

"I'm *bored* out here," she wailed.

"I guess. How long's your dealer been floating you?"

"A year. At first he was all like it's all right sweetie, pay me when you can, now he's like I really, really want my money."

"Dealers are funny that way. What's his name?"

"He has this Muslim name, Molefi or Motefi, or something like that, but everyone calls him Shaboo."

"Shaboo?"

Miriam Plumbeck shrugged her frail shoulders, reaching her right shoulder up childishly to brush her ear.

"I don't know, I think they gave it to him in a fraternity."

"A fraternity? Miriam, next thing you'll be telling me is good old Shaboo graduated from Berkeley."

"I don't know if he graduated."

"What, they have a major in dealing dope now?"

"Asher," she snuffled, "it's really really scary. He's threatening to do these things to me if I don't pay."

"Like what?"

Miriam Plumbeck sat upright; her face was disorganized and her brimming eyes had left dark smudges below them.

"He says if I don't pay he's going to put me in some awful place and peddle my white ass."

Down These Mean Streets

I LEFT MIRIAM'S HOUSE and drove up one of the leafy side streets toward University Avenue and parked in the shade of a flowering fig tree and sat there for a few moments, letting my hands rest on the bottom curve of the steering wheel. After a while, I got out and walked over to the Doggie Diner on the corner of University and Elm. The place was empty. A strong smell of Clorox came wafting up from the floor. The young man behind the counter had a thin ring in his eyebrow; he had an enormous Adam's apple.

"What'll it be, sir?"

"I'll have a burger and fries," I said, swinging my rump onto one of the red revolving seats.

"Grill doesn't open till six," he said apologetically, looking over his shoulder at the empty grill behind his back.

"Pretty temperamental, your grill?" I asked. "Doesn't like frying up a burger unless there's a crowd?"

"It's that the owner doesn't want me working the grill by myself."

"You're right," I said. "Frying up a burger's definitely a two-man job. Let me have a tuna on toast, then."

The young man shrugged his thin shoulders again.

I said: "What, you need a couple of guys for that too? One guy scoops out the tuna, the other guy holds out the toast?"

"It's not that. It's that something sort of fell into the tuna."

"It's probably the guy supposed to work the grill."

"I think it's still down there at the bottom somewhere. I mean I'll make you the sandwich if you still want. I just thought you should know and all."

"I'll pass," I said. I pointed to the Lucite pastry container on the counter. "How long those crullers been sitting there?"

"A week? Maybe a little less. Five days? They're really for decoration."

I told the kid I'd pass on *everything* but black coffee.

After a while, I wandered back toward the rest room and dropped a quarter into the pay phone and punched the number into Shaboo's pager. No more than five minutes later, the phone began to ring.

"That'll be for me," I told the kid.

"The owner doesn't allow anyone to use the phone for business."

"It's probably Stockholm calling," I said. "Your boss'll be thrilled."

I let the phone ring a few more times and then slid off my stool.

"Yo," said a thin tenor voice. "Who this?"

"It's Nelson Mandela. I'm in town to talk about paying off Miriam Plumbeck's note."

Whoever was answering the telephone paused to collect his thoughts. There didn't seem much to collect.

"How come you paying off her note?"

"Government wants to show its appreciation. A lot of people in Berkeley divested, Miriam Plumbeck, she divested more than anyone else. Paying off her drug dealer's least we can do."

"You disrespectin' me?"

"Does it *sound* like I'm disrespecting you?"

"Don't know what it sound like. *Who* you say you was?"

"Nelson Mandela."

"And you talking about this white bitch? You some guy wants to pay off her note?"

"Me and Winnie," I said. "Thing is, though, I'll have to speak to Shaboo himself."

"You got the money with you?"

"No."

"Then why you think my man he want to talk to you?"

"Talking to me's the *only* way he's going to see the money."

"I'll get back to you," he said. "You be at this number?"

"Sure. It's the Presidential Suite over at the Doggie Diner."

When I returned to the counter, the kid looked at me expectantly.

"It *was* Stockholm," I said. "I've won the Nobel Peace Prize."

I didn't feel conspicuous standing there on the mean streets of east Oakland, no more conspicuous than a nudist at a fashion show. I eased my back and trudged up the walkway toward the front door. Someone had left a child's red Schwinn lying carelessly on the walkway. I stepped over the bicycle and knocked heavily.

A large square woman opened the door with a tremendous jerk and glared at me. "What you want?"

"I need to see Shaboo," I said.

"You the po-lice, he ain't here."

"I'm his portfolio adviser."

"You got an appointment? Everybody say they got an appointment, he don't say nothing about no appointment to me."

"Do I look like I'd show up here *without* an appointment?"

The large square woman looked at me with some amusement glinting in her steady brown eyes. "Don't suppose you would," she said.

She shifted her bulk against the door frame to allow me to squeeze past her; she was wearing a strong perfume and smelled of lilac and cooking oil.

The house was one of those old-fashioned jobs that people put up in Oakland in the early part of the century. It had looked decrepit from the outside, but these houses have a lot of ruin built into them. The circular foyer just behind the door was almost the size of a small room. I stood there for a moment, admiring the ornate wet-plaster fixtures in the ceiling and on the walls.

"Shaboo, he in the back probably with one of his Muslim ho's," said Ms. Hospitality. "You get to the back of the house yourself or you figure on getting catched up by the bogeyman?"

I said I'd manage and set off down the long hallway that exited from the foyer. Whoever had designed the house one hundred or so years ago must have been haunted by the immensity of the wilderness they had crossed to reach California. There was absolutely nothing open about the place. The ceiling of the hallway was low. No natural light. The doors leading off the dark hallway were locked, but you could sense that the rooms behind them were small and protected.

I reached the end of the hallway, which abutted at the perpendicular onto another hallway. A young boy of no more than ten or so came charging down one of the arms of the perpendicular; he was running a toy red car along the wall and making roaring noises. He stopped when he saw me standing there.

"You the Devilman?" he finally asked.

"That's me," I said.

The child edged against the wall and stood there. Just then, a tall handsome woman dressed in Moslem robes opened one of the doors that led onto the hallway with her hip; she was carrying a laundry basket heaped with clothes. "What you doin' here?" she asked the child. "You supposed to be watchin' TV front of the house."

"He said he the Devilman," the child said reproachfully, still shrinking against the wall.

"He white, he the Devil on account of he white," said the woman, adjusting her robe slightly with her free hand.

Turning to me, she said: "What you want?" But she said it in a soft melodious voice.

"I've got an appointment, see Shaboo."

"He in the back working."

I shrugged apologetically. "I can't seem to find the back."

"Big old house. I get someone take you there." She lifted her leonine head and shouted: "Girl, you come over here."

Another of the hallway doors opened. A very young and very pregnant girl dressed in Moslem robes walked softly toward us.

"Girl, you take—what you say your name was?"

"I didn't. It's Asherfeld."

"You take Mr. Ashefeller on back see Shaboo. And don't you be lollygagging with the others when I come back. You got laundry to do."

The young woman lowered her eyes and nodded. I followed her swaying hips down the hallway and up a short flight of stairs to another hallway. The whole house held the warm somewhat dirty smell of women and children.

Shaboo's office was at the end of yet another hallway and down a full flight of stairs.

I knocked on the handsome old oak door and let myself in softly.

Shaboo was sitting at a large oak desk; he was staring at a computer screen. He was dressed in a flowing red dashiki, one that seemed to hang on his wiry body, and he wore a series of braided gold chains around his neck. He had let his hair grow out into a wild profusion of curls. He wore frameless gold spectacles, fastened together by an elaborately plaited lanyard; and he carried gold and onyx rings on almost every finger. He lifted his head from the screen to peer at me over his spectacles.

"Aaron Asherfeld."

"I know'd you wasn't Nelson Mandela." He inclined me to an old-fashioned plush chair by tilting his head. The room was small and close and windowless, the only light coming from a black stand-up lamp. I eased myself into the chair and stretched my legs out in front of me. Shaboo turned from me to resume looking at his computer screen. "Can't find my old data files," he said sourly.

I must have arched my eyebrows skeptically.

"I use Quicken," Shaboo said with great dignity. "Just like everybody else."

The door opened by a fraction and a light-skinned woman poked her intricately braided head into the room, saw that Shaboo was in conference, and closed the door immediately.

"Lot of women out there," I said.

"They ain't women. They my wives."

"Wives?"

"Koran says a man can take four wives."

"You believe everything you read, Shaboo?"

"Used to."

"You're sitting here with four wives, how many children?"

"Be ten this summer. And four dogs. Don't want to forget them neither."

"No *wonder* you're selling drugs."

"Yeah, well, sometime Allah He ain't as merciful He cracked up to be."

"I guess."

Shaboo adjusted himself in his chair so that a barely perceptible wave of tension spread through his body. "Ain't no one say you could call me Shaboo."

"What should I call you?"

"You call me *Mr.* Shaboo, same as everyone else come here wants something from me."

"You sure that'll be enough? I don't want to miss a point of protocol."

Shaboo scowled briefly and then relaxed. "You say your name *Asherfeld?"*

I nodded.

Shaboo nodded knowingly. "Husband, *he* sent you. Doesn't have the balls come over here hisself."

"You're right," I said. "Or maybe he just doesn't have the time."

"You got the time, though. You one white dude got all the time in the world. You here just *burning* up the time."

"You're wrong," I said. "I don't have the time either. Miriam Plumbeck needs to have her account cleared. How much you willing to settle for?"

"Settle? Did I hear that Jew-word 'settle'?"

"That's what you heard, all right."

Shaboo looked balefully at me. He got up gracefully and opened the heavy door to his study and shouted "Yo" into the corridor beyond.

Directly, two large men filed into the room; they carried the smell of beer and pretzels and cigarettes with them. Shaboo waved them over with a suave and practiced roll of his head. They had evidently been playing pool. It was obvious that they had spent most of the day drinking. They stood beside his chair on either side, holding pool cues, weaving slightly.

"Asherfeld," he said, "I tell these boys to bite the head off'n a chicken, they going to bite the head off'n a chicken. You can figure out what they likely to do to your little lady."

He looked up toward the man standing at his left. "That right?" he said carelessly.

The large dark man looked dubious. "Bite the head off'n a chicken?" he said uncertainly. "You mean a *live* chicken, cluckin' and all?"

Shaboo looked up in consternation. "Course I mean a live chicken. What be the point in biting the head off a dead chicken? Chicken's dead ain't got no head anyway."

"You wrong there, boss," said the other large dark muscular man, who was now swaying unsteadily on his feet. "Lots of them dead chickens still got their heads."

"Those not chickens," said the first man. "Them's more 'n likely turkeys or gooses."

Shaboo turned in his seat to look first at one and then at the other of the drunken men flanking his chair.

I tapped a finger on my watch face. "Guys," I said. "We could be here all day discussing poultry."

"You right there," said the man to Shaboo's left. Turning to Shaboo, he asked: "You need me for anything more, boss?"

Shaboo looked up and waved his men away. When they had left the room, he put his head theatrically into his hands.

"I know how it is," I said. "Those guys probably eat more than a pair of Dobermans."

"I tell the Dobermans bite someone on the ass least off they go an' bite someone on the ass." Shaboo sighed again. "Never mind what they say, Asherfeld. I tell them, they gonna lean on your lady real good."

"You're wrong."

"How'm I wrong?"

"She's not my lady and they're not going to lean on her."

"White man ain't about to stop them," he sneered. "Especially white man like you."

"Me? I'm not going to *do* anything. You're the one'll figure things out, decide it isn't worth the hassle."

"Why'm I about to do that?"

"You're too intelligent to take on a hysterical white woman." I watched Shaboo swell with pride at being called intelligent; I didn't mind extending the flattery. I figured it was true.

"Hysterical is right," Shaboo said. "I tell her I wants my money and right away she's boohooing her eyes out."

"Sounds like Miriam Plumbeck," I said. "Listen, you got a family, lot of little drug dealers out there to support. Last thing you need is a well-connected white woman in Berkeley telling the police that you threatened to peddle her white ass."

"Skinny white ass like that, ain't no one gonna buy a piece of that."

"Could be, Shaboo, but who the police going to believe? You or the owner of that skinny white ass?"

Shaboo required a moment to appreciate my remarks. Then he said: "You're right, Asherfeld, I give you that. Black man tries to run an honest business, he gets it comin' and goin'."

"Swell speech, Shaboo, only you're not trying to run an honest business. You're out here peddling drugs."

Shaboo looked at me in consternation. "Nothin' dishonest about that," he said. "Ain't no one told anyone they got to sit at home and stuff anything up their nose."

Shaboo released another long sigh and slipped his thumb underneath one of the gold chains around his neck. "What'll your man give me on the dollar?"

"It's not my call," I said. "I'll see what I can do, have him get back to you."

"Whatever it is," Shaboo said bleakly, "I'm gonna lose money."

"Could be."

"You get a choice, someone be asking you whether you rather be black or white, don't say black."

"I'm not about to."

Shaboo nodded his head again. Then he said: "Suppose you'll be wanting taxi take you back to Berkeley."

"You don't think I'm going to *walk* through east Oakland?"

Shaboo got up heavily from his chair. "I'll take you out front," he said. "Can't get no yellow cab come out here. See if I can get you a gypsy."

When we were out on the street, Shaboo watched me slide into the front seat of a decrepit Chevrolet gypsy cab. I slammed the door shut and then rolled down the window. Shaboo looked into the car.

He said: "Say hello to Winnie, Mr. President."

Scheming

I DROVE BACK to San Francisco in the late afternoon. The fog had already collected over the bay, leaving only the tops of the Golden Gate Bridge visible from the Bay Bridge, the rust-colored towers glowing in the sunlight that streamed over the heavy wet air. I got back to Greenwich Street in time to watch the local news. After a while, I stripped off my clothes and took a long shower. No matter what time of day you take a shower, you never feel worse for having taken it. I toweled off in the hall, leaving a puddle at my feet. One of my wives had always been adamant about drying off in the bathroom. We had very expensive hardwood floors. The architect had ordered them cut in an elaborate herringbone pattern, with light and dark wood alternating. "Asher," my wife had said in that tone of voice that suggested she was calling attention to child molestation, "please, not on the floor, please." Now I toweled off where I wanted; the floor never seemed to mind.

I got dressed in a pair of baggy shorts and an old sweatshirt. Then

I called Plumbeck and let him know what his ex had been up to.

"You're telling me fifty thousand dollars went up her nose, Asher?"

"I don't know where it went. It's what she told me."

Plumbeck sighed theatrically to give me a sense of his burden in life. "I don't pay, what are the chances they'll be using Miriam for Handi Wipes some crack house over in east Oakland?"

"What are the chances? Probably zero."

"What are you telling me, Asher? These people are always killing each other, every day you read about the police how they found some drug dealer in a dumpster or something."

"It's intramural," I said. "White woman they pretty much figure it's not worth the trouble."

"This is something you *know,* Asher, or something you're just telling me?"

"Professional judgment," I said.

We let it go at that. I felt for Plumbeck. He had crossed the line between being generous and being foolish; he knew it and he didn't know how to step back over.

A couple of days went by. The weather turned golden the way it sometimes does in early summer in San Francisco. The days opened without fog and the air was still, calm, clear and bright. Elderly Chinese women came to St. Mary's park in the late morning to sit on the splintery wooden benches and let the sun bake their arthritic joints. The Maudit across from the park set up tables on the sidewalk and served latte and double espressos to the thin women who lived in the sleek condos on top of Telegraph Hill. In the late afternoon, teenagers would chase one another up the flanks of the hill, the girls shrieking in the warm golden sunshine.

A firm in Bend, Oregon, had asked me to find out whether there would be a demand in San Francisco for Bend, Oregon, loganberry juice. It seems that loganberries had all sorts of striking virtues. "This could be very big, Mr. Asherfeld," the director of marketing had told me on the telephone. They had sent me a sample of their stuff. It tasted sweet and bitter all at once. I wouldn't have used it to dress a wound. The chains wouldn't touch the stuff, but I found a few specialty stores willing to take the gloop on consignment. When I had finished up with my report a few days later, the fog had come back.

It was late in the afternoon. The fog had been rolling up Greenwich Street since almost two o'clock, sending cold wet fingers up the street and over the top of Telegraph Hill. The telephone rang.

"You've heard," Irene Ergenweiler said in her urgent this-can't-wait-a-minute voice.

"Heard what, Irene?"

"You *haven't* heard? Where have you been, Asher?"

"I've been trekking in the Himalayas, Irene. You know that."

"Very funny. Just put on your TV and watch the news, not Dan Rather, the local news with that woman whose hair looks like it's been lacquered? Call me back right away, as soon as it's over."

It was a minute or two before five; I caught the woman whose hair looked as if it had been lacquered just as she was midway through a trailer for the news. She stared earnestly into the camera, her pudgy co-anchor by her side, nodding like an imbecile. She finished up her trailer and said: "Another Bay Area firm rocked by sexual-harassment charges, that story coming up."

The Imbecile turned and said: "They never learn, do they?"

I sat through a string of commercials and then the news itself came on. They like to do a lot of self-promotion in San Francisco when it comes to local news. They've got an award-winning team in place just to tell you how the gay and lesbian community feels about these terrifically important local issues like unisex toilets. The lead story was all about a shooting in Orinda in which a seventy-eight-year-old woman managed to disarm a burglary suspect one-third her age and shoot him in the buttocks. The film clip caught her crowing into the camera, her speech a rich stream of profanity, excised at every turn by the network. Finally, Lacquer Hair turned directly to the camera and said: "A twenty-four-year-old administrative assistant at the upscale firm of Plumbeck and Ergenweiler is claiming today that she was set up in a posh apartment and forced to serve as the firm's mistress."

The camera panned to a still photograph of Alicia; she looked radiant as she smiled her gorgeous smile. The Imbecile allowed himself to lift his eyebrows in a tic of appreciation. Then he took over the story from Lacquer Head. It was pretty much the same story that Plumbeck had told me, except that it was told from the perspective of a woman who had been brought to realize how badly she had been used and figured that all that pain and suffering was worth at least seven million dollars.

The tight take on the Imbecile dissolved and Lacquer Head said: "An exclusive interview with Alicia Tamaroff—next!"

I muted the TV for the five commercials that followed and picked up the sound as the screen opened up on the little garden behind Maxine Stuntvesal's house in Marin. I recognized it right away. Stuntvesal was standing there; Capo Titus was behind her. Alicia was sitting on an iron chair by a white metal table. She had on large dark glasses and she was wearing an elegant silk scarf over her thick blond hair. She looked like a movie star hiding from her fans.

Stuntvesal made sure that the world knew how tough it had been for Alicia, servicing an entire firm of uncaring men up there on Russian Hill; she had a lot to say, but no one at the studio was much interested in having her say it. The camera kept drifting off to Alicia, who sat there on the bench twisting her hands in her lap.

When Stuntvesal paused for breath, the camera drew in tight on Alicia. The thin spidery woman who was supposed to be conducting the interview touched the remote in her ear and then thrust the microphone toward Alicia's face.

"How are you taking it all?" she asked sympathetically, as if the harassment were already a foregone conclusion.

"I really just want to put this behind me," Alicia said. There was a kind of brush-soft accent to her voice.

"You're saying you want to put it behind you?" the Spider-Woman asked.

"I need get on with my life."

I wasn't certain, but it *sounded* as if Alicia had made a mistake in English grammar.

The interview went on for another few seconds. The whole thing was sordid and corrupt and cheap, but it was also the sort of thing that anyone with an IQ of more than fifty might have anticipated.

"Can you *believe* it, Asher?" Irene Ergenweiler asked when I called her back. *"Seven million dollars.* The *gall* of that woman thinking that what she had was worth *seven million dollars."*

"It's pretty galling, Irene," I said. "Knesterman in on this?"

"Oh, Mr. High and Mighty this is too too sordid for my delicate sensibilities knows all about it. He was the one that told Eddie this afternoon what was coming down."

"He probably told the boys they were going to have to post a bond to keep him in the picture."

"Can you *imagine?* Seybold Knesterman *offended.* Knesterman! It's all we need. First that *insane* business with Maison Jarr and now this, this bimbo just throwing mud at everyone. *Why,* Asher? Why would a person *do* something like that? I mean no one *forced* her to take those charge accounts and live up there and like pretend it was nineteen thirty-five. How am I going to look anyone in the eye ever again? It's so unfair."

"Irene," I said, "trust me on this. Your friends will think you're fascinating. The tennis pro over at the club'll probably slot you in for ten free lessons."

Irene Ergenweiler snurfled a wet angry snurfle into the telephone.

Then I said: "The boys have decent liability, you know?"

There was a long dreadful pause. "That's the worst, Asher," Irene said. "Just the minimum. If they lose a court case, it's all coming out of their pocket. We'll be ruined. That's all there is to it."

I said: "I'm sorry." I had nothing else to say.

A Russian Beauty

GEARY BOULEVARD GOES from the heart of downtown San Francisco out to the Pacific at Land's End. No part of the avenue looks like the Champs-Elysées. It's a big, wide, open boulevard with a straggly weed-covered divider running down the middle. The sides of the street are lined with banks and discount bedding stores and places to have film developed in two hours and lumber-yards and small, smelly pizza parlors and a lot of Chinese and Vietnamese restaurants. The farther out you go, the colder, wetter, and foggier the avenue gets. Close into town, the upscale side streets are named after trees. Young brokers move there before they can afford the move to Pacific Heights; but out where the avenue is bisected by streets with numbers instead of names, the side streets are filled with small pink and white stucco houses, places where immigrants live on their first stop after Ho Chi Minh City.

I sat in the back of the Geary Avenue bus and watched the avenue roll by in the fog. I like this part of town. I like the cold hard utilitarian light that sifts over the streets. I like the way the fog keeps things dark when the rest of northern California is blazing with light. I like the way the somber evergreens in the park above the avenue have all been bent over by the wind. The place still feels like a city, not a boutique. The markets sell stuff someone actually needs. No one worries much about their image. No one ever hits the streets in running shorts to huff and puff their way through six miles; no one glides into the stores on in-line skates.

The Russian community starts somewhere around Thirty-fifth Street, close to the ocean. The light has a glinting quality, despite the fog. The smell of salt and the sea is in the air. San Francisco has always had a Russian community. A handful of refugees from the revolution made it out here in the twenties. Some of them spent their lives dreaming of Odessa and counting out the tiny diamonds they smuggled out of Russia in their underwear; others never gave up being aristocratic and discovered that they could get by in San Francisco just by being snooty. During the Brezhnev era, a lot of tough, determined Russian immigrants took one look at Brighton Beach in New York and figured anything had to be better than that. They took over the pink and white stucco houses on the side streets and made sure that the bakeries sold Russian bread. They spent a lot of time complaining about what a cheap soulless city San Francisco was. Now the place is filled with Russians who are just beginning to figure out that San Francisco is a better place to live than Minsk.

I got off at Thirty-second and walked past a Russian bakery, catching the heavy smell of fresh bread. I could see that the woman behind the counter had beefy red forearms and a tough squeezed-together face. She stood there somberly as I walked by.

I didn't know just what I was looking for, but it didn't hurt to look. I kept walking down Geary, past a hardware store selling Russian military medals and past a grim little sandwich shop with a lot of unappetizing blintzes mounted in the window.

The city's largest Russian Orthodox church is on Thirty-eighth. It's a real Russian church, with narrow white clapboard siding and an onion dome covered in gold foil. The windows are all stained darkly, in cut purple and rose glass. The façade is actually finished in some sort of glinting mosaic; the attenuated saints are composed of tiny colored circles. They seemed to wink and shine in the brilliant late afternoon sun.

A little glass-covered bulletin board mounted on the wall of the church indicated that a miracle worker from Shanghai named Troubetskoy was scheduled to work a few miracles that evening. It said that Father Ephriam Zozima would conduct evening services afterward.

The worn marble steps were divided by a polished brass banister. I walked up them, letting my hand trail over the cool of the brass, and stepped into the back of the sanctuary. Afternoon services had been concluded; it was too early for vespers. Except for one or two heavyset women kneeling at pews at the front of the church, the large room was empty. The place was dark and spooky and somber, the wooden walls old and the decorative white plaster pillars streaked, as if someone had run their fingers down through the fluting. The stiff little statues mounted on wall pedestals looked as if they had been carved by someone without a firm grasp of perspective; they were covered with gilt. A heavy smell of incense drifted in the air. From far away, some part of the Orthodox liturgy was being chanted. It must have been a recording. When I looked up to the nave, no one was there.

At the side of the church, a staircase turned in a spiral away from the main floor. The sign at the bottom of the steps said Refectory. The staircase turned in a half circle and ended suddenly on a black wooden door. I knocked with the back of my hand so that the rap sounded as dull as possible.

"Da?"

"I'd like a word with the Father."

A young boy of no more than twelve opened the door; he was dressed in a silk cassock and surplice. His cheeks were blazing like two cherries. Behind him, I could see Father Zozima, sitting at his desk. The boy asked me something in rapid-fire Russian. I shrugged my shoulders.

"The Holy Father speaks no English."

Father Zozima got up from his desk and shambled over to me. He had a full white beard stretching almost to his chest. He seemed immensely old, almost prehistoric, his face deeply lined. He looked at me curiously. He was smoking what I could see was an unfiltered cigarette, holding the cigarette upward in the Russian style between his thumb and forefinger. A powerful reek of stale cigarette smoke and decay enveloped him. He volleyed something in Russian to the boy.

"The Father asks if you're a believer?"

I shook my head.

Father Zozima continued to look at me curiously. His study was low-ceilinged, the walls paneled in heavy wood stained almost black by the close cigarette smoke. Zozima shambled back to his desk and resumed his seat.

He waved me toward him. *"Da?"*

"I'm looking for someone. I thought you might help."

"The Father says that many people seek but that only the Church gives men sight to see."

Zozima smiled, revealing a set of blackened stumpy teeth. He reached over to pat the top of my hand.

"I'm looking for a *person*. I've got all the spiritual satisfaction I can handle."

Zozima's face took on a faint brittle edge; the warm fuzzy glow disappeared from his eyes.

"Who is it you are looking for, the Father asks?"

"A woman. An especially beautiful young woman."

"The Father inquires if perhaps you have come to the wrong place? This is a church."

"I know it is."

Zozima sat there, looking at me with his smoke-reddened eyes.

"Why you are pursuing this thing?"

"It's what I do. People pay me to find things."

"And do you? Find things? The Father asks."

"Sometimes."

"The Father says you should be a fisher of souls, not women."

"Tell the Father that I'm looking for this woman to protect her soul."

"Protect her soul from what?"

"Vanity."

Zozima nodded as if it all made sense to him.

"The Father says that it is very difficult to protect the souls of beautiful women."

"I know."

"Impossible, maybe."

"He's probably right. Tell the Father he's probably right."

"He says that beauty is the devil's snare."

"Absolutely."

Zozima nodded again and then said something abruptly to the boy. "You may check the register of the church."

The two of them watched me edge out of the dark little room, the bearded Zozima and the boy with blazing cheeks.

I spent an hour looking through the register in a windowless dusty little room in the basement of the church. The names were written in Cyrillic, but someone had added a Roman transliteration underneath each name. No Tamaroff had been born in any of the years between 1965 and 1975; no Tamaroff had died during those years either.

I put the heavy cloth-bound books back on the shelves and slapped the dust from my jacket.

Then I started checking the confirmation records for 1979 to 1983, the years when Alicia might have been twelve. The first two years were a wash. The confirmation records were written entirely in Cyrillic, but in 1981, the church had added small snapshots to each page of the records. I found Alicia staring out of the last volume I had taken from the shelves. The other children whose photographs lay on the page were still childlike, with children's ringed wreaths of baby fat about their face. Alicia stared out from her picture, the full force of her beauty visible already at twelve, her cheekbones flared, eyes already almond-shaped and wide and staring, and her twelve-year-old lips large and lustrous and lovely. She had worn her hair demurely for her confirmation photograph, the top cut in bangs, but there was simply no mistaking her face. I put the book underneath my arm and trudged up the steps to the lobby that ran from the church bookstore to the sanctuary itself.

The main entrance to the bookstore was out on the street, but a pair of glass doors let on to the back of the store. It was half-light inside, the only illumination coming from badly streaked windows.

A disheveled priest in a black cassock stopped shelving dusty books behind the counter to regard me with suspicion. I thought he might be put out because I had come through the back doors. He said something in Russian. I spread out my hands. He nodded comprehendingly.

"Something I can help you with?" he asked in perfect English. He seemed to have been put together from layers of pudgy flesh: everything about him was soft. I noticed that his cassock was actually held together at the waist by a length of brown rope.

"I'm interested in the lives of the saints."

The priest looked at me with a steady derisive expression in his dark black eyes.

"I do not think so."

I put down Alicia's confirmation picture. "What about her?"

"Etta krassavitza," said the priest, slipping into Russian. "She is a beauty."

"You tell me who she is?"

"No, I cannot."

"I mean just tell me her name," I said, pointing to the Cyrillic letters.

"I am unable to read Russian," said the priest imperturbably; he drew his head back as if he were concerned to maximize the distance between us.

"Must be a real problem, your line of work," I said. The books behind him all had Russian titles.

"Not at all," said the priest.

I tucked the volume underneath my arm and walked out the glass doors and crossed over to the vestibule of the church. I stood there for a while, feeling the dense atmosphere of the place, the light gathering in a dust-filled space high above the church floor. Just before it emptied into the street, the vestibule gave out onto a little alcove. A stout red-faced woman stood there behind a card table carrying pictures of various saints.

"Do you speak English?"

"Da," she said energetically.

I showed her Alicia's photograph and asked her to transliterate the name from the Cyrillic. She beamed with pleasure. "Iss Vybotskaya." She looked slyly at me. "So pretty."

The afternoon had gone by the time I got through putting the confirmation records back in place; long strands of fog had advanced down Geary Boulevard, giving the storefront windows a washed-out look, as if someone had emptied the color from a picture. I walked east for a few blocks, away from the ocean, feeling the immensity of all that water at my back. At Twenty-ninth or so I stopped in a little restaurant called Bunin's. It wasn't much—just a counter with a row of counter stools and a few booths against the wall—but I was hungry and it didn't seem any worse than any other place I might have gone in the late afternoon. The place had an old comfortable smell of fried onions and cabbage.

I eased myself onto one of the revolving seats. The small man in a white shirt who had been soaping glasses in the iron sink wiped his hands delicately on a clean towel in a curiously surgeon-like gesture; he nodded precisely to me, his clipped pointed beard jerking downward.

I ordered a burger and fries. "Chum fries," said the little man. "Bread, no rull."

"Whatever."

I watched him cook; he had the deft movements of someone used to working with his hands. The food was pretty good, though. The potatoes were cut with onions and green peppers, and the burger was a large slab of well-done beef mounted on a thick-cut slice of what was obviously homemade bread, the taste of yeast still pungent.

"Pretty good," I said.

"Of cawse," said the little man, "I train sixteen years to be cook."

"And look how it paid off."

He looked at me closely for a moment.

"So what do you really do? With all that training, I mean?"

"I am doctor," he said sadly, pointing to his chest.

"Can't make a go of it here?"

"No," he said decisively, wiping the counter behind the plate with a damp towel. "Everytink fency, fency machines, fency tests, only fency tinks." He shrugged his thin shoulders eloquently.

"You could go back?"

"Nawbudy go back."

I nodded: "Leaving is forever."

"Whad you know?" he asked bitterly. "Sometime in afternoon, I stend and watch fawg. My life, stending and watch fawg."

"It could be worse."

The little man stopped wiping the counter and fixed me with an unavoidable stare. For a long moment, he said nothing. "How?" he finally asked. "How could be worse?"

I finished up my meal in silence and slid off my stool and looked through the telephone books that were mounted on a steel platform underneath the pay telephone.

There were three Vybotskayas in the San Francisco directory, but only one lived in the Sunset. The woman who answered the telephone answered with an enthusiastic *Da* followed by a gabble of Russian.

I cupped the receiver with my hand and motioned Bunin over, pantomiming translation by looking perplexed and forming a talking mouth with my fingers. It's tough to do without a language.

Bunin took the receiver from me and introduced himself; he

spoke calmly, with a kind of hauteur that I could hear without understanding what he was saying. He held up his finger and looked at me.

"Tell her I need to speak with her daughter."

There was a complicated exchange and then Bunin turned toward me: "She asks if you Meester Teetus?"

"Exactly."

"She work tonight," Bunin translated. "Already at clob."

"Where?"

"Where? Where always."

"Tell her I forgot the address."

Bunin listened alertly and then said: "She no know, somewhere Broadway. Big clob, fency, like always."

"That's fine," I said. "I remember now. Tell her thanks."

I had coffee at Bunin's and watched Bunin clean the counter with his deft precise strokes and tried to imagine what San Francisco must look like to someone from another world.

"Iss like Odessa," Bunin said, reading my thoughts, "only in Odessa, no fawg."

Sorrows of the Night

CENTERFOLDS WAS an upscale strip club in North Beach. It featured good food and a lot of glitzy decor and very pretty women who wandered around in low-cut dresses making small talk with Japanese businessmen. It opened after the last of the topless bars closed in North Beach. Everyone said it would be a flop. Everyone was wrong.

I got there at a little past eight. The big tough-looking maître d' standing at the reservation desk looked at me appraisingly.

"Monsieur will be dining with us tonight?"

"I don't know about Monsieur," I said, "I plan on sitting by the bar."

The maître d' nodded severely. "As you wish," he said. "The

cover is twenty dollars." He motioned me to a young woman standing behind a glass counter.

I paid my twenty dollars and walked up to the horseshoe bar. Two women were onstage, dancing their way through a set that involved a lot of fancy action with a fire pole. One woman would wrap her long lovely limbs around the fire pole and slide languorously up and down the thing while the other woman would stand on the stage and try to sway in time with the music, popping her fingers with the beat. Then they would switch off. After a while, they left off climbing up and down the fire pole and got down on their hands and knees in a position calculated to suggest a cat stretching. They were both very young and very pretty in the kind of way that shows you what a difference there is between being very pretty and being beautiful.

I ordered a vodka Collins from the bartender and sipped it as I looked over the lounge. I didn't much want to drink anything but I figured an order for diet Coke wouldn't be terrifically appreciated. Almost all of the tables were filled with men trying to eat huge steak and lobster dinners without missing any of the action onstage. There were young women everywhere, all of them dressed in long black evening gowns held up by spaghetti straps and corny white gloves—the kind that were popular in the fifties. Some of them were elegant and had elegant high cheekbones and fine hair and some of them looked fragile and lost and some of them were hefty and looked like they worked out a lot, but they were easy to look at and they all looked like the kind of girl you could take home at two in the morning without having the neighbors call the vice squad.

The two women onstage finished up their set with a flourish that involved removing their brassieres simultaneously; covering their bare breasts childishly with their hands, they scampered from the stage. Soft wispy music replaced the driving beat on the stereo; the harsh stage spots dimmed and the room filled with a soft muzzy light. It was all pretty slick.

A young woman with large caterpillar eyebrows and deep fine brown eyes came up to me and said, "Hi."

I said hi right back.

She asked me what my name was and where I was from and what I did for a living—all the hopelessly canned questions that girls at bars ask before asking someone to buy them a drink or take them home.

"Would you like to dance?"

I smiled and shook my head. "I don't dance," I said. "Not since high school."

"No, silly. *I* do the dancing. *You* get to watch. It's very private and very, very stimulating." She licked her dry red lips to show me how stimulating things were going to be.

"I don't think so."

She was obviously someone's pampered baby, doing time at Centerfolds to make money for a trip to Florence or to cover the down payment on a new fire-engine red Miata. For a moment she looked at me in astonishment.

"Why'd you come here then?" she asked in a tone of voice a small step from incredulity.

"To escape the sorrows of the night."

"That is so poetic," she said happily. "Is it like *from* somewhere? I mean it sounds like it's from Maya Angelou or somebody."

"No, I made it up all by myself."

"That is so outstanding."

My little speech rekindled her enthusiasm for dancing. She said: "Oh please, you've got to come watch me dance."

"Not tonight, honey."

A triplet of Japanese businessmen settled themselves into a booth at the side of the room. She caught their eye or maybe they caught hers. "Got to go," she said instantly, slithering off her bar stool and leaving behind some sense of confident youthfulness.

I ordered another vodka Collins and sat with my back pressed against the smooth railing of the bar. A tall cocoa-colored woman who had been keeping a trio of men company at the far side of the room wriggled out from her side of the banquette and smoothed down her tight dress. She had a show-girl figure, a tremendous sense of herself. Swaying slightly, she walked directly over to the bar, and leaned her elbows on the countertop so I could appreciate her cleavage. She had incredibly fine flawless skin and well-made fleshy lips. It was hard to avoid looking. She caught my look and transferred herself from the edge of the bar to the stool next to mine. She gave off a dense complex smell of soap and shampoo and perfume and beyond that of something thrilling.

"I love dancing for men," she said, just slightly slurring her words; she was drunker than she seemed.

"Lot of men out there love having you dance."

"But not you?"

"Not me, not tonight."

"It's because you're afraid to see a proud African woman dance."

"That must be it."

"You don't have to be like that. My father was Swiss."

"I'm sorry," I said, sipping from my drink.

"I know your kind," she said.

The bartender caught the slurring in her voice and nodded down toward the steps in that vague minatory way bartenders have of nodding. In a moment, the maître d' had swum up from his station. He took her drink and said something crisply to her in French. She looked at him contemptuously for a moment and then shrugged her beautiful round shoulders. "No one," she said, enunciating her words carefully, "appreciates a proud African woman." She walked from the bar with dignity, rounding the horseshoe and exiting by the side door.

"I am sorry about that," said the maître d'. "She should to know better."

"It doesn't bother me," I said. "A woman that good-looking can do whatever she wants."

"The maître d' looked at me inquisitively. "You want that I make the arrangement for you?" he asked.

I shook my head.

"Because if you are inclined, I can arrange the thing."

"It's a swell offer. Some other time."

"As you wish."

At a little past nine o'clock Alicia came into the lounge from a side door. She stood there at the back of the room not three feet from me and lit a cigarette. She had the same high forehead, the same mass of disorganized blond hair; the same warm rosy flush to her skin as the girl I had seen at Plumbeck's office. She had the same shocking presence, that ability some women have to dominate the very space they occupy.

Only she wasn't Alicia.

Her face retained some purely human irregularity, a kind of narrowness that made her eyes seem set together and her nose too long. She was taller than Alicia and thinner, without Alicia's overpowering voluptuousness. She *was* a striking, well-put-together woman, but Alicia had been a great beauty.

She caught my look, stubbed her cigarette into the sand-filled standing ashtray by her side, and with a kind of shrug calculated to suggest reinvigoration, walked over to the bar where I was sitting.

"You shouldn't drink alone like that," she said. "It give ulcers."

"You're probably right. Have a drink with me. That way we can drink to my health and your career."

She ordered a gimlet from the bartender.

"Prost," she said, lifting her glass.

"Whatever."

"So Mr. Whatever, you have name too?"

"Aaron Asherfeld."

She held out her hand; it felt firm and shapely in my palm.

"And you."

"Tiffany," she said.

"Nice Russian name."

She lifted her eyebrows in mock astonishment. "How you know I Russian?"

"It's your soulful Slavic look."

"What you know, Aaron Asherfeld?" she asked. "What you know from soul?"

"Why don't I tell you what I know someplace a little more private?"

Tiffany lifted her eyebrows up in a feigned gesture of astonishment. "I like how you think, Aaron Asherfeld," she said. "Is twenty dollars for fifteen minutes, one hundred for hour. You like hour, I think. Maybe we drink champagne, talk about soul, other things maybe."

"Let's start with fifteen minutes."

She shrugged her shapely shoulders and slid off the bar stool, motioning me to follow with a nod of her head. She led me around the back of the lounge and out the side door from which she had entered the room. The corridor beyond had three fire-engine red doors. Tiffany withdrew a small key from her bosom and unlocked the first door.

The room beyond had something like a low bunk bed against the far wall; a large mirror was mounted above the bed.

Tiffany switched the light by the door, suffusing the room with a red strobe light.

"What kind of music you like, Aaron Asherfeld?"

"Your choice."

For a moment she fumbled with the controls of the stereo system that was built into the wall by the door. Ravel's *Bolero* came pulsing softly into the room.

"Make comfortable on bed," she said; she couldn't get the edge out of her voice. She probably didn't realize she had it.

I sat down heavily, my upper shoulders leaning against the wall. Tiffany perched herself at the very edge of the bed and dropping her blond head forward slipped a spaghetti strap from her shoulders. She was about to stand. I put my hand on her bare warm shoulder.

"I'm not here to watch you dance," I said.

She turned to look at me.

"What you here for, baby?" she asked. "What you think you here for?"

"The truth."

I hadn't taken my hand from her shoulder.

"What kind truth you want?" She ended her question with a seductive sigh.

"Why are you pretending to be someone else? That kind of truth."

She swiveled her head to look directly at me; I dropped my hand from her shoulder.

"Who tell you I somebawdy else?"

"It doesn't matter. I know. I'm not here to frighten you."

She stood up abruptly. "I no have time for games," she said, stabbing at a red panic button beneath the light switch on the door.

There was a heavy muffled tread outside the door and then the door swung open. The club bouncer stood there in the doorway, a large gorilla dressed in a black silk suit and a white silk turtleneck sweater.

"Trouble?" he said sourly, looking at the two of us.

"Not for me," I said, standing heavily. Tiffany moved over to the mirror and began running a brush indignantly through her fluffy blond hair.

"I think maybe you made a mistake about where you think you are," said the gorilla. "We don't appreciate sexual harassment here. This is a caring environment."

"Sure," I said. "Anyone could tell that right away."

The maître d' who'd been so happy to make an arrangement swam silently up to the gorilla's shoulder and looked into the little room.

"*Ça va,* Carl," he said. "Call the gentleman a taxi. He'll be leaving us as soon as he settles his bill."

I took a half step toward Tiffany's back. "This isn't Odessa, Tiffany. You don't know the rules of the game here. You may think you do, but you don't."

Carl stepped directly into the room and put a heavy hand on my shoulder, digging his fat thumb into the tissue under the muscle. "I don't think you heard the man, dufus," he said. "You're leaving."

"I heard the man and I *am* leaving, but if you don't take your thumb out of my shoulder I'm going to tell the world that this really *isn't* a caring environment after all."

Tiffany snorted into the mirror.

The gorilla and the maître d' escorted me to the front desk and watched as I paid my bill. I put the tab on my American Express and when the chit cleared they both drifted away. I took a twenty from my wallet and wrote *AA* on the margin, together with my telephone number. "You'll make sure this gets to Tiffany," I said to the girl manning the desk.

"Whatever," she said, taking the bill and tucking it into her décolletage.

Basque Food

I TOOK MY DINNER later that night in an old-fashioned Basque restaurant on the corner of Broadway and Montgomery. The place had been old when I had first arrived in San Francisco; now it was older still, with ruined paint on the walls and deep cracks in the faded leather of the banquettes. The owners really were Basque. They stood behind the counter gabbling to themselves in their harsh incomprehensible language; they were both of them very old but not decrepit. They did all the heavy work in the restaurant by themselves, the old woman cooking in the back from four in the afternoon till well after midnight, and the old man emerging from the kitchen carrying a full tray of food, wheezing as he struggled, his legs bowed out.

Neither of them could speak a word of English. Dishes on the menu were written in Basque and English. When someone ordered in English, the old man could just about guess at the meaning; and when someone tried to pronounce the Basque, he would snatch the menu away in disgust, muttering as he departed for the kitchen. The food was simple and the prices hadn't changed much in ten years. You got a salad with dinner, and a carafe of red wine. The bread was chewy. Dessert was always the same—some sort of custard.

Neither of the owners had ever bothered to learn my name, but after five years, the old man nodded to me when I came into the restaurant.

I had the chicken with rice, and when I had finished, I mopped the thick brown sauce up with the chewy bread and drank a second glass of the coarse red Spanish wine.

The high June sun had set an hour before I started climbing the Montgomery street steps up the slope of Telegraph Hill, but the night was clear and the western sky was shot through with pinks the color of peeled peaches and a lot of deep purple. It was a terrific night. Walking up the hill, I could smell the deep disturbing fragrance of the night flowers that were opening up their petals to the evening air. Here and there, a few people had turned on their living room lights. I could see a dark-haired woman in one room, bending low to light a purple candle. For a moment, I wondered what it would be like coming home to her, having her hold my head in her long-fingered hands. I thought it might be wonderful, but I didn't want to do anything to make it happen.

I got back to Greenwich Street at a little past eleven; the fabulous pinks and peaches had gone from the sky, but there was still that deep purple left. We get that sometimes in summer. I collected my mail and trudged upstairs; inside, I opened up the living room windows to let in the smell of the little garden underneath the window, that and the smell of the sea.

I got myself comfortable on the couch, with the remote lying on my chest, but I must have dozed off. When the telephone rang, the television was off.

"Aaron Asherfeld," said someone I recognized as Tiffany right away, "I want thank you for twenty dollars. Iss very nice."

"Don't mention it."

"No, I think maybe we have drink and talking."

"Now?"

"Why not now, Aaron Asherfeld?"

I couldn't think of a reason why not now; I told her where I lived and how to get there; I told her not to make a racket coming up the steps.

It was a little after three in the morning when the downstairs buzzer rang; something should have warned me that it was an odd hour for a social call, but the sort of things that are supposed to warn you generally don't. I buzzed the buzzer, punched up the pillows on my living room couch, and splashed some Old Spice on my face.

When I opened the door, Tiffany was standing there. She wasn't alone. The man standing next to her was about forty or so. He wasn't much taller than Tiffany, but he looked mean and he looked tough. He had thinning sandy hair and a boxer's face, the nose smashed down the center and flattened. His skin was coarse and thick. I didn't think he'd even register an ordinary punch. He was wearing a black leather jacket and standing there with his hands thrust into its pockets.

I stood there by the door and for a moment looked at the two of them. Tiffany put her hand on my chest and pushed me into my own apartment. She closed the door behind her.

"Aaron Asherfeld," she said. "This my bradder, Yuri. He has something for you."

Tiffany's brother extracted an old-fashioned blackjack from his leather jacket pocket—the kind with a flexible handle wrapped in tape. He looked at me appraisingly and said something in Russian to Tiffany.

"My bradder says you to mind own busyness."

I looked again at the man's tough, creased face; his eyes were far away.

"It isn't any good, Tiffany. He used it up long ago."

"Why you call me that name?" she suddenly exploded. "My name Tatiana. You want speak to me, you call me Tatiana. What my bradder use up?"

I motioned the two of them into the apartment and pointed to the couch. They both sat down; Tatiana's brother kept smacking his blackjack into his palm but I didn't think his heart was in it.

"Your brother used up whatever it was that let him hurt people, Tatiana."

"How you know that?" she cried out indignantly. "You no mind your busyness, you see how he hurt people." She brushed away a tear furiously. "You see," she said.

"It's not something I want to see," I said. "And it's not something you want to show me."

"Why you doing this think? You know noffink about what happen."

I was about to say something, but all at once Tatiana's brother dropped his blackjack to the floor; his face collapsed in on itself, the cheeks hollowing themselves out. He opened his mouth soundlessly. Then he howled.

Tatiana looked at him speechlessly. He lumbered to his feet and walked directly to my living room wall and placed his hands at shoulder height on the wall; he began to beat his head on the wall with enough force to make the room itself shake. As he struck his own head, he kept right on howling.

It was terrifying to watch.

Almost immediately, the Dutch sisters at the other end of the building began banging on the walls of their apartment; and directly thereafter, the one dog in the building, a large, balding, fearful Rottweiler named Diane, began to howl in sympathy.

"Christ, Tatiana, he's going to wake the entire neighborhood."

Tatiana moved to her brother's side and put her arms across his shoulders, talking to him in a brisk, soothing tone of voice, as if she were addressing a child.

All at once he left off banging his head against my wall and lashed out against Tatiana with a flat open-handed slap that sent her reeling backward almost across the room. She stood there speechless by the far wall, her face already reddening; her brother resumed methodically banging his head against the wall. His forehead was covered with blood.

I picked up the blackjack from in front of the couch. Tatiana saw what I was doing and screamed, "No hurt him." I didn't see how anything I could do would hurt as much as what he was doing to himself. I got behind him in one step, and as he rocked backward, clubbed him on the base of his neck with the blackjack. He stiffened and crashed down onto the floor. Tatiana screamed again. The Dutch sisters raised their banging to a crescendo; the building dog howled. But when they heard that the banging had stopped in my apartment, the sisters left off banging and after a few more halfhearted howls, the dog stopped too.

My wall was completely streaked with blood. Someone was now knocking on my apartment door; with the bloody blackjack in my hand, I lumbered over to the door and opened it. It was the Chairman, the building's Chinese owner who lived in the first-floor flat. He stood there, his face impassive but his eyes red-rimmed.

He immediately entered a volley of glottal Chinese into the apartment. Tatiana had regained her feet and came storming over to the door, responding to the Chairman's Chinese with an explosion of indignant Russian. She pointed to her brother and swung her index finger to her cheek. The Chairman continued to remonstrate in fluent Mandarin.

Just then one of the Dutch sisters came paddling down the hall in her bathrobe and slippers, her thin hair in old-fashioned iron curlers; she was smoking a clove cigarette. Stabbing at the Chairman's chest with her own bony forefinger, she addressed him in Dutch.

The Chairman stopped his tirade and turned to look at the woman who was now lecturing him. It must have been daunting: two women were addressing him in two languages he could not understand. He looked uncertainly at both and then pantomimed placing a telephone call. "Po-ice," he said as clearly as he could without the use of the letter *l*.

Tatiana said: "You want police I call police." She turned to look for my telephone, but her brother had by now risen to his knees, his head lolling from side to side, and within an instant began vomiting copiously on both my hardwood floor and the margins of my Rya area rug. That was enough to clear the hallway. Alarmed no doubt at even the *thought* of being asked to help clean up, the Dutch sister spun on her heel and with a parting shot in Dutch retreated to her apartment. The Chairman looked uncertainly at the mess inside my apartment and said something that may actually have involved one or two imitation English words. Diane, the building Rottweiler, took the occasion to resume her howling.

I closed the door and leaned against the frame. Having emptied his stomach, Tatiana's brother had managed to seize a pillow from the couch and slide it under his vomit-tinged mouth; he seemed now to be sleeping rather than unconscious. He was snoring peacefully.

Tatiana stood there, her face still red. She surveyed the scene.

Then she placed her long-fingered hands on her hips and chuckled. "He come back from Afghanistan," she said, "something not right here." She pointed in her own temple.

I said: "I guess."

At the Silver Pissoir

SEYBOLD KNESTERMAN STOOD GRAVELY by his silver and porcelain urinal and tried to urinate. I stood by the elaborate French imitation sink and waited for him to begin. The partners at Knesterman's firm all had their own washroom, with ornate urinals, their names carved in silver above the bowl, and elaborate sinks and even a small redwood sauna. It didn't do much good for Knesterman: he stood there waiting.

"Prostate giving you trouble, Knesterman?" I said.

"It's the size of a cantelope, Asherfeld, and of course it's giving me trouble.

Just then Knesterman's flabby stream started; he rocked back a little on his heels and stared into the wall above the silver fixture on his urinal.

"You don't think that having your name mounted on a urinal is just a bit tasteless, do you, Knesterman?"

"Not at all, Asherfeld," said Knesterman happily, luxuriating in actually being able to relieve himself. "Which reminds me," he said, "this business with that grotesque lawsuit isn't going to make our job any easier this afternoon."

"You mean the harassment thing?"

"Harassment," Knesterman sniffed, shaking his member. "A grown woman allowed herself to be set up in an apartment and now she's claiming she was harassed. What is this world coming to? There are dozens of women in this city who would be delighted to accept such an arrangement, Asherfeld. We both know that. This isn't a legal issue, it's a shakedown, pure and simple."

Knesterman finished up at his silver urinal and rearranged himself. Then he pushed his cuffed sleeves upward on his thin wrists and delicately washed his hands.

"You think they'll settle?"

"*Of course* they'll settle, Asherfeld. I've already gotten a call from counsel."

Knesterman slid a silver panel above his sink to the side to reveal a row of colognes in fancy glass bottles. He opened one, shook a few drops of cologne onto his palm, and began effetely patting his cheeks.

"Must take a lot of discipline to live this way, Knesterman."

"A good deal," Knesterman agreed. "What worries me, though, is what they're asking."

"What do you mean? I thought they were asking seven million."

"That's the figure they entered. But they have no intention of going to trial, Asherfeld, you know that. Ergenweiler and Plumbeck are a partnership. They have as much chance of paying off a judgment as, oh I don't know, you do."

"Then what's bothering you, Knesterman? Offer them what the insurance will carry."

"Ultimately, I intend to. Right now their opening figure is two point five million. Of course, Marvin Plumbeck simply doesn't have that kind of money. I don't know that *I* could raise it."

"For sure, Knesterman," I said. "If he had that kind of money, you'd have first dibs."

"Yes," said Knesterman gravely, "there is that."

"What'll his insurance pay?"

"Possibly half that amount if he stipulates to harassment."

"So what's the problem?"

"The problem, Asherfeld, is that Marvin Plumbeck will never stipulate to harassment."

After straightening his starched cuffs and checking the seam of his trousers to make sure he hadn't dribbled, Knesterman prepared to resume his schedule. He swung open the door to his private bathroom with grave courtesy, motioning me to precede him, and walked down the hallway toward his office like an ocean liner approaching port.

Eddie and Irene Ergenweiler were waiting for us in Knesterman's office. Eddie was standing by Knesterman's library; he had taken a leather-bound volume from the shelves. He held the book cradled in his left hand and was flipping the pages with his index finger; he was chewing gum in a furious preoccupied way. Irene Ergenweiler was sitting in one of the two formal leather chairs that

Knesterman had facing his desk. She was dressed in a ribbed sweater and tight-fitting designer jeans. Her tense face was tightly drawn. She had put too much lipstick on her lips. It made her mouth look like a wound, the lips themselves red and fleshy.

Knesterman bustled into his office, nodding to Eddie Ergenweiler and pausing before Irene to offer her his hand. Then he took his seat behind his immaculate desk. I nodded to Eddie and Irene and sat on the expensive French oak bench beside the door, resting my elbows on my knees.

Knesterman fastened Eddie Ergenweiler with a disapproving stare. "Put the book away, Eddie," Irene Ergenweiler said. For a moment, Eddie Ergenweiler looked startled, as if he couldn't quite figure out the direction of the room's sympathetic currents. He closed the book and rubbed the spine gently on his suit jacket sleeve to remove his fingerprint smudges; then he put the thing back on the shelf. I could see that the book was part of a set—*Great Naval Battles of Antiquity.*

"I didn't know you were interested in naval battles, Knesterman," he said.

"They're first editions," said Knesterman, as if that explained everything. "Quite rare."

Ergenweiler nodded comprehensively. Irene Ergenweiler tried discreetly to tap the face of her elegant Movado wristwatch with the reddened nail of her index finger in order to remind Eddie that Knesterman billed by the hour; I saw the gesture and so did Knesterman, who frowned with displeasure.

"Let's cut to the chase, Seybold," said Irene.

Knesterman regarded Irene with a vacant milky look. "You *have* seen today's issue of *The Investor's Target,* Irene?"

Irene Ergenweiler shook her head, her dark features suffusing themselves with blood; she was preparing for a blow.

"What about it?" Eddie Ergenweiler asked.

Knesterman picked up his white telephone and said: "Bring in three copies of the *Target,* Frieda."

Within seconds, Frieda came flowing into the room like a cold wind; she handed a copy of the newspaper to Irene and Eddie. The newspapers had already been folded to Itchak Bupkiss's column, the column head circled with red Magic Marker. I noticed that the copy of the newspaper she placed before Knesterman had been ironed; it lay perfectly flat on his walnut desk.

"Will you be needing your own copy, Mr. Asherfeld?" Frieda asked.

I shook my head. "I'll just sort of do a mind-meld with Knesterman over there, Frieda."

I had already read Bupkiss's column. I said: "You got the time, maybe you could do a couple of shirt collars for me, though."

Frieda snorted through her thin compressed lips. She looked inquisitively at Knesterman and then stalked from the office. Eddie and Irene bowed their heads over their newspapers. Eddie Ergenweiler finished first; he looked up and groaned theatrically.

"What does it mean, Eddie?" Irene asked, the paper lying in her lap.

I got up and walked over to the back of Irene's chair and picked up her copy of the paper. " 'Unbilled receivables boost Maison Jarr revenues,' " I read aloud. "It means that Itchak Bupkiss kind of figured that someone made a fifteen-million-dollar company look like a twenty-five-million-dollar company by shady accounting."

"But this stuff is old," Eddie Ergenweiler said, flapping his arms in consternation, working the gum vigorously in his mouth. "It's just a rehash of the indictment, failure of due diligence, this, that, the other thing. It's totally Mickey Mouse."

"Eddie," said Irene Ergenweiler carefully, "this is different." She tapped the paper with the tip of her nail.

"How's it different?"

"This is *public,* Eddie. It's going to affect the price of the stock."

"I've already had a call from Armstrong Hrska," said Knesterman gravely. "I do have some influence with the boy, but he was simply adamant about this. It is a very serious matter."

"What are you saying, Knesterman?" Eddie Ergenweiler asked.

I straightened up behind Irene's chair. "He's saying that if you have any plans to save your ass you'd better use them now."

Irene Ergenweiler crossed her legs and wrapped her arms around her knees. She stared at the worn red oriental carpet in front of her. "What do *you* think we should do, Seybold? I don't even know *what* to think anymore."

"I'm afraid I don't think you have many options. A full disclosure, a very substantial fine, perhaps even a suspension of the firm's license. It's the only way."

"The only way, Knesterman?" Eddie exploded. "What happened to the slap on the wrist, pay a little fine, the whole thing goes away? I mean a week ago it was like hey Eddie mellow out, pay a little fine upfront, it's the cost of doing business."

"It's not an option anymore, Eddie," I said. "Knesterman's right. Somehow this thing went public. Stock's going to drop like a hot potato. The SEC finds out there was even a suggestion of accounting impropriety you could be looking at criminal charges."

"I *knew* it wouldn't work out. Didn't I say it wouldn't work out, Irene? I mean we're talking George Raft here, only the guys asking protection are working for the government."

"You were right about that, Eddie."

"So what are you telling me my options are?"

"You can tough it out," I said, "in which case you get to pay Knesterman here every penny in your 401K and in the end you're going to lose in federal court anyway."

Irene said: "Maybe they really should fight it out to the bitter end. That way Eddie at least he can sleep at night."

Knesterman shook his head as if Irene's unwillingness to face facts were personally distressing him.

"Give it up, Irene," I said. "It's over."

"How can you be so sure, Asher?" Irene asked plaintively.

"I don't know how a 10Q got screwed up," I said. "I don't really want to know. The fact is it did get screwed up. I know it, you know it, and now everyone with a dollar to buy *The Investor's Target* knows it. A week ago, if Eddie over here acted quick as a mouse, he might have gotten away with it. Now it's too late."

"It's not *fair,* Asher," Eddie wailed.

"Lot of things aren't fair. This is one of them. I'm telling you as one of your friends, do what Knesterman says. Take the hit. You can rebuild your career. You can't come back from jail time, even if they suspend your sentence."

Irene Ergenweiler lifted her face to look at me directly. I thought I could see the white scars by her ears where the surgeon had tightened her skin. "One of our *friends?"* she said.

Knesterman coughed decorously. "Whatever you decide, it ought to be decided quickly," he said. The cough was his signal that the meeting was at an end.

The three of us left Knesterman's office together. In the hallway facing the elevator, Eddie placed his wadded-up chewing gum in a piece of paper he fished from his pocket; pretending that the silver ashtray was a basket, he hooked the chewing gum over his head. It fell to the floor.

"Typical," he said, picking it up. Irene looked at him fondly, as if to suggest that no one that childish could be capable of doing anything really reprehensible.

We rode down together in the elevator. Irene stared straight ahead at the door and Eddie looked up at the ceiling, rotating his head.

When the elevator stopped, Eddie bounded out and executed an imaginary jump shot in the plaza. "Eddie," Irene said.

Ergenweiler managed to contain his twitching feet until we reached the building's revolving glass doors. Irene swung through the door but Eddie halted the turnstile before swinging through himself.

"You know how Bupkiss comes up with this stuff, Asher?"

"No idea. He's probably got a lot of contacts."

"You think?"

Eddie Ergenweiler stood there for a moment, his wife on the other side of the revolving glass door. He seemed lost in thought.

The day after Bupkiss's article appeared, Maison Jarr's stock dropped by half its value. It had been offered at 10 and had climbed to 24½ within six months of its public offering. By the end of the week it stood at a little under 4.

Firestorm

NO ONE EVER CALLS at two in the morning to tell you that you've won a million dollars, and no one ever calls you at two in the morning to tell you that the operation was a success.

I had lain in bed for a long time, listening to the foghorns sound out on the bay and feeling the damp summer fog come sliding into the city from far away.

Then I drifted off into one of those confusing dreams in which my wives began exchanging their identities so that one woman's habit of clanking her fork against her teeth attached itself confusingly to another woman's small red mouth.

I had just finished surveying the scene and was about to slam a dream-door shut in disgust, when the telephone rang.

I picked up the cool Princess. "Asher, it's me. Please, please, please don't hang up."

"Miriam? It's two in the morning. What's the matter? Discover that fat *isn't* a feminist issue?"

"Asher, I'm so frightened I'm peeing in my pants. He's trying to kill me."

I sat up and tried to rub the sleepiness from my eyes.

"Who?"

"Who do you *think?*" Miriam exploded. "I *told* you he wanted his money. I *told* you he was going to do something terrible to me. I *told* you and you wouldn't listen."

Miriam Plumbeck was a hysterical woman under the best of circumstances, but now she was becoming dangerously unhinged.

"What's he doing, Miriam?"

"He keeps calling, he's like calling me every fifteen minutes, he just says *bitch* into the telephone in this snarly voice. Asher, it is *so* scary."

"Take the phone off the hook."

"That's even scarier, Asher, then I have no way to call anyone."

"Miriam, listen to me. Call the police."

"I *did* call the police. Don't you think that's the first thing I did?"

"What'd they say?"

"They said they couldn't do anything. It's what they always say."

"Who'd you speak to?"

"The desk sergeant."

I hoisted myself up into a sitting position.

"Asher, please, can you come out here and stay the night, please? Tell me you'll come out here, Asher, please. I'm begging you."

It wouldn't have done a lot of good saying no to her and I didn't try.

I called the police in Berkeley before I even got out of bed. The night clerk put me through to the desk sergeant right away. "I understand your concern," he said, "but calling a woman up and saying *bitch* isn't a crime."

He paused for an awkward moment.

"It should be, though," he added handsomely.

"Could you at least send a sector car over to the house, Sergeant, just show the flashing red lights?"

"Sure," he said affably, "I have a sector car in the neighborhood. I'll have them cruise on by."

I got up and trundled into the bathroom and splashed cold water on my face and tried to brush my hair. It didn't do much good. I dressed myself in the same clothes I had taken off an hour ago; then I rubbed some toothpaste over my teeth just to cut the night taste in my mouth. I collected my keys and my blue windbreaker and turned off the lights in the bathroom. Just before I left my apartment, I called Miriam in Berkeley. I wanted to let her know about the sector car.

The telephone rang and rang and rang. Miriam never answered.

There's not much traffic in the city at two in the morning. I whipped around the Embarcadero without stopping once. The Bay Bridge was almost empty. I got to Berkeley in under fifteen minutes and took Ashby off the freeway; I could see revolving red lights pulsing in the night sky even before I turned on Milvia.

There were two fire trucks parked in front of Miriam's house: a big hook and ladder and a smaller dispatch truck. The police department's sector car was pulled in front of the fire engine, its revolving light flashing. The street was already full of people, standing there gawking, the women with their arms folded somberly across their chests, a few teenagers, a couple of squat-looking Latino types just in from the late shift. The fire was pretty much over. Miriam's house was blackened on one side and it looked like the roof was gone. A couple of firemen were manning one of those big two-man hoses and sending a stream of water on the sides of the house, which were still smoldering. I parked on the diagonal in someone's driveway and walked over to the fire chief standing in front of the lead truck.

"Tell me what happened, Chief?"

The chief pushed his slanted helmet back on his head; he had an enormous creased, tired face, with soot-blackened eyebrows and red eyes. He stopped entering ticks on the form he had mounted on a clipboard and looked at me.

"Now what do *you* think happened here, fellah?" he asked. "You got a hook and ladder over there and a whole bunch of guys shooting water at a house and a lot of smoke still coming up from the house and this is a tough proposition for you?"

"Forget I asked. We need an interview, we'll ask the cops."

A look of alertness creased the chief's tough features. "Hey, no offense. Why didn't you tell me you was with the media?"

"You didn't ask."

"When you're right, you're right. Color me insensitive. So what can I do you for?"

"Tell me about the woman lives here, she hurt?"

"Smoke inhalation," the chief said professionally, "lot of superficial burns on her butt, the reason being she tried to put the fire out herself, some second-degree burns, she'll be all right."

The chief removed his helmet to show me his fine head of iron gray hair.

"Where's she at now?"

"Over at University hospital on Shattuck."

"Any idea what happened here, Chief?"

"We're definitely treating this as a suspicious occurrence," said the chief, nodding gravely.

I thanked the chief for his time and told him to wait for the camera crew; I told him they were stuck in traffic. He was still standing there by his truck nodding affably when I got back into my car.

I got to University Hospital just as the bells on the Berkeley campus were tolling three in the morning. Serious cases they take over to the huge county hospital in Oakland; here in Berkeley, University hospital takes in the druggies, and the kids who overdose, and the girls who forget to say no and are hoping they can say rape.

The fluorescent lights threw an evil glow over the ambulance port, where two green ambulances were parked, waiting patiently for the action to begin.

There was no one at the reception desk inside the main lobby; I was about to reach over and help myself to the telephone when someone shouted, "Asher."

It was Marvin Plumbeck. He came hustling on over to me, carrying a burnt smell with him.

"Jesus, you are a bud," he said; he shook my hand and put his other hand on my shoulder. "Can you believe this? Can you absolutely unbelievable believe this?"

"You see Miriam, Plumbeck?" I asked, steering him to the empty wooden bench in front of the reception desk.

"I just got down. They're scraping skin from her behind, Christ only knows why she thought'd be a good idea to sit on the fire. She'll be all right. She's still groggy. Hell of a close call, though. Let me tell you Asher, she came this close to losing it."

Plumbeck held up his thumb and forefinger to show me. He sat down heavily on the bench and held his head in his hands. I put my hand on his shoulder. "Asher," he said, "she came this close." A series of sobs sent his chest into spasms. After a while, he stopped sobbing. He pulled a clean handkerchief from his pocket and blew his nose noisily. Then he looked up at me.

"Asher," he said. "This shit has got to end. You go out there to wherever this slimeball lives, tell him *I'll* pay him whatever he wants, just lay off Miriam. You understand what I'm saying? He wants fifty thousand, check is in the mail. This is too heavy for me."

For a moment, I stood there like that. Then I said: "How'd you know about the fire, Plumbeck?"

"Police called me, Asher," he said. "Miriam had my phone number in her purse." Then the same thought occurred to Plumbeck. "What about you, Asher?"

"Miriam called me. Told me she was spooked, asked me to come over."

"Good old Asherfeld," said Plumbeck, "always a bud."

Business Call

SPEAKING ON THE TELEPHONE, Elbert Trudelwein sounded the way all policemen sound: he sounded tired and he sounded suspicious. He called me at home the day after Miriam Plumbeck's house was firebombed.

"You don't mind," he said, "we'd kind of like to take a statement from you, get your fix on what happened."

"I mind," I said. "It's not going to do me any good, is it?"

"Your call," he said. "It's a free country."

"Lieutenant, I don't give you a statement, all that's going to happen is that two weeks from now I'll get a supoena."

"Make it easy on yourself, then. Talk to us now."

I sighed heavily into the telephone. "Any chance you could come here, save me a trip?"

"Sure," said Trudelwein agreeably. "Actually, we're parked in front of your house, be up in two minutes, maybe less."

They were knocking heavily at my front door in thirty seconds, two large, shopworn men. Trudelwein must have been a few years past sixty. He had a full head of gray hair and a sheepdog face that looked as if it were constructed in layers and a great ruined mesomorphic physique.

"You Asherfeld? This here's Detective Swentin Swoboda."

He motioned me to his partner. Swoboda was half Trudelwein's age; he wore his brown hair cut short. He looked trim and fit. He extended his hand for me to grasp, taking the opportunity to look over my shoulder into my apartment.

"Good place to grow a lot of drugs here," he said, letting go of my hand and more or less sliding by me to enter my apartment. "Now that you got some serious federal heat coming down, lot of freaks grow pot inside. You know that, Aaron?"

Trudelwein had followed him in, leaving me by my own door; the two men gave the impression of filling the whole of my living room.

"That a fact?" said Trudelwein; he was looking over the books on the shelves I had mounted over my desk.

"You got your freak, he's in the rack, all he has to do is reach out grab some hemp, he's lit."

I said: "You got welfare mothers selling their babies for crack cocaine and you guys are still worried about horticulture? Get real."

"Drug's illegal," said Trudelwein. "What's wrong is wrong. Wouldn't you say what's wrong is wrong, Detective?"

"Absolutely, I'd say what's wrong is wrong." Swoboda was looking out my living room window, peering into the little garden down below. "Course a garden like that, probably grow poppies there you want to. Wouldn't you say that'd be a terrific place grow poppies, El? Man could satisfy a serious habit little garden like that."

I sat myself down on my desk chair and put my feet up on my desk.

"What is it? You guys take the House and Garden training over there on the force and want to show me how much you learned? You can't make heroin from *California* poppies."

"This any good?" Trudelwein asked equitably, ignoring my question. He had taken a volume from my shelf; a client had sent it to me in the mail. It was entitled *Rediscovering the Light*.

"It's a hard read," I said. "No pictures."

Swoboda had turned from the window. "You making snotty remarks to my partner over here, Aaron? That your style?"

Trudelwein put the volume back on the shelf upside down. "I'd hate to think you were making snotty remarks, Aaron. It would get our relationship off on the wrong foot. Isn't that a fact, Detective? Man gets his relationship off on the wrong foot with us, hard to get straight again."

"I'd say it be pretty near impossible," said Swoboda, leaning his trim hip on my windowsill. He was playing with the venetian blind cord, batting it aimlessly with the back of his hand.

"Our relationship, now that's a real worry to me, guys. I'll tell you what *would* make me feel we were working through a lot of stuff that's making us all sort of tense."

"What's that, Aaron?" asked Trudelwein.

"You ask your questions and haul yourselves out of here in five minutes. You want to poke through my books, come back with a warrant."

"Touchy," said Swoboda; he was still batting at the cord. "Wouldn't you say that Aaron is touchy?"

"Very definitely touchy. Course, it could be that time of month. Is that your problem, Aaron? Hormones got you out of sorts?"

I didn't say anything; I didn't have anything to say and I wouldn't have said it if I had.

"Now that you're all through making snotty remarks, Aaron, you want to tell us how come you were out in Berkeley just after suspicious fire breaks out?"

"Miriam Plumbeck's a friend of mine. She called me, asked me to come out."

"Pretty upset, was she?" Trudelwein asked.

"Hysterical. Of course, that might have been because she just got through talking with you and figured a Doberman be better protection than the Berkeley police."

Swoboda said: "You go out there, you figure this is your lucky night, Aaron? Woman's frightened, little of the old in and out?"

"Man's blushing," said Trudelwein. "Pay dirt. Wouldn't you say we hit pay dirt?"

"Exactly, Lieutenant. Big-time pay dirt."

"Only by the time you're out there, she changes her mind, one thing leads to another, you're out there on the streets, you figure *hey* this isn't right."

"Not right at all."

"That the way it went down, Aaron?"

"Sounds like the way it went down to me, Detective."

I said: "You guys are out of your minds."

"Not what we hear, Aaron. What we hear, we hear you got a serious craving."

"Like a sugar addiction, Aaron. Wouldn't you say it's like a sugar addiction, Detective?"

"Exactly like a sugar addiction."

"Eat a lot of Froot Loops, Aaron? Don't feel right in the morning until you get that sugar high?"

"Miriam Plumbeck called me at *this* number, two in the morning. Phone company'll have a record of the call. By the time I got to Berkeley, the fire was over."

"We got you talking to the fire chief three-oh-seven, Aaron. Man's busy putting out a fire, tells us you show up talking snotty to him. What is it with you and uniforms, Aaron?"

"It's a definite thing, Aaron and uniforms, wouldn't you say, Detective?

"Definitely, I'd say definitely. Aaron here wasn't so busy taking care of business with Miriam Plumbeck, I'd say definitely there's something kinky."

"You do a lot of serious freakiness, Aaron?" said Swoboda, still batting the venetian cord aimlessly.

"Thing is, Aaron," said Trudelwein, "you got more than a sixty-five-minute window of opportunity, get yourself dressed, splash on some after-shave, and haul your sorry ass out to Berkeley. No traffic that time of night."

"No traffic at all. You're probably in Berkeley no more than twenty minutes. Leaves you plenty of time to strike out, you know what I mean?"

I got up heavily from my chair and walked over to the hall closet and took my blue windbreaker from its hanger.

"Going somewhere, Aaron?" asked Trudelwein.

"Me? I'm going out."

Trudelwein and Swoboda both tensed slightly.

"No one said we were through, Aaron."

"No one has to. You guys aren't even in your own jurisdiction.

You got a complaint to make, file it with the DA. You can help yourself to a couple of beers. I see your car in front when I get back, I'll file for trespassing."

"No need to get touchy, Aaron."

"Absolutely, no need. We were just leaving," said Trudelwein. Then he said: "Aaron, you know it's a crime to lie to the police. You know that, don't you, Aaron?"

I shook my head. "In Bulgaria, maybe. Not in this country."

Trudelwein didn't miss a beat. "Maybe you're right, Aaron. Maybe it's not a crime. It's definitely not a good idea."

"Not a good idea at all," said Swoboda, the two large men seeming to flow together as they left my apartment.

Backside in the Air

THE WEATHER TURNED COOL at the beginning of the week. All over the city, flags were flapping in the stiff wind that blew in from the ocean. Tourists in Bermuda shorts and T-shirts hugged themselves as the wind whipped across their bare legs and thin arms. It wasn't cold, but it was cool enough to confuse people from the East who thought of summer in terms of barbecues and hot hazy humid days.

"I really thought I missed the seasons," my dentist once said. "I grew up in Boston, you know."

I waited in the chair, my mouth full of hardware, and tried to encourage my dentist to get on with it by making a glugging noise.

He held up his diamond-tipped drill meditatively. "Just last month, I went back for a conference on periodontal disease, wouldn't you know, and it was unbearable."

I tried to glug sympathetically. I had never been back but I thought it would be unbearable, too.

I spent the next few days at the San Francisco airport, trying to find out what happened to a shipment of extra-large women's running shoes for an importer named Borge. He had only just set up shop in the Bay Area; he still spoke with a Danish accent. The running shoes had been shipped from Thailand; they had never arrived in San Francisco. I checked the main cargo terminals. Nothing. The shoes had disappeared.

"Looks like the fatties won't be running on these shoes, Borge," I told him.

"Ja, ja," he said indifferently; his stuff was covered by insurance and he didn't seem too worried. "Maybe you try Oakland?" he added as an afterthought.

It was something I should have thought of myself. Oakland gets almost as many of the big cargo flights as San Francisco. I gave myself the afternoon to check the main hangers; I figured I'd check on Miriam Plumbeck before I did anything else.

I drove out to Berkeley with the driver's side window wide open and listened to a fruity therapist named Wendy give her callers grief. She did a lot of on-the-air diagnoses. She had a low seductive voice. She said "I hear where you're coming from" a lot. She was about as perceptive as a waterfall.

I parked in a splash of sunshine outside the hospital. The place had the languid feel a lot of hospitals get when the real emergency stuff goes somewhere else. Except for a few stiff old parties sitting on a wooden bench, the reception area was empty. No one was running a gurney down the hall; no interns were beating on anyone's chest. A nurse waddled across the reception area, carrying a clipboard.

"Know where I can find the burn ward?" I asked.

"Burn ward? Burn ward? We got no burn ward here. Someone tell you we got a burn ward here? Over County, *they* got a burn ward."

I finally found Miriam in a private room on a ward that was supposed to handle cardiac patients. She was lying on her stomach on one of those special beds that break in the middle. Her rear end was hoisted into the air. The skin on her behind had been covered with something that looked like tissue paper; I could see that underneath it had been blackened. She was hooked up to an IV by her left wrist.

"Asher," she said, her voice muffled by her pillow. "It's so sweet of you to come."

I pulled up a chair and tried to sit so that I wouldn't be facing her blackened behind. "How you feeling, Miriam?" I said.

"It hurts," she said in a faraway spaced-out voice; she was pretty doped up.

I patted her shoulder awkwardly. She reached her hand from underneath the sheet and put it over my hand. "A week ago someone wanted to peddle my white ass, Asher," she said. "Look at it now."

"I'm sure it'll heal."

"Scars," she said vaguely; she really was pretty spacey from the painkillers.

"You remember what happened?"

She curled her hand over her shoulder so that she could actually slip her hand in mine.

"I heard something bang into the house, next thing I knew, boom, there was this explosion and all."

She ruffled her face into her pillow as if she were wiping her nose.

"How'd you manage to *sit* on the fire, Miriam?"

"I don't know," she said sleepily, "pretty silly, I guess."

Then in a cool clear focused voice, she said: "Marvin saved my life, Asher."

I sat by the side of the bed holding her hand; I didn't say anything.

"He hates me, Asher. I knew he was angry, Shaboo, but I never thought he hated me, but he does. He really does."

I could feel the tension and the anger begin to rise in her. She reached her left hand from the sheet and depressed a little plastic button that ran up to the IV drip. "Demerol," she said. "I'm self-medicating. Can you believe?" The drug hit almost at once, relaxing her body and washing away the tension.

"Go easy on that stuff, Miriam."

"Why?" she asked dreamily. "It's so nice."

Her breathing became regular. I thought she might have fallen asleep, so I disengaged my hand from hers and stood up carefully.

From someplace far away, Miriam Plumbeck said: "You know what I think?"

I waited to hear what she thought, but she didn't say anything more.

"Get some sleep, Miriam. I'll come out again in a couple of days."

She made a muffled noise into the pillow. I tiptoed from the room. I was glad to get out of there.

I found Borge's shipment of extra-large women's sneakers at the Oakland airport. They must have gotten lost somewhere in Southeast Asia. The transit tickets showed that they had been seized by customs in Singapore and Hong Kong before being routed to Oakland. It was like the Flying Dutchman: a cargo of fat women's shoes making its mournful way from port to port.

I had dinner at the airport's hot dog stand, washing down two franks with a root beer soda, and afterward I killed an hour playing video games so I wouldn't have to kill an hour sitting in traffic. I got back to Greenwich Street just after ten. One of my wives had left one of her sad and lonely messages on my machine. She had thought that anything would be better than being married; now she thought that anything would be better than being single. "Asher," she said, "you have no idea what jerks there are out there."

Marvin Plumbeck had left a message. I called him back, waking him up. He sounded confused and tired.

"Do Fior d'Italia tomorrow night?" he asked.

I told him that'd be fine; I told him to go back to sleep. Then I caught the late news and afterward I stood by my living room window watching what would have been the bay if I could have seen anything. I thought of the thousands of fish out there, living their own lives, happy to feel the cool waters swish along their silvery backs.

An Old Italian Restaurant

THE WAITERS ALL HAVE silvery hair at the Fior d'Italia, that and terrific manners. They glide over to your table; they never tell you their name. They manage to look bored and attentive all at once. It's the oldest Italian restaurant up in North Beach, a great smoky place, with soot-covered ceilings, and a lot of pictures of old-fashioned baseball players on the walls. It's the sort of place that caters to the *other* San Francisco, the one home to prosperous undertakers and men who made a fortune dealing in plumbing fixtures and drywall and women with tendon-ruined necks and smoke-thickened raspy voices; dentists with a practice out in Forest Knolls come here on the weekends and so do a couple of minor league baseball players who managed to spend years on Telegraph Hill living off a small portfolio and whatever they could make gambling.

Plumbeck and I had both ordered the house specialty, a kind of veal dish, something tarted up with a ton of cheese and a thick gooey sauce. Our elegant silver-haired waiter raised his eyebrow by a hair when we ordered.

"What's the matter?" Plumbeck asked. "No good tonight?"

"Very good, sir," the waiter answered professionally. "Maybe a bottle of Chianti, go with your dinner?"

"Whatever," said Plumbeck morosely. He usually took a great deal of interest in his food.

An enormous Italian family moved into the dining room like a herd of caribou; our waiter managed to seat them expeditiously at two tables that he had moved together. Watching him direct the family's stout father and sclerotic grandfather and assorted wives and children to their places was like watching an expert lion tamer in action. The noise and commotion distracted both of us. When the clan had finally quieted down, I took a breadstick and for no reason at all held it like a laser pointer.

"They're squeezing you pretty hard, Plumbeck?"

"They all want something, Asher. Sometimes I ask myself what I did, wind up being squeezed this way."

"It's just bad Karma. Former life you got to figure you neglected the rights of the disabled, something like that."

"Asher, the way I figure, I must have been *kicking* cripples some former life, positively knocking the crutches out from under their arms."

"That bad?"

Plumbeck sighed theatrically, but there was something behind the sigh, some secret sorrow.

"I'm going to have to take the heat on the Maison Jarr thing," he said.

I was flabbergasted. "Take the heat? Plumbeck, you told me Maison Jarr's Eddie's problem. Who's pushing you up front?"

The waiter arrived carrying a tray of antipasto and the bottle of Chianti, which he opened expertly.

"You wan' I should let it breathe a little, gentlemen?"

Plumbeck looked up amused. "Mix this stuff with oxygen, it's likely to catch fire. Just pour it out."

We sat there for a while, munching at the little slices of ham wrapped around gherkins and sipping the harsh red wine.

"Worse than dog piss," Plumbeck said.

"Drink a lot of dog piss in your time?"

"My share, Asher. My share."

Our waiter came over to our table carrying a tray balanced on his shoulder; he deposited our veal dishes and a mountainous plate of pasta. A tiny Mexican busboy swam up in his wake holding a plate of ungrated Parmesan cheese. I shook my head, but Plumbeck had him cover his pasta with the stuff: it looked like snow as it drifted down.

I thought Plumbeck would go at his food with gusto—he generally did—but after poking at the veal and taking a desultory mouthful of pasta, he took a long swallow of the Chianti and crossed his silverware ostentatiously on his plate.

I looked at him curiously.

"Eddie's nuts," he said finally.

"What else is new?"

"I'm not talking nuts as in he's married to Irene Ergenweiler nuts. I'm talking nuts nuts."

"Plumbeck, you're talking about your partner."

"He's nuts anyway," said Plumbeck. "Told Knesterman he's decided to go to the mat on this thing. Asher, he screwed up, should never have filed that weirded-out 10Q. He goes to the mat, we're going to be facing criminal charges, I'm lucky I don't find myself in some federal penitentiary hoisting up barbells. I come out I'm likely to find myself a born-again Christian, go on all the talk shows tell people how spending twenty-two months in the slammer was this positively *terrific* thing happened to me."

"Plumbeck," I said, "nobody's going to put you in prison." I pushed my own food away; it was no fun eating if Plumbeck was going to just sit there.

"You think I want a *suspended* sentence, Asher? Be one of these guys can't even cash a check because the computer flags you in some grocery store?"

"So you take the hit for Eddie, what's Knesterman figure you're going to have to do?"

"Court date, big upfront fine for sure, reprimand from the SEC, I'll probably have my license lifted for two years. I'll survive."

Our waiter returned to our table and looked inquiringly at the food we had left untouched.

"You want I should bring you something else?" he asked.

"Sure," said Plumbeck. "I want you should bring me back the last couple years. I need to do them over."

I left Plumbeck at the corner of Broadway and Columbus and walked back over to Greenwich, the dark wind off the bay blowing in my face. When I got halfway up my block, I could see that a dark sedan was double-parked in front of my house; two heavyset men were silhouetted in the front seat.

As I turned toward the concrete steps leading up from Greenwich, the passenger-side window rolled down noiselessly. I turned on the steps, but I didn't walk over.

"Aaron," said whoever was in the front seat. "We've got to talk."

I recognized the voice right away: it was Swentin Swoboda.

I walked over to the sedan and squatted down beside the window and looked at the two of them sitting there. "Why?" I said.

"Why what?"

"Why do we have to talk?"

From behind the wheel, Trudelwein said: "I'd say it was strikeout time again for our boy Aaron. Wouldn't you say that, Detective?"

"Absolutely. We sit here all this time, we figure Aaron is pulling the chain some yummy little number, looks like we were wrong."

"What is with you, Aaron? A man of your abilities, you still can't score."

"Outstanding abilities."

I stood up heavily.

"Don't go away mad, Aaron," said Trudelwein, looking straight over the steering wheel. "Reason we wait for you is on account of we got good news."

"Terrific news."

"What's that?" I asked.

"You're in the clear on this Plumbeck thing."

"This is something I already know."

"No, Aaron. What you know, you only *think* you know. It's only when we *tell* you you didn't do the crime you know you didn't do it."

"You following us on this, Aaron? See, the crime isn't what you do, it's what we think you do. Isn't that right, Detective?"

"Absolutely, it's right."

"It's for your own good we talk to you like Dutch uncles, Aaron, you know that."

"You're right. I needed to have two meatheads abuse me for half an hour. Clears the sinuses. It's something every citizen can use."

"There you go. Any rate, reason I'm telling you this is we got this boogie from over in east Oakland cold on this one."

"Shaboo?"

"What a small world, Aaron. The very one. This someone you know socially?"

"Sure, we're both members of the Bohemian Club. Every fall

we go up to the Grove and get wild. What do you have on him?"

"On your boy? Plumbeck, she tells us that he's over there earlier in the evening, making all kinds of threats, we go over dust the house, and sure enough, it's his prints everywhere."

"Doesn't prove he threw a Molotov cocktail at the house, Trudelwein."

"Doesn't prove he didn't either, Asherfeld."

"You ever hear of the idea that a man's innocent until proven guilty?"

"Sure, Aaron, we hear of it. Only thing is we don't believe it."

Tick Tock

I SPENT THE AFTERNOON OF JULY FOURTH walking along the waterfront, watching the predatory gulls swoop down on unsuspecting tourists, actually snatching food from their hands. A lot of the Embarcadero is landfill, but the Barbary Coast came down almost to where I was walking. The place was full of hookers and pimps and tough cops; men would wander into the cribs and seedy bars, take a drink, and wake up far out on the Pacific, their heads throbbing and a six-month voyage around the Cape ahead of them. It must have been a tough, brutal world. It was still a tough, brutal world, but it was tough and brutal in a different way.

I got as far as the foot of the Bay Bridge and looked over the *Jeremiah O'Brien,* tied up at anchor at one of the rotting piers. It's the last of the Liberty ships. A couple of years ago, the city turned itself inside and out to retrofit the thing; someone actually sailed it to Europe in time to celebrate the fiftieth anniversary of VE day. Now it's back at harbor, rotting away all over again.

I stopped by a little shack at the foot of the pier called Java House and ordered a greasy burger and fries for my dinner.

"What do you think?" the counterman asked me, nodding his head toward the ship at anchor outside his shack. He didn't wait for an answer. "Sailed on one of them over the Aleutians," he said.

"Colder than hell, get up on the deck do your watch four in the morning, some sub's down there, you could be *in* that water no more than two, three minutes. Hell of a thing."

He paused to flip my burger and press out some grease with his spatula. "Think we ought to have nuked them Japs?" he asked philosophically. "Or you one them shits thinks it was this terrific crime?"

"You're giving me a lot of room to maneuver on this," I said.

"Had some kid in here the other day wanted to tell me casualty estimates for an invasion of the mainland and all were this crock, would have been a cakewalk, our guys go on, get it over with in a couple of days. I'm telling you, a lot of guys I know fought over in the Pacific, not *one* of them ever said them casualty estimates were too low."

He whipped my burger from the griddle and placed it steaming on an open bun; he stood there, holding the platter in his hand.

I said: "The way I figure it, casualty estimates are *always* too low. You going to give me that burger or just let me admire it from a distance?"

"What say?" said the counterman, putting my food in front of me.

Later that evening, I watched the fireworks go off over Crissy Field. The fog had come in during the late afternoon, and by evening it had covered the city completely. The great pinwheels and fire rockets left the field with an explosive puff, but the fireworks themselves exploded up in the fog, leaving only a kind of smeared burst of color in the night sky.

I caught a taxi that had been creeping along in traffic and told the driver to take me over to Sixth and Market.

The driver was a big hulking blonde; she had rings through her earlobes and rings through her eyelids and her nostrils. She turned down the meter's arm with that resigned gesture all the cabbies use, and edged the taxi into the far lane so that she could make a U-turn.

"Like getting yourself pierced?" I asked.

"What? This is something that offends you?"

"Me? No. I think it's terrific you've got yourself pierced in so many places. It makes a statement."

We drove for a few moments along the Embarcadero, back along the way I had walked earlier.

"What kind of statement you figure it makes?" she finally asked. "I mean my being pierced and all?"

"Hey," I said, "you got earrings hanging from your nose, that's got to say you *like* being pierced."

She thought this over for a while, driving carelessly and fast against the flow of traffic.

"See," she finally said, "way I figure, piercing's my way of being me, you know what I mean?"

"Sure. It's your way of being you."

"Exactly."

"Hurt much?"

"Nose hurt a lot at first. This guy did the piercing told me rub some alcohol over the spot. I think the tissue is sort of dead or something now. It's like I go blow my nose, I can't feel a thing anymore. It's kind of weird. I mean a part of your body is like just *dead.*"

"It's not weird. One of my wives used to say the same thing."

"One of your wives was pierced?"

"Not exactly," I said. "It was always an argument we had, though."

"Bummer," she said, as she swung the taxi onto Market Street, the wheels rattling on the old trolley tracks.

"You going over the Palace?" she asked when she had stopped at Sixth. She didn't wait for an answer. "I know how it is. Sun goes down you figure you're just going to die you go back home alone again."

I waited for her to make change. "What about the guy that did the piercing? He's not waiting for you?"

She shook her head sadly. "He's up in Seattle, selling coffee. Can you imagine? He got this like little tin truck, stands out there in the rain, sells this espresso. I mean it's unreal."

"What isn't?" I said as I started to get out of the cab.

"Really," she said emphatically.

* * *

I crossed Market, my collar up against my neck, and took a look at the vestibule of the Palace Theater. Miss Independence was giving a special performance. Her photograph showed her separating herself from a red, white and blue bikini. The vague and muddied beat of the stereo system reached out to the street. I gave Miss Independence a mental salute and walked around the corner to the little alleyway that ran from Market Street over to Mission. Chico-Chico kept his books and accounts in a little room in the theater's cellar. He had been an enforcer for some Mexican street gang when he took over management of the theater. He had taught himself accounting and scheduling and made a profit for whoever owned the place without stealing anyone blind.

I knocked on the door and slipped into the warm puddle of light thrown by an old-fashioned accountant's lamp. Chico-Chico was sitting at his desk; he was cutting a whole series of checks by hand. He looked up at me sourly.

"What you doin' here?" he asked. "You suppose be watching them firecrackers go off."

"I did that, Chico," I said. "Fourth of July, I figured I just had to come by and pay my respects to Miss Independence."

Chico-Chico snorted. "Tha's ain't Miss Independence up there. Miss Independence, she started leaking silicone one of her tits, had to go to the hospital out in Hawaii. Cow up there some local stripper from Oakland. Cos' me time and a half get her down here tonight."

"Regular outrage," I agreed. "Miss Independence, she probably figured her health was more important than taking her clothes off in front of a bunch of winos. Can you imagine?"

"Hey," said Chico-Chico, "don't be calling them *winos*. They *clients.*"

"You're right," I said. "Guys haven't bathed in weeks sitting around sipping Gallo Mountain Dew from paper bags—hell, no reason to call them winos."

It was warm in the little cellar room; I unzipped my windbreaker and eased my back against the door frame. "Aren't you going to ask me to sit down, Chico?" I asked.

"No," said Chico-Chico, "I ask you to sit down, next thing I know you sittin' down. I got checks to write. Cows upstairs, they finish up they wan' get paid, you know what I mean?"

"Sure," I said, sitting myself down. "You mean you want I should sit down *and* get out of here in a hurry."

"You got that right, Asherfeld. Now what you want?"

"Ever have anything to do with any Russians, Chico?"

Chico-Chico stared at me in bafflement. "Who?"

"Russians."

"I ain't never been to no Russia, man," he said. "You know that."

"I mean here in the city."

"Onliest people I know are them cows upstairs and clients they come in an' watch them cows. I go home, get some sleep, come back here do it all over again. You understan' what I'm saying to you?"

"Sure, Chico. How about this, then? You get me ten minutes with Gentian, let me ask him what I need to know."

Gentian Violet was an adviser to various political figures in the city; he was also part owner of the Palace.

Chico-Chico looked up at me in astonishment.

"Strictly professional, Chico. I just want to ask him a few questions."

"How'm I suppose get you ten minutes with Gentian? Far as he concerned, I'm just some greaser works his place."

"Ask Tick Tock to set it up."

Chico-Chico looked at me coolly for a moment. "It's a favor, Asherfeld," he finally said. "You gonna owe me one."

"I know that, Chico," I said.

It was past ten o'clock when I left Chico's basement office. I could still hear the muffled booms of the city's elaborate fireworks, disappearing up into the fog and clouds; from time to time, I could see the gray sky pulse for a second with a burst of muted color. I didn't much want to go home. I thought of spending a few hours watching Miss Independence salute the flag, but I figured that would make me more depressed than ever, so I walked aimlessly down

Market, toward the Ferry Building. Under the best of circumstances, Market Street looks like a sewer: now it was sad and cold and lonely.

At the corner of Market and Sixth, a beggar shambled up from his sleeping bags and out of a doorway and stood in my path. He looked at me fiercely.

"Spare change for a dermatological emergency?" he asked.

I looked at him quizzically; I didn't want to find out that he had some horrible skin disease.

"I require a hair transplant," he said, sweeping his weathered hand over his scalp. The one thing he didn't seem to need was more hair.

"Looks like you got more hair than you need, fellah," I said.

"It's a *prophylactic* transplant," he said. "I wish to avoid inconvenience in my sunset years."

I reached into my breast pocket and fished out my wallet. "How much you figure this transplant's likely to set you back?"

"At least five dollars, possibly more."

"I'll go for a buck," I said, handing the beggar a dollar bill. "Make sure you get the micrografts, have them blend in with your own hair."

"I intend to," he said. "Did I mention that I am also requesting assistance for a tummy tuck?"

He pulled up his ratty jacket to reveal his grime-encrusted midriff. I could see that he was covered with louse bites. I held up my hands; he caught my gesture.

"I can see," he said, "that you are suffering from compassion fatigue."

"You got that right," I said, pulling up the collar of my windbreaker. "When I get over it I'll start worrying about your tummy."

I walked until Market met New Montgomery Street. I could see Plumbeck's office building standing in the middle of the block. It looked like some sort of Egyptian monument—blank and empty. I thought of heading farther down Market and stopping in at some of the bars on Spear Street, but I got tired in a flash. Going home didn't seem like such a bad idea after all. I flagged a taxi that had been cruising the wrong way down Market and crossed the street to clamber in.

My driver was dressed entirely in black; the skin on her face had been pancaked dead white. Her hair was piled on her head and her large lips were colored a dark liver red.

"Halloween?" I said, after I had given her my address.

"Goth," she said indifferently. "Be over at Death Guild later, no time to change."

"Who's playing?"

"Fear and Loathing," she said. I could see on her hack card that her name was Tirzah.

"Probably how the audience feels after the first set."

"Yeah, well, the music speaks to me. I can find myself in it, you know what I mean? A lot of people run from fear and sadness. We kind of delve into it. It's kind of like pain worship."

I must have grunted encouragingly.

"Course most of your club scenes, what you get is a lot of pretentious little shits running around. Over at Bedlam, no ambiance, but absolutely. The place is crawling with people don't really understand what goth is all about."

"Hard to imagine."

"Over at Death Guild you get a crowd that's drawn toward the dark side."

Tirzah half turned to drape her arm over the seat back and face me. "We don't try to minimize the painful aspects of life by putting a mask over them, you know what I mean?"

"No."

For a moment, Tirzah looked perplexed. Then she found the key to her own thoughts. "It's like we recognize the beauty in tragedy," she said, turning onto Greenwich Street.

"Or the tragedy in beauty," I said.

The puzzled look returned to her features. "Right," she said. "That too."

I counted out the fare and placed the worn dollar bills into her none-too-clean palm. "Face a lot of tragedy in your life?" I asked, looking at her unlined face. She couldn't have been more than twenty-two.

"Me personally?"

I nodded.

"Well, it all like sucks, doesn't it?"

"Absolutely," I said, exiting from the taxi.

I trudged quietly up the stairs to my apartment. Inside, everything was quiet and dark and empty. Far away, the foghorns were sounding on the throat of the bay, where the waters of the Pacific surge into the Golden Gate. I stood by my window for a long time, looking out at the gray sky and listening to the sounds of the night.

Juice

CHICO-CHICO LET A WEEK GO BY, and then he called me late one afternoon. "Tick Tock be on a line over Trocadero tonight. He say he speak to you then."

I said: "Thanks, Chico," politely.

"Hey, Asherfeld, I need some free legal advice, I'm gonna call you, right?"

I thought for a tiny moment of what I should say. Then I said: "Anytime, Chico, day or night."

"I figure you be saying that, Asherfeld. I need you, I'm gonna call you."

Dumb guys have it tough.

I hung up with Chico-Chico and spent an hour reading a book a client had sent me. It was entitled *Inner Peace.* The author was someone who called himself Sawatikram Sanesh. He was posed on the back cover dressed in saffron Buddhist robes. His inner peace didn't get as far as shaving. His face had a three-day stubble and his eyes were red. The biographical notice on the bottom of the page said that he had been born in Akron, Ohio, and that his birth name was Lester Thurgood. Sawatikram Sanesh was enthusiastic about centering yourself. It seems that not being centered was this terrific problem. A lot of times not being centered had led him to take drugs and treat women as means and not ends.

My former client had been charged with child molestation by his adult daughter. She was a large, tubby woman with very long feet; she had recovered the memory of her abuse while driving home from a weekend at Reno. She was so excited by her discovery that she called her father to tell him. He had read *Inner Peace* while in jail; he had given me his own copy of the book, the one that he had marked up with a lot of exclamation points and *how trues*.

Sawatikram Sanesh thought it was important to get right down into the lotus position and meditate for at least an hour a day. Anytime he had a bad thought, he would whip right down onto his heels and meditate away. It was supposed to work like gangbusters. I slipped off my shoes and sat down on the hardwood part of my floor. I could still smell the faint smell of vomit from Yuri's visit. I tried to tuck my heels over my thighs. Nothing doing. I couldn't get both my heels up where they were supposed to be. I figured I was stuck with my bad thoughts.

I gave up after a couple of seconds and stripped off my clothes and took a shower instead, letting the hot water stream against the back of my neck. I don't know how things are over there in India, but up here on Telegraph Hill, a long hot shower does a lot more for clearing out bad thoughts than sitting in the lotus position.

Afterward, I put on a ratty blue bathrobe and sat at my desk, listening to the foghorns sound over the bay. Alicia's face came unbidden to my mind. I had only seen her once, but I could still see her bright blond hair tapering down to fine fuzz over her temples and the way her large square shapely teeth looked when she smiled her glistening smile. I thought of all the perky young women bouncing around the city in their Reeboks or working out their dimpled thighs in all the exercise clubs or ordering chaste vegetarian dishes in trendy little restaurants. *Can you like tell the cook to hold the oil?* I thought that Alicia when she went out to eat would order ribs and a mound of fries. A beautiful woman is different.

I got dressed after a while and polished up my teeth and combed my hair. I walked to my bedroom and turned on the light by my bedside table. Then I stood by my own front door, the darkness seeping into the apartment, full of strange somber nighttime colors. I tried to listen for something. I knew I wouldn't hear it.

The Trocadero is a big sloppy South of Market Street club. It was supposed to be a very hip and very tony place, but six weeks after it opened, the hip and tony people who spent their weekends in Tahoe and their summers in Saint Paul de Vence decided that they really had better things to do with their time than snort lines of coke in the bathroom of some converted warehouse. The place began to attract sullen adolescents from Vallejo and Benicia. The kids spent a ton of money and began taking all sorts of new drugs, like Ecstasy and crystal meth; the newspapers began to write up the loud bands that played there, and the Trocadero became hip and tony all over again.

I had taken a cab over from Telegraph Hill. My driver was someone named Manny. When I told him where I was going, he gave me a long sober look. "Trocadero?" he asked. "You figure on scoring you're wasting your time."

"Why's that?"

"On account of the place is full of kids, eighteen, nineteen years old. I'm telling you, these kids are hard as nails, scoring with one of them be like scoring with ice."

Manny waited for a moment, timing his story to the light that had turned red on Broadway. When it turned green, he said: "I'm telling you this for your own good, pal. I got a daughter, she's nineteen. Pity the guy who looks twice at her."

He gunned his beaten-up Chevrolet across Broadway.

Manny thumped himself on his chest. "In here, it's like there's nothing there, only this cold, you know what I mean?"

I told Manny I knew what he meant. I did.

It was only ten in the evening—still early for the Trocadero; but a long line of teenagers had already formed in front of the club's red rope, stretching like a disheveled snake back down Folsom almost to the corner of Eighth. SoMa is still a neighborhood of body shops and Salvation Army outlets and stores selling made-in-Korea designer knockoffs from long metal racks; there are still two- or three-story redbrick apartment houses on some of the blocks, places where you can rent a room for a week and sleep off an awful hangover; a lot of ratty losers disembark the sad panting buses at the Greyhound Station and wander around the cool sun-baked streets until they score enough change to buy something from the bodegas lining the avenue. There are trendy little restaurants here and there, places with zinc countertops and menus written in French and places serving weird food. There's even an English chophouse somewhere, as if English food were any great recommendation. At night the winos cadge change from the upscale crowd; every couple of months, someone on line somewhere looks cross-eyed at someone else and there's a shoot-out.

It's a terrific part of town.

I walked slowly up the line in front of the Trocadero until I came up to the red rope that had been mounted on two brass stanchions in front of the club's steps. I thought Tick Tock might be manning the rope, but there was no one there.

The two kids who were first in line eyed me suspiciously. They couldn't have been more than twenty or so; they were both dressed in leather jackets and slovenly oversized pants that looked like pantaloons and heavy Doc Marten shoes. They looked filthy and vicious somehow, the way most kids look.

"Hey, man," the boy finally said, "line forms all the way in the back."

"I know," I said. "I'm with the band."

Both kids looked at me incredulously, their smudged eyes widening.

"You're with the band?" the boy said.

"Drummer," I said, "snapping my fingers in the air."

"You're full of shit," said the boy emphatically.

"No, really. I was born to drum. It's genetic. My mother was black."

"Hey, man," said the boy, preparing himself to be angry, "why don't you just take all that rhythm and move to the back of the line?"

Just then Tick Tock emerged from the doors of the club; he hitched up his pants and spotted me right away.

"Asher," he said with as much warmth as he generally put into things; he walked over to the rope and lowered it, motioning for me to pass through with a drop of his shoulder.

I edged past him; as Tick Tock reclipped the rope to its stanchion, I heard the young girl hiss at her companion. "You idiot," she said. "He really *is* with the band."

Tick Tock paused on the club steps; he must have been well into his fifties. He still had a thick boxer's body and a boxer's way of balling his fists unconsciously over and over again. He wasn't about to let me into the club without making sure he had a good reason for the favor.

"So I understand from Chico you be needing a favor or two, Asherfeld," he said, with his pleasant west-country lilt. Boxing had been his passion. It had taken him a long time to realize that his vocation lay in service.

I could hear the band running through a warm-up set inside the club.

"I'm interested in a couple of Russians, thought maybe you could tell me where to look."

Tick Tock regarded me professionally, his heavy beaten-up eyelids raised. "You're talking now about the outer Richmond and such stuff, are you?"

I nodded.

"There's a lot of trash out there," he said dispassionately. "People sell their own mother, you gave them half a chance. Mistake letting that crowd in, Asherfeld, if you don't mind me telling you."

"Not like the Irish," I said.

"Not like the Irish at all," he said calmly. "What sort of information you be needing?"

"The usual," I said. "Where, when, how come."

Tick Tock nodded gravely. "I can't say as *I* have anybody you could call. Someone at the consulate do you any good?"

"The *Russian* Consulate?"

"Well now, Asherfeld, I'll not be thinking that the Chinese Consulate would be doing you any good."

"Russian Consulate be great," I said.

"I'll be looking after the Borg up in Pacific Heights this evening. I'll ask Gentian Violet."

The Borg was a well-known lesbian activist named Roberta Borgenbanger; Gentian Violet was acting as her political adviser for as long as she could afford him.

"I appreciate the favor," I said.

"No need, Asherfeld, you'll be repaying it sooner or later. Now party's supposed to end at two or so. You be there a little before. I'll see if I can't get you a minute with Violet himself."

I left the Trocadero at a little before eleven and walked the long dark blocks from Eighth over to Market and then over to Geary. I wanted something to eat and I didn't want to make a big deal of it, so I stopped at Lefty O'Doul's, which is a kind of brauhaus and tavern, with a big steam table and a lot of good-smelling cuts of turkey and pastrami. The place used to be a famous sports bar, O'Doul holding court by the black piano in the front. Pictures of him pitching are all over the walls. They show a young, somewhat beefy-looking man with a squared-off blue jaw. Now the place attracts a lot of the sad sacks from the Tenderloin—old hookers on Social Security, number runners trying to figure out where the action went, ferryboat captains. They go there because the food is good and cheap and because the place is still lively.

I ordered a pastrami on rye and ate my food in the back, watching the enormous color TV. Everyone around me looked to be in their seventies or eighties. Years ago, I had taken one of my wives into Lefty O'Doul's. She looked around at the peeling wall and sniffed at the cabbagy smell of the place. The woman at the table next to us was eating her food in that meditative way people have of eating when they wear poorly fitting dentures. My wife hugged herself and shuddered. "What do these people *live* for, Asher?" she asked earnestly.

I hadn't known what to say to her; now I figured that coming into Lefty O'Doul's each evening and gumming a turkey sandwich on white bread with mayonnaise might be all the reason for living anyone might need.

I caught a cab from the stand in front of the St. Francis Hotel.

"Where to, sir?" the driver asked; he was a young black. He was freshly shaven and he was wearing a starched white shirt and tie.

I told the driver to take me up to Pacific Heights.

The interior of the taxi was clean and smelled of something like lemon; there was a little fur cover over the armrest, and a white doily to rest your head against. "A little music, relax you, sir?"

"What do you got?"

"You name it. We've got R and B and we got soul and we got Motown and we got rock. You want country, we got country. You a brother, we got rap. You want classical, we got classical."

"Tell me what you got in classical."

"Classical, we got Marvin Gaye. That do you?"

I said that'd be fine. Marvin was singing one of the great sad songs of the seventies. I remembered hearing the song for the first time and realizing as I heard it that I no longer loved the woman who had hugged herself and shuddered in Lefty O'Doul's.

We drove up Geary, past the fleshy hookers in hot pink pants by Leavenworth and Hyde, and passed the tall sleek transvestites standing on the streetcorners at Polk.

"Pretty nice cab you've got here," I said. "You own it?"

My driver shook his head and turned to flash me a smile. "You're asking on account of all this extra service I provide. Beginning of each shift, I clean out the car, put in the doilies and the armrest, stock the CD. Black man get ahead, he's got to work twice as hard. Couple years I'll be able to buy a medallion."

"That what you want? Own your own cab?"

"What I want, what I can get, them's two different things," he said evenly, without turning his head.

"I know what you mean."

"You think you do anyway."

The conversation seemed to darken his mood; he didn't say another word until he dropped me off at the corner of Pacific and

Fillmore. I counted out the fare and added a tip. "Good luck," I said.

He grunted in response and gunned the car from the curb after I got out.

The mayor had purchased a beat-up old Pacific Heights mansion when he was elected; his wife spent a couple of years fixing it up. Now it was a showcase. It was a big imposing house right on the corner of Pacific and Fillmore with crenellated turrets on each side of the building and a lot of fancy paint work in the front. It wasn't a Victorian, but like a lot of large expensive San Francisco buildings, it had been painted to look like one. There was a file of official Cadillacs in front of the mansion.

Tick Tock was leaning against the lead car; he was wearing a wire in his ear, which he pulled out when I approached.

"Asher," he said genially.

"Keeping the faith?" I asked.

"Trying to. Course the company I'm forced to keep would try the patience of a saint."

"The Borg giving you grief?"

Tick Tock consulted his watch ostentatiously.

"Among other things. His Honor was supposed to be finished up with speechifying an hour ago. Still going strong, so far as I can tell."

"Man has a lot to say."

"Almost all of it pure wind, Asher, pure wind. I'll go in and see if I can't persuade Gentian to have a word or two with you."

Tick Tock walked briskly up the steps to the mayor's house and came out thirty seconds later.

"He'll be right out," he said officiously, fastening his earphone back into his ear.

A second later, Gentian Violet flew out of the mayor's house in that busy self-dramatizing way public officials have. He was a trim, carefully barbered middle-aged man; he was wearing a very well cut powder blue suit.

"You Asherfeld?" he asked, scowling at me.

"Yup."

"Let's make this short and sweet. Only contact I can give you at the consulate is a man named Litvinov. He's got a real weakness for unripe fruit, if you know what I mean. You might try calling him."

"Can I use your name?"

"Of course you can't use my name," Gentian Violet exploded. "What kind of fool question is that?"

"I appreciate the delicacy of your position," I said, "but if I can't use your name, why do you think this Litvinov be likely to see me in any case?"

Gentian Violet looked at me inquisitively. He had a good deal of confidence in the power of his stare. He said: "Christ, Asherfeld, use your imagination. Tell him the mayor sent you. How's he going to know? His Honor's in such a fog learning how his zipper works, he's not going to notice anything." Then he turned to Tick Tock, who whipped his earphone from his ear alertly. "Borg'll be coming out in ten minutes. She'll be going over to Wolfies in the second limo, Mayor's wife'll be in number one." Tick Tock nodded professionally. Of a sudden, a quick alert smile crossed Gentian Violet's face. He stuck his hand toward me and shook my hand with a single downward jerk. "I never met you, Asherfeld, but you owe me one."

"What a deal," I said, watching his well-tailored back as he moved quickly back up the steps to the mansion.

"I don't suppose they'll be inviting us in for champagne," I said to Tick Tock.

"I don't suppose, Asherfeld," he said musically. He withdrew his earpiece from his ear again and looked at me sympathetically. "You gettin' on all by yourself with those heathen Italians up on the Hill?" We had never been friends, but we had known one another for a long time.

"I'm getting by," I said. "What about you?"

"Rosharon, bless her heart, she'll be gone seven years ago this month, Asherfeld."

We stood there for a moment without speaking; we were both embarrassed by what we felt.

How You Say? A Good Soul.

THE DOWNSTAIRS DOORBELL rang once and then it rang twice again in a sharp staccato. I had been somewhere between wakefulness and sleep, the images and moods moving calmly through consciousness. I got up and buzzed open the downstairs buzzer, and then stood by my own half-cracked door, waiting to see who was clicking up the steps.

It was Tatiana. She was dressed in a blue raincoat, which she held fastened against her throat. She stood on the landing in front of me, swaying just slightly on her absurdly high heels.

"Shotakoy, Aaron Asherfeld," she said.

"I don't speak Russian, Tatiana," I said, pressing against my own door so that she could come into my apartment.

"I know, but you have *dusha naraspashku* anyway. How you say? A good soul. I feel you have good soul."

I told Tatiana to sit down and went back to the bedroom to put on a pair of slacks and an open shirt. My eyes were gritty and I felt unshaven. When I came out, Tatiana was sitting on the couch, her legs crossed at the knee. She had taken off her raincoat; she was wearing the same low-cut dress she had had on at Centerfolds. At the club, she had been one pretty woman in a roomful of pretty women; sitting there in my living room, she blazed erotic energy into the air. She must have come from work. She looked blowzy and her eyeliner was smudged, but she filled her dress with soft swaying curves and the black smudges underneath her eyes gave her a sad provocative look. She caught my mood right away.

"Kashu maslom ne isportish," she said, shrugging her brown shoulders. "Iss impossible to translate."

I sat myself at my desk and tried to look at her without seeming to look at her. It's not as easy as it sounds.

"So, Aaron Asherfeld," she said, her body rotated so that her bosom was aligned with her knees. "I think maybe we friends, *da?"*

"What kind of friends you have in mind?" It was a stupid question to ask.

Tatiana gave me a long, low, level, and very amused stare. *"Veshat lapshu na ushi,* Aaron Asherfeld," she said.

I had no idea what she had said, but I knew what she meant.

"We're going to be friends, Tatiana, why don't we start by you telling me why you're running around pretending to be someone you're not?"

"Questions, questions, Aaron Asherfeld," she said, leaning over to rest her forearm on her nyloned knee so that she could show me more of her cleavage. *"Radi boga,* I no here to answer questions."

I shrugged my shoulders.

"Alicia my soul sister. You understand what means? We like this." She held up her hands and allowed the fingers to lock. "She in trouble, I there to help. These people she with, bad peeple."

I figured she was talking about Marvin Plumbeck.

"Maybe so," I said. "Still doesn't tell me why you're out there pretending to be her. Why don't you tell me where she is, let *her* answer these questions."

"Aaron, she—how you say?—in denial." She circled her finger around her temple.

I burst out laughing: it was hard not to, hearing those words uttered with a Russian accent.

"She start out on this busyness, then she change mind. She say this, she say that. Who knows? Is for me *raskhlyobyvat kashu.* Clean up mess."

We sat like that for a moment, both of us feeling the deep quiet stillness of the night seep into my apartment.

"I not here talk," Tatiana said.

I must have arched my eyebrows.

"I like you, Aaron Asherfeld," she said in a low throaty voice; she ran her thumb under the spaghetti strap of her silver lamé dress. I could see the shadow of her dress fall against the smooth flushed skin of her bosom.

"Why?"

"Why I like you?" she asked in astonishment. She shrugged her shoulders. "I no need reason like someone."

She sat there, fingering her strap. I could see that she had licked her lips; they were glistening. Then she said: "What you like, Aaron Asherfeld? What make you happy?"

I kept looking at her: my throat was tight and I could feel the moisture on my palms.

"I woman need firm hand. You understand? How you say? Dizipline. You like tie me up?" she asked softly. "I think maybe you like tie me up. Put me on bed, tie me up. You like that, I think. Then take your pleasure. *Otche charascho*—very good. That what I think, Aaron Asherfeld. That what I think you like."

She got up from the couch in a very practiced fluid gesture, shaking her hair out as she stood; then she came over to my chair, swaying as she walked. She leaned over my chair, grabbing the arms with her hands; her face was level with my own. She threw her head back and whipped her hair over the top of my head so that the hair dragged over my head and ears. I could smell the shampoo she used and the smell of her skin. "You like what I do, Aaron Asherfeld?" she asked, her lower lip glistening. She stood there, still holding the arms of my chair but leaning over, her arms straight, elbows tight against her rib cage so that her bosom was pressed high. Her face was close enough to mine so that I could see the fine crumbs of eye shadow that had formed on her lashes and the faint line near her ears marking the farthest reach of her flat pancake makeup. Her perfume had become mingled with the night smell of cigarettes and sweat. Just below the open threshold of her dress I could see a small discoloration in her skin, a kind of mole.

I reached up and grabbed both her wrists and twisted them from my chair, holding her arms together in front of her.

"Aaron Asherfeld," she said huskily, swaying in front of me. "You take me now, take me into bed."

"I don't think so," I said, trying to make the words come out evenly.

"Don't think, Aaron Asherfeld," she said, still swaying. "You feel." She tried to lower her clasped hands; I wouldn't let her.

"It all for you," she said. "Don't you want?"

"No," I said.

For the first time, she opened her eyes wide. I could feel the soft sponginess go out of her body. "You telling truth?"

I looked up at her. "What difference does it make?"

She looked at me without blinking. The hardness that I had seen at the club came back into her gray eyes; it was like watching ice re-form.

"I think maybe I make mistake come here, Aaron Asherfeld," she finally said, as if she had decided something.

"Maybe."

"I think you a man not like woman." She disengaged her hands from my grasp and walked over to my living room window, holding her right elbow cupped in her left palm, looking out at the inkiness of the night sky.

"You know what I think, Aaron Asherfeld? I think you *ni bogu svechka no chyortu kocherga.*"

"I'm guessing that's not a compliment, Tatiana."

She shrugged her shoulders and snorted; then she walked over to the couch and put on her raincoat.

At the door she said: "*Dosvidania,* Aaron Asherfeld. I no see you again. Don't worry about tonight. *Snyavshi golovu, po volosam ne plachut.*"

I sat there and listened to her hard brittle footsteps clacking down the stairs. Then I got up to go to the bathroom, but it took me a long time to adjust myself to a routine call of nature.

Counselor to the Tsar

IT WASN'T HARD to reach Maxim Litvinov. I called the Russian Consulate on Green, asked for the second deputy, and presto, there he was, saying "Litvinov here" in a deep musical bass.

"This is Aaron Asherfeld, Counselor," I said.

"Who?"

I told him who I was again and told him that I needed a few minutes of his time.

"You need time?" he said, his voice narrowing with suspicion. "What for?"

"The mayor asked me to check on some things with you, Counselor."

"The mayor? He tell you about me?"

"Yes he did. He said you were the most capable man at the consulate."

"He say that?"

"Absolutely."

Litvinov gave out a huge rumbling chuckle. "I no can lie," he said. "He right."

"It's well known, Counselor, San Francisco political circles, you have a problem, Litvinov's man to call."

"Maybe I call mayor, find out what *he* say," Litvinov said slyly.

"Probably can't get through, but why don't you check with his assistant? I can hold for you."

I figured Litvinov wouldn't know who the mayor's assistant was and would be embarrassed to admit it.

Instead of calling the mayor's office, Litvinov said: *"Charascho,* you know where is?"

"Yes I do."

"You come over, maybe four o'clock."

I spent what was left of the morning drawing up a list of coffeehouses in the city. A client of mine named Schlothauer had started a real-estate empire by putting together people without enough money to buy anything solid on their own and having them own their building jointly. The scheme was called tenancy-in-common. Schlothauer had married a pale-skinned Croatian refugee named Nané. She was a terrifically intelligent, hardworking woman, the real brains in their partnership. She showed Schlothauer how to finance a new building from the sale of an old one, and how to keep borrowing money against the expectation of new partnerships. During the eighties, they made money hand over fist. They bought an enormous mansion out at Sea Cliff and had an incredibly expensive Romanian painter named Josef paint the inside of the house. Schlothauer took me out there when it was all done. He pointed to the ornate stippled ceiling and the hand-rubbed pastel walls. "You know what this is, Asher?" he asked with snobbish innocent pride.

"A lot of paint?"

"What do you know, Asher?" Schlothauer said. "You're so busy getting divorced, you'd probably turn up your nose at the Mona Lisa."

"Not if I could get Josef to give it a good stippling," I said.

"This is class, Asherfeld," he said with satisfaction. "Real class."

He almost beamed.

"I'm glad you like it, Jack," I said. But six months later, the real-estate market collapsed in the city, and like so many others, Schlothauer learned that the magic of leverage works in reverse. He lost his business and then his house; he had to move his wife into a flat above a hardware store on Fillmore. If he hadn't been able to prove he was destitute in court, the DA would have brought charges against him for fraud. He had read somewhere that Seattle was full of little trolleys serving espresso; he figured what would work up there might work down here. Somehow he managed to get someone to back him in a new scheme. He wanted me to check on the competition.

I had lunch at the Balboa Café over on Fillmore—it's kind of a yuppie shrine; and then I walked through the posh sunny streets of Cow Hollow, up Fillmore and then over to Green. The police had placed barriers on the street between Steiner and Vallejo in order to let the schoolchildren from Saint Paul de Venice run up and down the middle of the street in their parochial-school uniforms, chasing one another and shrieking. I threaded my way through the younger children. At the head of the block, a group of older boys was kicking a soccer ball, chasing the ratty thing intently after they had kicked it and trying out all sorts of fancy moves. They looked young, and lithe, and indefatigable. One of the boys gave the ball a mighty kick. It lofted in the air and sailed upward toward me; I stuck out my hand and managed to stop it midair, batting it down. Then I cupped it in an underhand grip and flipped it to the boy who had kicked it. He blocked the ball on the fly with his forehead and then picked it up. Looking over toward me with a fierce, somewhat menacing glance, he said "Thanks."

I got to the consulate at a little past four. I didn't have the feeling that things were hopping over there. In the bad old days, the place was rumored to be a center of espionage. There was an enormous satellite dish on the roof of the building and a lot of official-looking Zil limousines parked out in front. But ever since the end of the cold war, the old mysterious life seemed to have gone out of the place. The limousines disappeared and the people who had watched the consulate reported that the satellite dish was pretty much used to track CNN broadcasts.

There was no guard at the front of the enormous brick building and no receptionist behind the enormous semicircular desk. The interior seemed full of ghosts. The gilt sign above the reception desk said, CONSULATE OF RUSSIA, in heavy block letters, but whoever had put up the sign hadn't quite gotten rid of the old sign: I could still see the outlines of the words *Union of Soviet Socialist Republics* behind the new words. The far wall from the reception desk held a large picture of a beaming Boris Yeltsin. There must have been a dozen pictures on the wall before. I could tell because their shadows were still there.

I crossed the reception area; I was looking for something to tell me where Litvinov kept his office. Nothing. I reached over the counter for the telephone and picked it up. I immediately got a canned message. "You have reach Consulate of Russia," said a stale bored voice. "No one here to take message." There was a pause and then: "Goodbye." I tried punching in the last four digits of Litvinov's extension. All I got for my troubles was the dial tone, returning again and again.

A broad marble staircase ascended from the lobby to a landing on the second floor. A sign written in both Russian and English said, Entry Forbidden. I walked up the steps anyway.

The second-floor landing gave out to a series of offices, all of them with heavy varnished doors. At the end of the corridor, I spotted an open office. A very stout woman with a great many facial warts was sitting primly at a small walnut desk, her hands folded in front of her, thumb on thumb. She looked up at me.

"Maxim Litvinov?" I said. "Tell me where his office's at?"

"Puchimu?" she said unblinkingly. "Why?"

I backed away from the door. "Forget I asked."

"Da," she said.

I followed the corridor until it gave out on another marble flight of stairs. On the landing above, I spotted a middle-aged man exiting a room; he was wiping his hands with enormous deliberation as he walked, forcing the edge of a ragged paper towel underneath his fingertips. He looked up as I approached.

I said: "You know where I can find Maxim Litvinov?"

"Litvinov? *Litvinov napelvat v dushu,"* he said, scuttling rapidly down the corridor.

I finally found Litvinov on the third floor of the consulate. He was sitting in the only other office I had seen with an open door; but the door did have his name printed both in Cyrillic and Roman letters.

I knocked and said: "I'm Aaron Asherfeld."

Litvinov got up from his chair with an explosion of nervous energy. He was a large, powerfully built middle-aged man, with an enormous barrel chest; he had a shock of thick white hair and a lumpy face with a potato nose. *"Pahzhahlistuh,"* he said energetically, clambering around his desk, "Come in." He shook my hand with a tremendous show of vigor, pumping it up and down. "Sit, sit," he said grandly, pointing to a high-backed sofa mounted on bear-claws by the wall.

I sat myself down and leaned forward, resting my forearms on my knees.

I could see that Litvinov's desk was covered with foodstuffs: there were several jars of jam, and a little loaf of bread that he had been cutting with a silver paring knife, and a wedge of pale butter. *"Radi boga,"* he said, smacking his forehead theatrically with his open palm as he sat down again. "What I thinking? Take, take."

He pushed the bread and the jams toward me.

"I'm not here to eat, Litvinov," I said.

Litvinov cut himself a slice of bread and helped himself to an enormous scoop of what looked like red currant jelly; he ate the bread and the jam separately, licking the jam from the spoon directly. *"Otche charascho,"* he said. "Very good." It wasn't a terrifically elegant performance. He finished up with his bread and jam and wiped his lips and his fingers with a handkerchief that he had fished from his rear pocket. Then he blew his nose vigorously, cleaning each nostril tentatively with the handkerchief edge. He looked up at me, his lumpy face turning crafty.

"I call mayor about you, Asherfeld," he said. "He say he never hear of you."

"Litvinov, it's what you'd *expect* him to say, isn't it?"

Litvinov thought over my answer for a moment and then slapped his large palm on the tabletop, causing the jam jars to bounce; he laughed explosively. "You right. I like you, Aaron Asherfeld. So what's this hush busyness you want?"

"Mayor's concerned about a few problems over the Russian community out on the avenues. Kind of an unwholesome crowd seems to be moving in there. You know what I mean?"

Litvinov nodded sagely. "These people *malo kashi yel,* they eat too much." He ran his cupped hands a few inches from the surface of his own ample belly.

"Could be," I said. "Mayor asked if you could check a name for him?"

The sly look came back into Litvinov's eyes; he shrugged his massive shoulders. "I no policeman," he said. "No files. Everything now *demokrataya, da?*"

I stood up from the sofa. "You're right," I said. "Bad old days are gone. New Russia, I figure you probably read someone their Miranda rights before taking them down to the cellar and giving them a working over."

Litvinov looked closely at me; I could tell he hadn't understood what I had said. I put my hands on his desk and leaned over my own palms. "The mayor is a reasonable man, Litvinov. He's not asking for information for free."

Litvinov pushed out his lips. Then he rubbed his thumb and his forefinger together.

"Little business over on Polk Street, maybe that'd just disappear, poof." I paused for a moment to let Litvinov digest my remark.

"You understand the word *poof?*" I asked.

"Puf?" Litvinov rumbled. "What is *puf?*" But the word must

have triggered an odd Russian association. A wet smile suddenly creased his large lumpy face. *"Da,"* he said enthusiastically, clapping his hands together as if I had made him a present.

"The mayor's interested in someone named Vybotskaya," I said. "Yuri Vybotskaya."

Litvinov said *da* again and picked up the red Lucite handle of his rotary telephone and dialed a single letter. Then he said something in rapid-fire Russian. He sat there beaming. In a moment, a plump woman wearing a shapeless brown uniform entered the room; she wore a single star on her shoulder mortarboard. She deposited an old-fashioned manila file on Litvinov's desk. Litvinov nodded his head curtly and then with his fat fingers curled in on themselves shooed her out of the room by making a brushing motion. He opened the file, read the first page intently, and then flipped through the rest of the file rapidly, wetting his thumb to turn the pages.

"Your friend *napelvat v dushu,"* he said. "Someone with very bad soul."

"Is he legal?"

"Legal? He come here in eighty-five. Odessa. Before that Afghanistan. Very bad war, Afghanistan. Vybotskaya, he with Black One Hundred, you know about?"

I shook my head.

"Better you not know. People in Black One Hundred, they do bad things."

"Who's he living with here, you know?"

Litvinov held the file sideways.

"It says he living with mather, sister. He probably not even speak English."

"Sister?"

"Da."

For just a second, Litvinov opened the file folder so that I could see the stapled photographs. I could tell that it was Tatiana's face in the folder.

"You sure it says it's his *sister?"*

"They both Vybotskaya, Yuri he born nineteen sixty-one, Tatiana, she born nineteen seventy-one."

"What about his other sister, Litvinov? The one who's a real beauty?"

Litvinov looked over the first page of the file, chewing his lip meditatively.

"Krassavitza? A Russian beauty? Only one sister. She from Odessa. She come here in eighty."

"You sure about this?"

Litvinov nodded his large head and put the file on his desk. "Fadder dead."

"One last thing, Counselor," I said. "It say anything in there about what this Yuri does for a living?"

Litvinov gave me a low sly look. "I know what he do."

I waited patiently in front of his desk.

"He pimp," he finally said. He didn't have any trouble at all finding the word.

Do You Think I'm a Bad Person?

IRENE ERGENWEILER DROVE her silver Jaguar convertible with a kind of fast slangy expertness. Watching her behind the wheel reminded me of the times I had watched her play tennis at her club in Marin. She was really an accomplished athlete. She would spring up and down behind the baseline, her smooth, tanned, and polished thighs working rhythmically underneath her frilly tennis skirt, which kept bouncing from her legs, and then attack the ball with a long fluid stroke. In between sets she would smoke by the umpire's chair.

"You mind if we go up to the headlands, Asher?"

"Me? Why should I mind? Headlands be terrific."

She threaded the sleek car through the traffic on Lombard and up the long curving approach to the Golden Gate Bridge. She had a trick of anticipating traffic so that she never seemed to brake unnecessarily or get caught behind poky drivers.

She took the first exit off the bridge. It snakes underneath the highway and then climbs the headlands of the Golden Gate National Recreation Area. It's sensational open country, with fantastic views of San Francisco, white in the bright sun, and the bay in front of the city, and the incredible expanse of the open Pacific on the other side of the Golden Gate.

At the top of the headlands, Irene swung the Jaguar onto the side of the road and got out; she parked her trim rear end against the fender of her car and almost immediately lit a cigarette. She smoked the way other woman breathed, taking in the tobacco voluptuously as if it were oxygen.

I sat there in the open car, resting my forearm on the sun-warmed metal of the door, and watched the blue smoke from her cigarette curl around her face. When she had smoked her cigarette almost down to the filter, she ground it out beneath her sandal.

"Take a walk?" she asked.

I got out of the car and followed her trim rear end up a marked gravel path. At the very top of the headlands, there's an old ruined World War II fort. It's nothing more than a series of low concrete blocks meant to hold heavy artillery in place, but it's a nice place to sit in the midday sun and the views are fantastic—out toward the bay or the ocean or even the endless row of dun-colored hills behind the fort, stretching toward the horizon. We climbed to the top concrete emplacement. I sat with my back against the wall. Irene squatted in front of me on her knees, her forearms on her thighs, like an Indian. I couldn't have maintained that pose for more than thirty seconds. She didn't seem to mind. Her legs had a perpetual springiness. There was a lot of graffiti on the wall, but it was old stuff, some of it from the 1940s.

"It's pretty up here," Irene said vaguely.

I looked out over the city and the bay and ocean spread out below us. "It's one of the golden places," I said.

"I suppose."

"You going to tell me what's bothering you, Irene, or you figure on waiting till I worm it out of you?"

"It's Eddie."

"What's he do this time, go for a Ponzi scheme?"

Irene smiled a tight little smile; it was supposed to be rueful. It just looked curt.

"He's going to confess to this sexual harassment thing."

"Eddie?"

"He's going to ask Knesterman to plead it out, get the best settlement he can."

A chipmunk popped up from behind the jagged edge of the concrete abutment and looked at us intently. Far above, a red-tailed hawk was flying upward on a thermal current. When its shadow fell across the concrete, the chipmunk darted back down into the concrete.

"Why's he doing it, Irene?"

"God knows it's not because he's guilty of anything, Asher. This was Marvin's bright idea. Marvin's the one who was absolutely obsessed with that fat little tramp. Eddie never even slept with her. He went along with the whole thing because it was Marvin's idea!"

The mention of Plumbeck's name seemed to sound the deep well of bitterness that was as much a part of her personality as the dark color of her skin or the uncanny whiteness of her teeth.

"Can you imagine? *Marvin* says renting a mistress is this *wonderful* idea and there's Eddie saying 'Hey, let's rent a mistress.' Asher, if Marvin had suggested playing Russian roulette, honestly I think Eddie would have gone along with it."

"Aren't you being a little hard on him, Irene?"

"Am I? I don't even know anymore. I do know that give Eddie a choice, he'd much rather be shooting baskets than making small talk on satin pillows with some bimbo."

"You think."

"Give me that much credit, Asher. You can't live with a man for seventeen years without knowing these things. My God, I'm lucky if I can get him to pay attention to me once in a blue moon."

I thought there might be a difference between making love to Alicia Tamaroff and Irene Ergenweiler; it was nothing I wanted to bring up.

Talking about Eddie's lack of interest seemed to release some sort of dark mirth. "It's absolutely amazing, Asher, how a man can be too tired to make love to his wife, not too tired to bounce out of bed and shoot hoops for hours on end."

"It's pretty amazing, Irene, but none of it makes a lot of sense to me. To hear you tell it, Eddie never even *thought* of going up there to nine-nine-nine Green, he's the kind of guy that would rather curl up with a good basketball than a blonde any day."

"I'm not saying Eddie's a saint, Asher. All I'm saying is I know him."

"For sure, Irene, but then why's he taking the hit on this sexual harassment thing?"

"Because he has to."

"Why?"

"Marvin's *crazy,* Asher. You know that. You *know* that Marvin's crazy. He's not going to stipulate to anything. Asher, he's *in love* with that little bitch. I mean, he's so totally in denial he still thinks it's some sort of mistake. I mean, he thinks that just *admitting* it was a terrible idea to put that woman in an apartment is compromising his precious relationship. He doesn't realize she's only in it for the money. That's *all* she was ever interested in, the money. I mean, really. It's so obvious."

"I still don't get it, Irene. Why isn't this all Marvin's problem?"

"Asher, wake up and smell the coffee. They're a partnership, right? If it goes to trial, they're liable for punitive damages. They're asking *seven million dollars.* Eddie has something like one point five million in insurance. Do you think I want to face the rest of my life owing some little tramp five and one-half million dollars?"

"I don't suppose, Irene."

Irene Ergenweiler finally got off her thigh and sat herself down on the concrete abutment, her long legs in front of her. "This way, Eddie stipulates to sexual harassment, Knesterman thinks he can get the other side to settle for insurance."

We sat that way in the warm sunlight. Irene seemed to have emptied herself of her bitterness.

After a long while, she said: "I want to ask you something."

I looked at Irene inquisitively.

"Do you think I'm a bad person, Asher? I mean, really bad?"

"We've known each other a long time, Irene," I said.

"Come on, Asher, that's not what I asked."

I said: "No, I don't think you're a bad person." It was what she wanted to hear and I didn't think I could persuade her that the question didn't mean a thing. She sat there, her taut brown face turned toward the forbidden sunshine. She was like a lizard; she derived her energy directly from the sun. She held her face like that for five minutes or so, finally breaking her pose to light another cigarette.

"Cigarettes and sunshine," she said, "how could anything that feels so good be harmful?" She coughed her deep wet smoker's cough.

"Hard to believe, Irene, seeing how they agree with you."

"You're one to talk," she said, taking a deep drag on her cigarette and arching her neck so that the sun could bathe the skin of her lintigoed chest. "You probably still eat red meat."

I snorted.

"Do you work out, Asher?" she asked suddenly. "I bet you don't."

"I gave up cigarettes. I figure I don't ever have to do anything disagreeable again."

Irene wasn't really interested in my health habits. "I think so long as I work out I'm okay," she said, stubbing out her cigarette on the concrete, and then stripping it and letting the wind blow the paper away.

"Kind of like high school algebra? The negative and positive sort of cancel one another out, is that it?"

"It makes sense to me, Asher, but listen, as long as we're talking, can you do me a favor? Can you talk to Eddie?"

"About what?"

"Just reassure him, Asher."

"About what?"

"I don't know. He's all puffed up."

Jaguar Time

I WALKED DOWN GREENWICH later that afternoon and wandered over to Pier 39. It's an old pier that the city had renovated; now it's filled with novelty stores and stores selling Swedish knives and little gadgets to trim your nose hairs and restaurants promising fresh seafood and authentic San Francisco sourdough bread. The seafood is strictly frozen and the bread is awful, but the pier itself is pleasant enough. I like to watch the sea gulls swoop over the splintery wooden railings; sometimes the sea lions that congregate on the rotten and abandoned piers abutting Pier 39 get into slow-moving fights with one another. It's a great show. One of my wives watched a fight between two enormous old bulls, with yellow teeth. Almost all the fighting is a matter of seeing which old bull can make the most noise and roar the loudest. When things had more or less quieted down, with absolutely nothing accomplished and neither bull the winner, she turned to me and said: "It really is this biological thing with you, isn't it? I mean there is absolutely no difference between you and that sea lion out there."

"You think?" I had said.

My wife nodded vigorously. "Oh, I *know,*" she said.

I ordered a spicy Thai sausage from a little sausage stand at the head of the pier and washed that down with a bottle of Thai beer. Then I walked south along the Embarcadero. The Loma Prieta earthquake had more or less destroyed the old elevated freeway above the Embarcadero; the waterfront is open now, and even though the great ships are gone, the place is still old and wooden and splintery and full of ghosts. The enormous white wooden buildings stand there in the sun, the proud crests of long-vanished steamship lines still mounted over the front doors. Every now and then a sparkling white cruise ship comes into the bay. I can see it sedately passing by the Golden Gate from my living room window, but it's not the same thing at all. A cruise ship can never be a trans-Pacific ocean liner, one bound for Singapore, an elegant woman wearing a fox stole over her shoulders waving sadly from the upper deck.

Irene Ergenweiler had arranged for Eddie to take the Jaguar over to the British Motor Car showroom on Folsom. The thing needed its weekly tune-up; I thought I might take Eddie out for coffee while the masters changed his car's spark plugs. I walked around the Embarcadero as far as Mission, and then walked down New Montgomery until I got to Folsom. The Jaguar showroom takes up half the block. Up front, they have the new Jags on parade, and in the back, they've got the old Jags up on the service blocks. It's kind of a shrine for the guys in the Bay Area who own Jags. They like to hang around the showroom and tell one another how terrific they are for owning Jags and how boring it would be to drive a Mercedes even though the Mercedes never needs to be taken in for work.

Eddie Ergenweiler was out by the service bay; he was practicing his jump shot in the open air, jumping up and flipping his wrist over, and then crouching and breaking free and jumping again. He was dressed in a brown three-piece suit, but he had his shirt collar loosened and he had taken off his jacket. When he saw me coming through the service door, he stopped jumping and eyed me cautiously.

"Irene tell you I'd be here, Asher?"

"How else would I know, Eddie?"

"What, she figures that if you tell me it's okay to plead out this sexual harassment thing, all of a sudden I'm going to see the light, say, hey, no reason I shouldn't tell the world I'm guilty of harassment, empty out my insurance policy, ruin my name? Is that what she figures?"

"You tell me, Eddie. I don't know."

A mechanic dressed in spotless white coveralls approaches Eddie Ergenweiler. He was carrying a clipboard; he wore an industrial stethoscope around his neck.

"Mr. Ergenweiler," he said, "I'm going to recommend you change the rotor cuff. It looks to me like she's wearing a little."

"How much's that gonna cost me?" Eddie asked.

"I'm not going to tell you it's cheap," said the mechanic, "probably be between four and five hundred dollars. Course we *could* just leave it as it is. Thing is, little woman, she's out there on some road late at night, rotor cuff seizes up . . ."

The mechanic delicately left the consequences to Eddie's imagination.

"Hell with it," Eddie said buoyantly, "she freezes up, she freezes up."

"You're the boss," said the mechanic, turning back to the service ramp.

"I've got to come to some Jag showroom, hear that," said Eddie sourly.

I chuckled and said: "Take a break from shooting hoops, Eddie. I'll buy you a beer around the corner."

Eddie looked around the service bay for his jacket and found it draped over the back of the green Leatherette sofa that stood next to a sputtering automatic coffee machine. After checking to make sure his wallet was intact, he said mordantly: "What do you know, Asher, wallet is still where I left it. Nine times out of ten, I come down here, thing jumps right out of my pocket heads off for the cashier."

"It's what happens you buy a Jag."

"*I* buy a Jag, Asher? Me, I wanted a Harley. *Irene* needs fifty thousand dollars' worth of worthless British steel go from the house over to the tennis courts, she comes home first thing she tells me is her serve is off *and* the car's making this funny noise."

We walked out through the showroom, past all the thrilling new cars and out onto the grit of Folsom. Years ago the neighborhood was covered with waterfront saloons, tough places where sullen thick-necked men came to drink away the brilliant sunny afternoons while bartenders named Moe or Curly wiped down the polished mahogany bar with a damp rag. The bars are still standing, but most of them have gone upscale to accommodate the office-worker crowds from the downtown financial district. Some of them are still run by the same gruff characters, trying to move with the times by cutting back on the alcohol and cutting in a line of chicken-breast sandwiches.

I steered Ergenweiler to MacSorley's, on the corner of Folsom and Fourth. It used to be a terrific bar, something straight out of Eugene O'Neill. It was still low and cool and smoky in the late afternoon; but except for a middle-aged woman drinking sedately, the long bar was empty. We bellied up to the bar. I ordered two beers from the waitress and some chips, and Ergenweiler ordered a garden-fresh veggie burger. Then he retreated to the men's room.

I thought I remembered the short-order cook from the old days, but I couldn't be sure. He took what looked like a meat patty and slapped it on the grill. When it began sizzling, he covered it with fried onions.

"What makes that thing a veggie burger?" I asked.

The short-order cook looked at me intently.

"It's on account of the onions," he said. "Them onions veggies, ain't they?"

"Let me get this straight," I said, marveling at it all, "you fry up a *regular* burger, throw some onions on it and call it a veggie burger?"

"Mister," said the short-order cook, "ain't no one *ever* complained about my veggie burger."

He spatuled the burger onto a plate and scooped a huge wad of french fries from a fry basket that had been suspended in bubbling lard.

I pointed to the fries. "Nonfat?"

The short-order cook didn't miss a beat. "Them's *low*-fat fries," he said. "Them's low-fat on account of years ago I used to fry 'em twice. Now I don't anymore so as they got less fat. If they got less fat, they're low-fat. Am I right?"

Ergenweiler emerged from the men's room and took up his plate; I brought our beers to the table. Ergenweiler was already munching away by the time I slid into the booth.

"Want a bite?" he asked. "Thing tastes just like a real burger."

I waited for Eddie to finish up his veggie burger and wipe his face and clean his fingers carefully with his napkin. He had been happy while he was eating; his mood dropped as soon as he had nothing to do.

"I never slept with her, Asher," he said abruptly.

"Is that what you're telling Irene?"

"Is that what she told you?"

"It's what she wants to believe. It's the kind of thing *any* woman wants to believe, Eddie. Your wife catches you in bed with another woman, tell her you're taking a class in podiatry under the sheets, or studying astrophysics. Nine times out of ten she'll accept it."

"I'll remember that, Asher."

"Only thing is, I'm not a woman and I'm not your wife. *I* don't believe you."

Ergenweiler looked at me in that curiously innocent way he had of looking at people; he shrugged his shoulders indifferently. "She was pretty hard to resist," he said. "I mean maybe it *was* a little coarse and all, but Asher, it was like totally unbelievable. I would go up there, she'd have these old Knick tapes on the VCR, she'd be wearing these great outfits, I don't know, Lycra pajamas or something, cold beer, I'd watch these unbelievable games, you remember what a terrific starting lineup the Knicks had—Bradley and DeBuschere and the other guys—and then she'd do me while I was watching the game, it was unreal, Asher, you know it was like this is the way it's *supposed* to be, not this bicker, bicker, bicker. Christ, Irene can pick a fight about which way's the right way to floss your teeth, she comes in the bathroom, sees me standing there with the stupid tube of floss in my hand, she's like why don't you *cut* the floss before you use it, Eddie? Can you imagine? Why don't you *cut* the floss? This is my life. Me and the flossing dragon."

"What happened to spoil the good times, Eddie? Aside from running out of old Knick tapes."

"It was Marvin," said Ergenweiler despondently.

"Plumbeck?"

"He said he'd kill me if I ever went up there again."

"Pretty emphatic, was he?"

"Asher, trust me on this. He was completely serious. I mean me, I can take it or leave it, you know what I mean? But Marvin was just cuckoo about her. I mean, in the office, it was Alicia this and Alicia that, and hey, I'm going to run off to Paris with Alicia. I mean he had it bad, Asher."

"So you just cut out?"

"Had to."

"That's real sweet of you, Eddie. So how come *you're* pleading to sexual harassment and Marvin's not?"

Ergenweiler looked at me with a blubbery confused look. "Asher, I don't *know,*" he said. "Only thing is, every time I go over it with Irene, it comes out I take the rap. We don't settle, it goes to court, I could be in hock to this bimbo for the rest of my life. I mean, she's right about Marvin, God knows he's willing to go to the mat on this one, he's so burnt about the Maison Jarr thing."

"So what you're telling me, Eddie, Plumbeck bit the bullet for you on due diligence, you're going to bail him out on harassment?"

Ergenweiler shrugged his shoulders; his shoe-polish eyes were glistening in his long narrow face.

"It sort of looks that way, doesn't it?"

The Pimp's Diner

SEYBOLD KNESTERMAN WAS in rare good form when he called late the next morning.

"Asherfeld," he said with a snort of satisfaction. "I've just gotten off the telephone with counsel for Tamaroff et al."

"Who?"

"This woman who is suing Ergenweiler and Plumbeck for harassment," he said impatiently.

"Tamaroff."

"That *is* what I said, Asherfeld. Really, you are uncommonly dense this morning. In any case, they're going to settle for insurance."

"How much that come to, Knesterman?"

"I'm afraid it's a bit."

"You mean Eddie's whole policy is going down the tubes?"

"Asherfeld, *whatever* Mr. Ergenweiler has to pay, it is going to be less than what he would have to pay at trial. We both know that."

"They going to cancel on him?"

Knesterman snorted into the telephone to indicate his contempt for my question. *"Of course* they're going to cancel, Asherfeld," he said.

"It's going to be hard for him to work again, at least in any kind of corporate setting, Knesterman. He can't go back to work without insurance."

"I'm afraid that can't be helped. In any case, I just called to let you know. Send your statement to Frieda. I'll see to it that she cuts you a check straightaway."

I got myself showered and shaved after hanging up with Knesterman and hustled myself out of my apartment and down Greenwich and over to a hole-in-the-wall pizzeria named Omar's on Columbus. It was a late morning hustling kind of day. All over the city, guys were hustling to get to terrifically important power lunches and hustling back up to their offices on the thirty-fifth floor of the Bank of America tower and hustling to get in conference with a lot of other hustling kind of guys. I didn't much want to join them, but I felt like snapping my towel when I finished shaving and hustling anyway, even if I were only hustling to grab a slice of pizza. They serve New York–style pizza at Omar's, which means you order by the slice. The crust is thin and chewy and the only thing on the pizza is tomato sauce and cheese. Omar was an Iranian refugee. He kept a formal picture of the Shah on the wall of his pizzeria opposite his oven. He had never gotten over having had to leave Iran.

"My friend," he said with a kind of oily intonation in his voice. "I wasn't always this."

He pointed to the little pizzeria with a heavy gesture of his hand.

"What, then?" I asked.

Omar waved his hand again, this time in an airy gesture. "Better you not know what I do," he said.

"You're right," I said, turning my attention back to the pizza slice. "It's better."

Omar looked at me shrewdly through his narrow black eyes. His wife walked over from the far end of the restaurant counter. She was a short, dark, very domineering woman dressed in a kind of partial chador, which left her gnomic face exposed. She said something to Omar in Farsi. He sighed theatrically. "She tell me I have to learn to accept my fate."

"Could be worse, Omar," I said, looking up at the picture of the Shah.

I had an espresso at the Maudit after lunch, sipping the black bitter liquid at one of the outside tables. There wasn't a trace of fog in the sky. The light was an intense blue-yellow. When I had finished up wasting all the time I could manage to waste, I trudged down Columbus and up Greenwich to my apartment. It's a terrific street in a terrific part of town and every time I walk up it I think of all the mean crabbed streets in all the mean crabbed cities I could be walking up. My landlord, the Chairman, was standing in front of the house, reverently running a chamois over the fender of his enormous Chrysler. He spotted me and let go with a volley of Mandarin. He refused to accept my inability to speak Chinese as anything more than a whim. He pointed upstairs toward my apartment. I shrugged my shoulders helplessly, a gesture he habitually took as a sign of perfect comprehension.

When I got to my door, I thought I understood what he had been trying to tell me: the doorknob was warm and greasy.

Trudelwein and Swoboda were standing in my living room. Trudelwein was looking over my mail, and Swoboda was standing where he stood the last time he was in my apartment, by the window, which he had opened.

"Hope you don't mind, Aaron," said Trudelwein, "your landlord, he lets us in."

"My landlord doesn't speak a word of English," I said.

"Maybe so, but he certainly is respectful of the police. Wouldn't you say he's one very respectful slope, Detective?"

"Outstanding," said Swoboda.

"You guys are on the force out at *Berkeley?*" I said. "What happened, you miss sensitivity training or something?"

"We didn't miss it, Aaron. It just didn't take. Wouldn't you say that's right, Detective?"

"Didn't take at all."

"See, Aaron, we're the guys have to stand around some body

been in the water ten days gets fished out of San Pablo Bay. It generally takes the edge off our sensitivity."

"It takes it right off," said Swoboda.

I walked over to Trudelwein and took my mail from his hand.

"But, hey," said Trudelwein, "we're not here to talk about business, landlord, Aaron."

"Sure, it's a social visit."

"Almost, Aaron. We come by give you a message."

"Big boogie, set fire to Miriam Plumbeck's house? What's he calling himself, Detective?"

"Goes by the name of Shaboo."

"Shaboo, Shakalaka, Tuttifrutti, who knows? Only thing is, his name isn't Shaboo, it's Fred Williamson, man attended Berkeley. Can you believe it, Detective?"

"Hard to believe."

"Course even figuring he gets into Berkeley on account of the white guys have one hand tied behind their backs, you got to figure this boogie's just plain dumb."

"Dumber than dumb."

"Why's that?" I asked.

"Why's that, Aaron? On account of half of Berkeley hears this terrific argument he's having with Ms. Plumbeck, on account of he leaves his fingerprints all over the house, on account of he's a lowlife degenerate can't figure out that it's a bad idea boogie doing business with a white woman."

Trudelwein paused for breath. "Which brings me to my next point, Aaron."

"I can't wait."

"Shabootituttifrutti says he needs to speak to you, one lowlife to another."

"Be like a lowlife convention," Swoboda chimed in.

"You guys came all the way out here to tell me Shaboo wants to speak to me? Must be slow working out in Berkeley you have all this time on your hands."

"You're right, Aaron. It's not *exactly* like we're here on a social call. Wouldn't you say that's correct, Detective?"

"Absolutely. Absolutely, it's correct."

"We're also here to tell you something up close and personal. It's kind of this thing we do, it's like lowlife counseling."

"It *is* lowlife counseling."

"You see, Aaron, we figure we know what Shabootituttifrutti wants to talk to you about."

"What's that?"

"It's not affirmative action, Aaron."

"Not affirmative action at all."

"Way we figure it, Aaron, Shabootituttifrutti's probably going to offer to deal with you. Now I know what you're going to ask me. You're going to ask me, why would a fine upstanding citizen like myself want to deal with a lowlife like Shabootituttifrutti? The reason is, Aaron, in the first place, you're not a fine upstanding citizen, and in the second place, the way we figure it, you're a snoopy kind of guy and Shabootituttifrutti is the kind of guy trading in snoopy kind of stuff, if you get my drift."

"Pretty hard to miss, that drift," said Swoboda.

"Now here's the counseling part, Aaron. We think you'd be better off not dealing at all."

"We think it'd be a poor idea even talking to this Shaboo," said Swoboda.

"And this is for my own good, that what you're telling me?"

"No, Aaron," said Trudelwein patiently, "truth of the matter is what's good for you don't mean much to us. That's the kind of guys we are. We're not caring people, Aaron. Wouldn't you say that's true, Detective?"

"Not caring at all."

"What means a lot to us, Aaron, is we got this big boogie tight on felony one, we'd like to see he gets to spend a little quality time over at Folsom, last thing we want is someone like you trading information with Shabootituttifrutti, putting all sorts of poor ideas into the head of the district attorney."

"Perish the thought," said Swoboda.

"You guys all through?" I asked. "Or you figure I could use a little advice about how to deal with my ex-wives?"

"We're all through, Aaron," said Trudelwein, moving heavily toward the door. "Take a couple hours, get all indignant about how the police gave you a rough time, then concentrate on what we're saying."

Swoboda started from the window and moved to follow Trudelwein through my front door.

Standing at the door, Trudelwein said: "Wives, Aaron? *Wives?* You must use them up like Kleenex. Wouldn't you say that's true, Detective?"

"Like Kleenex," said Swoboda, crossing my living room.

For some reason a police matron brought Shaboo up to the shabby third-floor interrogation room. He was dressed in prison grays and he was manacled. He hadn't been in prison for more than three days, but he had already acquired the puffy look that everyone in prison acquires. He sat himself down awkwardly at the chipped elliptical conference table. The heavyset matron pointed toward the video camera mounted on a metal ceiling flange. Then she thrust her clipboard at me and said in a single breath: "Conference videotaped at all times, prisoner remains seated, hands facing table, manacles visible at all times, visitors remain seated in assigned seats, no recording instruments, no dictating machines, no laptops, no Walkmans, no smoking on account of Berkeley facilities now smoke free, no food allowed in conference room, no physical communication between prisoners and visitors, no sexual contact, contraband any form be immediately seized by duty officers, you understand all this signify you understanding sign on the bottom line."

I signed. The matron withdrew from the room.

"How come you're not out on bail, Shaboo?"

"Friday, I got a hearing Friday morning in Superior Court."

He leaned himself forward so that he could rest his forearms on the table. There was a long awkward pause between us. Then Shaboo said what everyone in prison always says. He said: "Asherfeld, I didn't do it."

"I didn't figure you asked me here to confess, Shaboo."

"Throwing a bottle of gasoline against some dumb white woman's house, that just isn't my style."

"No, I remember. Your style is to threaten to peddle her ass in some cheap whorehouse. You're right. That's a whole lot classier."

Shaboo made a visible effort to control himself; I thought for a strange moment that he was going to weep with frustration.

"I'm going to tell you how it happened, Asherfeld. You promise to listen to what I say, then I'm going to give you something you really, really want to hear."

I didn't think I had anything to lose. I crossed my legs and edged my back into the hard oak chair. Shaboo sat up suddenly, his manacles clanking. At once a metallic voice droned into the room: "Hands on table at all times, manacles visible."

Shaboo slumped slightly so that he could rest his forearms easily on the table again.

"Got a call that night from Miriam Plumbeck. Said she wanted to pay me off in full, she'd have the money up front, all counted, and could I just come over? I say give the money one my boys, she say I want to put the money in your hand so as I know it's over and done with. I get there, she's how about coffee, she's you want a piece of this cake, I'm like, lady, do I *look* like I'm here scoff up some pastry just give me my money, she's hold on, hold on, just have a cup of coffee, I drink the coffee, I tell her lady I don't *eat* refined sugars, she's like just taste it, I eat the cake, and I'm still out my money."

Shaboo paused and looked up at me. "You following me on this, Asherfeld?"

"It's not rocket science, Shaboo."

Shaboo plunged on: "So anyway, I'm sitting there, I'm already buzzed on account of all that white sugar I'm eating, I'm like lady I can't spend the night drinking coffee, eating pastry with you and all of a sudden she tells me, money's not here, it's on its way. On its way! I say lady you figure money is *walking* over here? She says no, my ex is bringing it. Asherfeld, I hear this, I'm like, lady, you get the money, you wrap it up send it to me FedEx, you think this civil servant's going to spend time dealing with your ex-husband, you crazy."

Shaboo leaned back again in his chair, but he remembered to keep his arms on the table.

"Shit," he said, "I saw that movie De Niro gets all wigged out an all."

"What happened next?"

"What happened next? Asherfeld, *nothing* happened next. Like I told you, I'm out of there."

"What Miriam Plumbeck say when you left?"

"I didn't give her a chance to say anything. I told you. I hear about her ex coming over, I'm *out* of there. Next thing I know, police roust me out of bed, tell me I firebombed her house. Now that's the truth."

"It's a nice story, Shaboo," I said. "Only thing is, no one's going to believe it."

"They will if you tell it."

"Why's that?"

"You're white," Shaboo said simply. "You an upstanding citizen, you tell the police you were out to see me, tell them I agreed to take money on the dollar settle this debt. Tell them I'm a businessman, tell them I ain't no no-account street hoodlum beat up on women. Asherfeld, I got *four* wives back home. They think I'm beating up on women, they gonna crucify me."

"It's rough, Shaboo, and my heart goes out to you. It really does. Only thing is, you left something out of your story."

"What's that?"

"It's the part about why I should do anything to help you. I seem to have missed that."

"You didn't miss it, Asherfeld. I didn't tell it to you."

"Why don't you do it now? It'll help focus my attention if I speak to the D.A."

Shaboo shifted in his seat again, clanking his manacles as he moved his forearms.

"Miriam Plumbeck? Her ex some dude named Marvin?"

I nodded.

"Marvin, he bad," said Shaboo, slipping into street slang. "He real bad."

"Marvin Plumbeck's an accountant, Shaboo. You talking badder than that or is this a social statement you're making?"

Shaboo smiled enigmatically. "Accountant, my black ass," he said. "He so bad he murdered a pretty white lady."

I sat stock-still. "Who you hearing this from?"

"Friend of mine in the city."

"How would he know?"

"He like you, Asherfeld. His business to know things."

"What else does he know?"

"He know where she buried."

At around eleven I called Yellow Cab for a taxi. I didn't feel like walking anywhere. My driver was heavyset and muscular; he was wearing a leather vest, his arms and shoulders bare underneath the vest. He carried a toothpick in his mouth, but that was his only large concession to cleanliness. The taxi held a rank feral odor. When he leaned forward to flip the meter, I could see he had a swastika tattooed on his biceps. Underneath the tattoo were the initials *WRL.*

"Swell tattoo you've got," I said, as he drove sedately down Greenwich and over to Columbus.

"Shows pride in my being a white man," he said in a flat uninflected voice.

"What's the *WRL?"*

"White Resistance League, man."

"What are you guys resisting?"

"Niggers."

We accelerated smoothly onto Columbus and drove down into the financial district without hitting a light.

"White race's greatest race in the world," he added unemotionally when we crossed into the Tenderloin.

"I can see why," I said.

I got out at the corner of O'Farrell and Polk and tried to amble inconspicuously into the Pimp's Diner on the southwest corner of the street. It wasn't easy. I didn't look much like a pimp and I didn't look much like a hooker, and except for the waitresses carrying food up and down the aisle, there wasn't anybody in the diner except for pimps and hookers. I thought the noise of conversation might have dropped when I entered the place; it might have been my imagination. I edged over to one of the waitresses who was manning the cashier at the end of the counter.

"Know where I can find Little Lulu?"

"You a friend of his?"

"I hope so," I said earnestly.

"Back table."

I walked to the back of the diner, past the working girls who were chowing down large plates of fries and talking loudly about lipstick or child care. Little Lulu was in the last booth. It wasn't hard to spot him. He had on a full-length white fox fur coat with a shawl collar, and he wore enough expensive gold jewelry to light up the polar night. A very pretty young black woman dressed in hot pink pants was seated next to him, her head resting demurely on his shoulder. There was a plate of half-eaten french fries in front of her.

"Little Lulu?"

Little Lulu looked up at me and smiled radiantly. He had beautiful even white teeth. "To my friends," he said elegantly, in a smooth whiskey-cured voice.

I slid into the banquette and tried to feel at home.

"I'm Aaron Asherfeld," I said, extending my hand.

"Aaron Asherfeld," said Lulu in the same whiskey-cured voice. "Now that's a fine name. Aaron, I'd like you to meet my number one lady." He shrugged his shoulder to prompt the young woman by his side to lift her warm pretty head. She looked at me and gave me a fuzzy smile. I could see that she was very sleepy. "LeeAnn, honey, this here's Aaron; Aaron, this here's LeeAnn."

LeeAnn blinked her eyes rapidly at me several times; she seemed to be searching for something to say. Finally she found what she was looking for. "Pleased to meet you," she said demurely, and replaced her head promptly on Lulu's fur-robed shoulder.

"Lady's been working since eight in the evening, she just all tired out. Ain't that the truth, honey?"

LeeAnn snuggled her head farther into Lulu's shoulder and murmured something into the fur.

"Course," said Lulu gravely, "for the right man, she could wake right up."

LeeAnn lifted her head for a moment and gave me her warm blurry unfocused smile.

"Go back to sleep, LeeAnn. I'm not here on a social visit."

Lulu looked at me indifferently. "What you here for, then?"

"Shaboo told me to look you up."

A slowly dawning smile of comprehension crossed Lulu's features. "Shaboo," he said, "now that man's plain unlucky."

"Yes, he is," I said.

"Sittin' in some jail over in Berkeley on account of some white woman got her house burned down."

LeeAnn lifted her head from Lulu's shoulder and said: "Who got their house burned down, Daddy?"

"LeeAnn, honey, your daddy's talking business now, you be quiet."

"Whatever," said LeAnn obediently, placing her head back down.

"Course, the way I hear tell it, Aaron, you just about ready to tell them police that Shaboo he got nothing to do with burning down some white woman's house."

Lulu had a wonderful voice: it was low, even, measured, and melodious.

"It'd be a lot easier telling the police anything at all if Shaboo hadn't left his fingerprints all over that house in Berkeley."

"Aaron, reason I'm even *talking* with you is that I know you got a hard road ahead of you."

LeeAnn shifted sleepily in her seat, stretching her supple young body toward Lulu.

"I can't make any promises," I said. "You know that."

"You can't be making any promises, I can't be divulging any information," said Lulu coldly.

I pushed myself up from the banquette and said: "Nice talking to you, Lulu. I'll just tell Shaboo we weren't able to have a meeting of the minds."

"Aaron," said Lulu evenly, "you know what happens I get angry?"

"Sure," I said. "You beat up one of your women. Probably evens the flow right out."

"You got a lot of nerve comin' in here and insultin' me to my face, Aaron."

"What? You *don't* beat up on your women?"

"He only hits me when I need it," said LeeAnn.

Lulu shrugged LeeAnn's head from his shoulder and rearranged his shoulders underneath his coat with a furious ruffle. Then he said: "I cut your heart out in two seconds, no one in this diner lift a finger to stop me."

I edged away from the banquette and shrugged my own shoulders in my windbreaker.

"Go ahead."

Lulu stood up unceremoniously, knocking the plate of french fries onto himself, the ketchup running along the fur of his fox in a long tendril.

LeeAnn said: "Aw, honey."

Lulu stared down in disbelief at himself. "Now look what you made me do," he said.

"What *I* made you do?"

"Asherfeld, this here coat cost me twelve thousand dollars."

"Cheap at twice the price," I said. "Of course, the ketchup looks sort of tacky, but hell, you can cut the thing up, make panty liners for your ladies. Just cut around the ketchup."

"Daddy," LeeAnn said, "you just let me blot it with cold water, stain'll come right out."

"Don't you be blotting anything," Lulu said, scrambling out of his coat. "Tomorrow morning, *first* thing, you take this coat over Peninou, tell them this here stain's ketchup. You got that? First thing tomorrow I'm over your apartment I don't want to see you lollygagging in front of no TV you take this coat on over and have it cleaned." He carefully draped the coat over LeeAnn's lap.

"Daddy," she said, "how I'm gonna work any more tonight I got to carry a coat full of ketchup around on the street?"

Lulu looked at LeeAnn as if he were contemplating an imbecile. "LeeAnn, you not going to work, you going to take your fat ass out of this booth and you going to take this coat back to your apartment and you going to watch it until Peninou she opens and then you going to take it over to Peninou and tell them get this stain out."

LeeAnn carefully bundled the coat in her arms and slid out from the banquette and walked down the aisle of the diner, her tight rear end shimmering in her hot pink pants.

Lulu sat himself down. His sartorial catastrophe had deflated him. "Now where were we?" he asked.

"You were about to tell me what happened up there on nine-nine-nine Green, Lulu. And who did it. And where the body went."

"Was that what I was going to do?" he asked, idly dipping an errant fry into the ketchup and eating it morosely.

"Yes, it was," I said. "It's what you *wanted* to do all along."

A German-speaking German Shepherd

THE NEXT DAY I spent almost ten hours tramping through the salt marsh at the northern end of the San Francisco Bay together with a policeman named Wurtleschein and a German shepherd named Reinhardt. We had gotten together at the northwest corner of the marsh. Wurtleschein introduced me to Reinhardt. "This here's a highly trained canine investigator, Mr. Asherfeld," he said. "I'd appreciate it if you didn't pet Officer Reinhardt, try to interact with him in any way."

"*Officer* Reinhardt?"

"We consider him a member of the force," said Wurtleschein somberly.

"Hey, it takes all kinds," I said.

"Officer Reinhardt's language of command is German," Wurtleschein said. "Any interaction in English is apt to confuse the officer."

"Probably send him right to the dictionary."

Reinhardt sank from a sitting position to his belly, resting his black muzzle on his tawny paws; he looked up at us both. I didn't think it mattered all that much to him whether we spoke in English or German.

Wurtleschein said: "Every thirty minutes, Officer Reinhardt gets a rest break, every two hours he gets hot broth, so we generally build our searches in two-hour intervals."

I looked down at the shepherd. "This pooch worth it?" I asked. "I mean underneath all that fur, he *is* just a pooch, right?"

Wurtleschein bristled. "Officer Reinhardt comes from a line of eleven champions. *German* German shepherds. He was born in Stuttgart."

"What? You guys hike over to Stuttgart buy a pooch? No wonder my taxes are so high."

"Department doesn't feel American shepherds measure up," said Wurtleschein. "The officer has outstanding conformation." He looked down at the dog and said: "Rheinhardt, *auf.*"

The dog continued to lie there, looking up at us with his melancholy brown eyes.

"Reinhardt, *auf.*"

Very slowly, the dog lumbered out of his lying position and took to his feet. He shook himself vigorously, sending fur flying on the rocky beach, and then immediately swiveled to stick his nose into his crotch.

"Reinhardt," said Wurtleschein. *"Achtung."* Turning to me, he said: "That means *pay attention.*" The dog had now sunk to his haunches and was busy licking his genitals.

"I know how it is, pooch," I said. "Four years of high school Spanish and I still can't order a tostada."

"Reinhardt," said Wurtleschein with just a note of irritation in his voice. *"Achtung."*

The dog left off licking himself, stood up, and looked up at Wurtleschein. *"Gut,"* said Wurtleschein. Then he said: "Rheinhardt, *setz.*"

The shepherd continued to stand, his long tail unfurled behind him waving like a banner.

"Let me get this straight, Wurtleschein," I said. "This chowhound here is an *asset* to the department?"

"He's having some trouble focusing because you're making him nervous."

I turned to the dog and said: "That true? I'm making you nervous?" The dog continued to wave his tail in the stiff morning breeze.

"Tell you what, Wurtleschein," I said. "Why don't we just skip the dog and pony show, have the pooch do his thing? I'm not exactly looking forward to finding what I figure we're going to be finding."

We set off through the tall reeds that came up almost to the edge of the beach. The water was shallow enough for wading for almost half a mile out into the bay. Wurtleschein had gotten me a pair of rubber hip huggers, but even so, it was slow, unpleasant going. There was real sand somewhere underneath the muck of the salt marsh, but you only got to it when your foot squished down half a foot of bay mud, so that each step sounded with a gross wet plop. After wading through the marsh for a couple of hundred yards, the two of us were winded. The dog thought it was all terrific. He looked like a big heavy animal to me, but he managed to muscle his way through the marsh by pushing off from his hind legs and gliding on his chest. He would bound out thirty yards for every thirty yards we covered and then come bounding back to Wurtleschein, his tail wagging.

After thirty minutes, Wurtleschein declared that Officer Reinhardt needed a rest break. We walked back to the rocky beach and sank down. My thighs were on fire. The dog sank to his haunches and laid his massive head across his paws. Small soapy waves were cresting onto the beach.

"Pretty frustrating work," said Wurtleschein, looking out across the salt marsh.

"Think we'll find anything?"

"Hard to say. Lot of people think they know something's out here, turns out to be some other place. Then again, someone really does dump a body in here, two weeks tops there's not much left."

I shivered involuntarily. "Doesn't seem like a very long time."

"You got your salt," said Wurtleschein, "that's like a natural corrosive." He paused meditatively and patted his dog's head. "And you got your tides, they'll tend to pull a body right out middle of the bay."

"Tides go both ways," I said.

"Tide goes out with a body, doesn't mean she comes back with a body," said Wurtleschein. "People got a lot of misperceptions about what happens to your average corpse. Don't get me wrong. Police too. We get calls all the time some department over in Novato or down Solano telling us someone's been in the bay couple months and could we keep an eye out. Not going to happen. Thing you got to remember is by the time your body hits the water it's not anyone's sweetheart or anything like that, just another part of the food chain."

I shivered again.

Wurtleschein checked his watch to make sure he had given Reinhardt his allotted rest and we shuffled to our feet again. *"Achtung,"* he said to the dog as the animal stretched himself languidly.

It went on like that for the rest of the day. We stopped regularly every thirty minutes to give the dog a break; and every two hours, Wurtleschein actually trudged back to his police car, which he had left up on the causeway, and poured something that looked like tomato soup from a large thermos into a doggie bowl.

"You got any coffee in there?" I asked once, pointing to the back of the car, which was separated from the front by a length of mesh fence.

Wurtleschein looked at me as if the very thought that *we* might need some coffee was outlandish.

We crossed the salt marsh walking from south to north and crossed it back again walking from north to south, walking a little farther out in the marsh each time. Wurtleschein carried a long flexible pole, which he rested on his shoulder. The first couple of hours, the dog let off a lot of steam, plowing through the marsh, but by late afternoon, he seemed pooped and strangely depressed by the whole business. He would trot out over the marsh for a few yards and then look back at Wurtleschein. Then Wurtleschein would shout out something in German and the dog would keep going. I didn't think his heart was in it.

"Looks like one pooped pooch," I said.

"Officer Reinhardt's been under a lot of strain," said Wurtleschein. "That foundry that collapsed over in Benicia? We had him on loan to local authorities, man he's working with didn't speak proper German, officer got confused, puts a lot of stress on a canine investigator when the chain of command isn't clear."

"What he do? File for disability?"

Wurtleschein looked at me with surprise. "No, no. Nothing that serious," he said. "We put him on antioxidants, gave him a lot of rest. I put in some quality time with him. He snapped right out of it."

Just then the dog stopped threading his way through the reeds of the marsh and stiffened.

Wurtleschein noticed it right away. *"Such,"* he said. Very slowly, the dog lowered his torso and began edging into the taller grass farther out from the rocky shore. He powered himself into the reeds. He wasn't quite swimming but he wasn't walking either.

I watched him muscle his way out from shore with a mounting sense of dread.

Wurtleschein looked over at me; he must have noticed that I had turned green. "You want to wait up on the causeway?" he asked.

"I'll be all right."

Far out on the marsh the dog raised himself from his crouch and began barking in short staccato bursts. His barks sounded curiously intelligent.

We both stiffened. "Reinhardt, *steh,"* said Wurtleschein. We made for the dog at a diagonal to the shore, sloshing through the salt marsh. By the time we reached the tall reeds, the water was up to our knees. I could feel its bone-numbing cold through the waders I was wearing. It must have been tough on the dog: the water came up to almost his shoulders. He stood there rigidly, barking in those short intelligent barks of his.

The dog held his pose until we got level to him and then all at once relaxed and began wagging his tail. Wurtleschein pointed back toward the beach and said: "Reinhardt, *nach Hause."* The dog turned with a great spring that shook a shower of droplets into the air and bounded back toward the beach. "Lot of things it doesn't pay to have a dog see," said Wurtleschein with dignity. I didn't say anything. We pushed way farther out into the marsh, the gentle waves lapping against our waders. Wurtleschein began probing the marsh bed in front of him with his pole. "Anything still here's going to be stuck in the mud," he said. "Be prepared for a lot of gas to come up I hit any soft tissue with the pole."

"What do we do then?"

"Use the pole as a marker, I'll beep Forensics," said Wurtleschein, patting his waterproof belt beeper with his free hand. He kept probing the ground in front of us with the pole.

We were as far out on the marsh as we could get by wading and we both saw it at the same time. It was suspended from one of the reeds and it looked like a whitish rag. It must have been what the dog spotted. Wurtleschein leaned forward, snaked it with his pole and drew it in toward us by sliding his pole hand over hand underneath his arm. "Probably nothing," he said.

I took the rag from the pole's tip. A lot of it was in shreds, but it was still clearly a woman's blouse. I could feel the texture of silk underneath the slime of water and the row of mother-of-pearl buttons running down the front was still intact. I held the blouse up so that the flat late-afternoon light shone through it. I could see that a name tag had been sewn onto the back collar of the blouse. I held the blouse by the collar and brought it to my face for a closer look. I could smell the deep fetid smell of the marsh on the blouse, and the smell of salt. I could still read the name all right. The dark blue letters that had been stitched onto a white name tag said *Alicia Tamaroff.*

The blouse didn't excite a whole lot of interest at the police department in Benicia. The desk sergeant greeted Wurtleschein and Reinhardt jovially, but when Wurtleschein told him what we had found, he seemed reluctant even to write it up. "You want I should tell the lieutenant you guys are filing on account of you found a blouse?" he asked incredulously.

"I'd be grateful," I said. I was cold and wet and tired and I had a cold wet tired dead pit in my stomach.

"Tell you what," the sergeant said, "*you* tell the lieutenant."

Wurtleschein disappeared into the back of the precinct with Reinhardt. The desk sergeant waved me through the wooden gates that separated the open floor space from the mounted podium holding his desk, and pointed with a pen toward a door.

"Lieutenant's second door on the left," he said amiably.

I didn't much expect the lieutenant to be perturbed by my story, and he wasn't. I told him everything I knew. The lieutenant was a sober civil-service type. He was reserved, quiet and efficient.

"Look here, Asherfeld," he said. "No one's filed a missing-person report, least of all not so we know about it here. And no one's showed up dead in the bay. I'm already out overtime for Wurtleschein and the dog." He held his hands up, palms outward. "It's like my hands are tied. I just can't justify anything more in terms of time and resources. You show me a complaint or a missing-person report, then maybe I could go with you on this, but as it stands, there's nothing there yet."

I got up heavily. "I understand, Lieutenant," I said.

The lieutenant looked at me shrewdly. "This someone special you're looking for, Asherfeld?"

"I only met her once."

A look of surprise crossed his face: he lifted his gold-framed spectacles just slightly from his nose.

"Why don't you let it go, then? Beautiful young woman like you say, you come out here, you spend a day tramping through the marsh. You done your duty. Let her father or her brothers go find her."

I said: "You're probably right."

Roll Back

IT HAD STILL BEEN LIGHT when I left the north end of the bay, but by the time I got to the Golden Gate Bridge, thick fog was streaming across the bay. Cars all had their headlights on. I had my windows closed but the cold seeped right into the car. By the time I got back to Greenwich Street, the city was covered with fog, the thick wet stuff drifting up every Telegraph Hill side street and meandering into all the Chinatown alleys.

I got up to my apartment and stripped off my clothes. The dark muddy smell of the salt marsh filled the little bathroom. I stood for a long time under a shower, letting the hot water beat against the back of my neck and listening to the foghorns. I could hear them even over the noise of the running water. When I finished up I lay quietly on my bed, still in my wet terry-cloth robe. The dark part of the night came and went.

I awoke at dawn and got myself dressed and showered and walked over to Columbus to a Korean pancake place that opened early every morning. I ordered up French toast. The stuff came with a little tub of imitation maple syrup and a wad of butter and a ramekin of blueberries. The Korean cook eyed me from his grill as I ate my breakfast; he had that look of distaste that all Koreans get when they watch what Americans eat. No one looks as malevolent as a Korean short-order cook.

When I had finished up, I walked slowly back up Columbus and over to Greenwich. Saint Mary's park was empty in the cold light. Even the pigeons were huddled on the trees, waiting for the sun to warm things up. The smooth sandstone facing of the church had an unpleasant sea green color, a trick of the morning light and the fog.

I got myself shaved and showered before the light had completely filled my apartment. I sat at my desk for an hour, watching the fog sift through the tangle of blackberry vines in the garden below my window. As soon as I heard the deep mournful bells of the church sound the next hour, I called Plumbeck at his office. His new receptionist answered the telephone. I told her I needed to see Plumbeck.

"Can I tell him what this is in reference to?"

"No."

"Hold, please," she said.

In a second she was back on the line. "He's going to be tied up this morning, Mr. Asherfeld. Can you check in with us later?"

I hung up with Plumbeck's receptionist without saying another word and shuffled on my windbreaker. I stood there by my door for a minute or so, looking at the walls and the hardwood floors and the windows that gave out over the bay. There was nothing out there but water now.

I got to Plumbeck's office at a little past ten. I had walked the whole way from Telegraph Hill at one of those dogged paces just under a jog, but when the elevator was slow in coming I found myself drumming my bunched fingers into my palms with irritation.

His receptionist was busy doing nothing when I swung open the doors with *Plumbeck & Ergenweiler* engraved on the smoked-glass front. She was a spidery woman in late middle age; she was dressed in one of those suits that made her look like a coat hanger stretching out a bedsheet. She watched me as I passed her desk and headed off down the hall toward Plumbeck's office; she didn't say a word.

I swung Plumbeck's door open without knocking. Plumbeck was sitting at his desk in his shirtsleeves. He was facing a man and a woman. The three of them looked up at me. Plumbeck said: "Asher, I'm in conference now. This is going to have to wait."

"It won't wait." I pointed to the man and the woman and said: "Get out."

The two of them rose obediently, collected the papers they had placed on Plumbeck's desk, and filed out without saying a word. They probably figured my next move would be to reach for an AK-47.

I closed the door behind me. Plumbeck looked at me steadily. "Whatever it is, Asher, it could have waited."

I crossed the four feet to the desk and dropped Alicia's blouse in front of Plumbeck. "Read the label," I said. Plumbeck handled the blouse delicately.

"I fished it out of the bay yesterday, Plumbeck. You remember the woman wearing this, don't you? Big beautiful blonde you were supposed to be crazy about? She's been out there for the better part of a month. Want to know what happened to her?"

Plumbeck held up his hand to stop me and then got up abruptly from his chair and made for the door; I followed him down the corridor and over to the conference room. The large picture windows gave out to the eastern part of the bay. Plumbeck stood there by the window with his hands over his ears.

I walked over to him and yanked them down. I held them by his sides while I talked into his face.

"She's part of the food chain now, Plumbeck," I said, letting go of his wrist and pointing to the water. "First week the fish must have thought she was pretty terrific, big bottom-dwelling mud sharks look up and see lunch seeping down. By now she's passing through the shrimp, little crustaceans. Another ten days, she'll be nothing more than a ripple in the water."

Plumbeck stood stock-still and then all at once his chest began to heave. I backed off from him in a big hurry. After giving out a few preliminary whoops, he vomited a filthy torrent of browns and reds against the picture window. I could feel my own stomach churn sympathetically as I caught the foul acrid smell. Then he doubled over to catch his breath. I could hear the terrible sound of the air being forced into his lungs. I let him stand like that for a moment and then I gave him my handkerchief.

"Clean your face, Plumbeck," I said, "you're disgusting."

He did as he was told. The act of vomiting seemed to have purged something in him. He straightened up slowly and walked stiffly back to his office; when he got there, he sank into his chair and held his head theatrically.

"I didn't know, Asher," he said, speaking to the desktop. "I just didn't know."

"Don't be so easy on yourself, Plumbeck."

"It's true. I *didn't* know."

"Sure you did."

Plumbeck looked up at me. He had already managed to convert some part of his shock into indignation. He was pretty good at it. "You want to explain yourself, Asher?"

"You helped kill her," I said. "That's the explanation."

Plumbeck waved his hand as if to shoo me away. "I loved that woman," he said emphatically. "I was crazy about her."

"I don't know what you felt. Maybe you loved her. You're not risking anything by saying it. Maybe you thought it was terrific keeping all that gorgeousness in an apartment. You've always had a tough time saying no to yourself. Maybe Alicia was just one more thing you couldn't say no to. I'm not here to take confession, Plumbeck. I don't know what's in your heart. I don't want to know. I'm here to tell you it doesn't make any difference to me. You still helped kill her."

"I didn't kill anyone, Asher."

"I never said you did. I said you *helped* kill her. I don't know what went on in your apartment. All I know, woman's dead and you were involved somehow."

Plumbeck looked up at me with a steady stare. He held up Alicia's blouse again. "Who put you onto this?" he asked. He had recovered enough of himself to regain a sense of his rights.

"What, you think cooking up some cheap scheme with Miriam to get out from under a drug debt is going to go *unnoticed* over there in east Oakland?"

"What are you talking about, Asher? We both know that lowlife took out after Miriam. Asher, you were *there.*"

"Get serious," I said, slapping the tabletop with my palm. "I was there because you and Miriam thought it'd look terrific if I showed up. But *you* got Miriam to put the ball in play."

"How am I supposed to have done that, Asher?"

"You had Miriam call this poor schnook up and tell him she was going to settle his debt. He comes over, leaves his prints all over Miriam's living room. Miriam tells him *you're* on your way, he's out of there and *boom!* you lob a Coke bottle filled with gasoline against Miriam's house. Only thing is, Plumbeck, urban terrorism isn't exactly in your line. I don't think you figured that Miriam burns off half her behind."

I had been standing in front of Plumbeck's desk, resting my weight on my hands; I backed off to walk over to his window. Down on New Montgomery Street, traffic had built up in front of an open manhole protected by a circular wire fence.

"Asher," said Plumbeck carefully, his voice hedged, "this guy was a lowlife. I can't pay off the whole world. I did what I had to do."

I turned from the window to face him again. "Is that what you say to yourself when you think about Alicia? I did what I had to do."

Plumbeck rose from his desk in a crouch, his face flushed. I could see the veins on his neck bulge.

"You don't have to answer that, Plumbeck. It's what everybody says. It's what Miriam's dealer said when he fingered you, told me to go look in some salt marsh for what was left of Alicia."

Plumbeck sat himself back down and slumped into his chair. "Asher," he said. "We've been friends for fifteen years. You taking some lowlife drug dealer's word on this thing? Is that what you're telling me?"

I walked back over to Plumbeck's heavy black desk and spread-eagled my palms on the surface. "Look me in the eye, Plumbeck, tell me you had nothing to do with Alicia's death."

Plumbeck brightened up. He said: "As God is my witness, Asher, I had nothing to do with that woman's death."

I straightened myself up. "God better not be your witness."

Plumbeck must have thought I was being facetious. "Why's that?" he asked with a faint smile.

"You're lying," I said flatly.

"Asher," he said in a slow threatening voice, "you've been a bud a long time, but I don't have to sit here and take this kind of crap."

"Sure you do. Anyway, righteous guy like you, crap'll probably bounce right off."

"This is fifteen years' worth of friendship you're putting on the line."

"Of course, some of that crap sticks, it'll probably be because you can't explain why you took the hit over that Maison Jarr thing for Eddie Ergenweiler."

"What are you talking about?" Plumbeck asked indignantly. "I *told* you, Eddie's crazy on this. It was plead it out or lose everything. Go ask Knesterman. He'll back me up."

"I don't think so," I said coldly. "You didn't plead out due diligence just because you thought Eddie was crazy, Plumbeck. You didn't wake up one morning and say to yourself, I'm just going to ruin my reputation, take a heavy hit because Eddie Ergenweiler's screwed up. I told you. You're not that kind of guy. You're pleading out due diligence, I figure someone's putting you in the microwave. You did it because someone was squeezing you."

Plumbeck looked at me as if he were for a moment enthralled with my story. "You're on a roll, Asher. I'm not going to stop you."

I wandered back to the window and looked out for a moment.

The scene hadn't changed. There was the same open manhole, and the same circular metal fence around it, and the same file of cars moving sedately around the impediment.

"What we need," I said, speaking again to the window, "we need a squeezer and we need something he can squeeze you with. The squeezer part is easy. It's got to be Eddie Ergenweiler. He's the one who needed you to commit professional suicide."

Plumbeck snorted derisively.

"Only thing is, we both know our Eddie doesn't exactly have the balls for a fancy job of blackmail."

"You got that right, Asher."

"Which pretty much leaves Irene. She's got the balls to blackmail a regiment. Wouldn't you say that's true? You don't have to answer. I know you agree with me. I figure Irene's pressuring you as soon as Knesterman tells me it's a done deal. What I didn't know is what she was pressuring you *with*. Now I do. She's telling you to fall on your sword because she knows you had something to do with Alicia's becoming fish food. And the reason she knows this is that she was there when she died. Isn't that about it, Plumbeck?"

"It's pretty close, Asher. I have to hand it to you. It's pretty close."

Politesse

THE BERKELEY POLICE believed in service: they took every opportunity to say so. The legend DEDICATED TO SERVING ALL HUMANKIND was carved above the entryway arch. The walls of the circular rotunda were filled with posters showing pasty-faced policemen showing ghetto types the intricacies of baseball, the policeman beaming as he held the bat and the sweatshirted young hoodlum looking on in a way suggesting that he couldn't *wait* until he was old enough to leave off mugging schoolchildren for lunch money and get into something serious like crack cocaine. The front desk was called the *service* counter. Signs everywhere were in English, Spanish, Vietnamese, and Braille. Anyone coming into the station speaking Urdu would probably be out of luck, but chances are the department would be so embarrassed by its lapse that they'd start a remedial Urdu program within twenty-four hours.

The large station room was divided into sections, each separated from the other by a Plexiglas partition. A file of beaten-down-looking women were waiting patiently at the partition nearest to me. A sign mounted on a chrome stand said Spousal Support. The women were waiting their turn with the patience of oxen. Light streamed into the open space from high windows in the ceiling. It wasn't a bad-looking room at all. It didn't look like a police station, and it didn't feel like one, but after a while it smelled like a police station anyway.

I found Trudelwein's name on the glass-enclosed personnel board. He was Lieutenant Elbert Trudelwein in raised white Lucite letters—the kind that stick into some kind of black crepe. His office was at the head of the third-floor stairway landing. The big oak door was closed. I knocked and walked in. Trudelwein was sitting placidly at an old-fashioned police desk mounted on a platform behind a little gate. Swoboda was leaning over the desk.

They both looked up at me just as I looked up and spotted a video camera in the ceiling.

"Hey," I said loudly, "you guys miss me? It's been a week and you haven't broken into my apartment."

I turned my face upward to the camera. "That's *broken* as in *breaking and entering.*"

I opened the little gate and rested my haunch on Trudelwein's desk. "You think I have to spell it, Trudelwein? Or will they know? What the hell. It couldn't do any harm: B-R-E-A-K—"

"Mr. Asherfeld," said Trudelwein courteously, "we certainly appreciate the humor, but is there a matter upon which we might be of service?"

"Service? Mr. Asherfeld? What happened to *Aaron,* or *lowlife?"*

Trudelwein said: "Mr. Asherfeld seems upset about something. Wouldn't you say that's true, Detective?"

"Very definitely upset."

"There you go, guys, few more minutes and you'll work right

into your routine, forget all about the video camera."

"I've forgotten about it already," said Trudelwein. "What about you, Detective?"

"No idea it's even there," said Swobdoa.

I straightened myself up and walked over to Trudelwein's small white plastic bookcase and fished out a book. It was a paperbound manual entitled *Police Procedures*. "Will you look at this," I said, bouncing the heavy manual on my palm. "*Police Procedures*. Somebody probably figures you guys need to be *told* what to do. Can you imagine?"

I opened the manual at random and looked at it briefly. "It says here you guys are supposed to be respectful to the public at all times. You double over when you read this stuff aloud in the locker room or what?"

Trudelwein continued to look at me with a benign milky expression. "Mr. Asherfeld," he said tentatively.

I held up my hand to stop him. "No, no, Elbert, we can kiss and make up later. I'm just here to tell you you've got the wrong guy locked up on this Plumbeck thing."

"You talking about Mr. Williamson?" asked Swododa carefully.

"Sure. That's who I'm talking about. Guy you kept referring to as that nigger lowlife." I looked up at the video camera again. "That's N-I-G—"

"Mr. Williamson was released yesterday," said Trudelwein. "Ms. Plumbeck dropped all charges."

I put the police manual down on the table. "*Miriam* dropped the charges?"

"Police can only perform their jobs effectively with the cooperation of the public," said Swododa sententiously.

"I know," I said, tapping the manual on the desk. "It says so right here."

"It's true anyway," said Trudelwein. "Wouldn't you say it's true anyway, Detective?"

"Absolutely," said Swoboda. "Absolutely, it's true anyway."

I stood there for a moment, thinking things over. Then I said: "Score one for the lowlifes."

I didn't have much to say to Miriam Plumbeck, but afterward I drove by her house anyway and decided to knock when I saw her beat-up old Saab in the driveway.

"Asher," she said with a warm fuzzy expression when she opened the door. She was dressed in a blue bathrobe and the kind of slippers that have a rabbit head popping up from the toes.

"If you want to grab my behind, do it very, very carefully," she said, as she leaned her face up to allow me to buss her warm cheek.

"I don't want to, Miriam," I said, "and even if I did, I wouldn't."

"Pity," she said. "Do you want coffee instead?"

"I don't want to grab your behind, I don't want coffee, I don't want any crullers, and I don't want to come in. I just stopped by to see how you're doing."

"I'm fine," she said decisively.

"That's good," I said, backing off the steps.

Enter Smoking

LATER THAT WEEK, I watched Irene Ergenweiler beat a young woman in straight sets at the Marin Tennis Club. Irene had been a junior national tennis champion her senior year at Stanford and she had been the club's woman's champion for three straight years in the mid-1980s. She was a calm and methodical baseline player, with wonderfully precise ground strokes and a terrific confident sense of the court. I was sitting in the club bleachers, the golden Marin sunshine sparkling in the calm clear air. Irene was up four games to nothing, and then she broke service again in the fifth game and won the final game at love, leaving her stocky young opponent simply gasping at her effortless passing shots.

The two women shook hands over the net. I sauntered down the stairs from the bleachers to the court and intercepted Irene as she was just finishing up packing away her rackets.

"Well, *hello,*" she said.

She was dressed in a white tennis outfit that showed off her tanned and polished and muscular legs. The skin of her face and neck was covered with a fine sheen of perspiration; her shoulders had been burnt into a dark mahogany color by the sun.

"Hello yourself, Irene," I said.

She leaned her rackets against a bench and bent over to shake her hair out. Then she fished her gold lamé cigarette pack from her purse and withdrew a Virginia Slims, lighting it up with an immense soul-satisfying drag.

"This something new, Asher?" she asked, blowing a stream of smoke upward into the air. "A love of tennis?"

"I'm not here to talk about tennis," I said.

"Well, I didn't think so," she said, inhaling again.

"I had a long talk the other day with Marvin Plumbeck."

"So?"

"The girl's body is in the bay, Irene. I thought Marvin would want to know."

Irene looked directly at me with her fierce predatory gaze. "What are you talking about, Asher? What girl?"

"Come off it, Irene. I'm talking about Alicia Tamaroff. Eddie admitted sexually harassing her, remember? *That* girl."

Irene continued to look at me.

"You're telling me that little tramp washed up in the bay? Is that what you drove out to Marin to tell me, Asher?"

She looked at me with a cold appraising defiant stare. She broke off the stare and said: "I don't know what happened to her. I don't *want* to know what happened to her. All I know is she was a scheming little bitch and if she wound up in the bay with her throat slit and her underwear wrapped around her neck, that's what she deserved."

"I think you know exactly what happened to her, Irene."

"And how would I know that?"

"Because you helped kill her."

Without missing a beat, Irene Ergenweiler slapped me hard across the face with her leathery right hand. The slap made a sudden cracking noise. My cheek went dead for a second and then felt as if I had been scalded."

I resisted the temptation to hold my cheek with my hand.

"A lot of people have a good slap in them," I said. "If they use it right, it can get them out of a very bad place. Trouble is, you used up your one good slap a long time ago, Irene, probably on something silly, like getting Eddie to use mouthwash. Now you're in the bad place, and you've got nothing to get you out of it."

She continued to stand there and stare at me, but her defiance had disappeared. "I don't want to talk about it here," she finally said. "Meet me on the terrace in five minutes, give me time to change."

She turned and maneuvered her taut muscular body into the women's locker room.

I left the tennis courts and wandered up to the lodge through the trim and well-watered club lawns. On the verandah, I took a table by the corner and looked out over the rolling hills of the golf course below. Marin is high-desert country and the only grass that grows naturally here grows in winter during the rainy season. To get the golf course to look as if it were Ireland in spring instead of California in late summer the club had to pump tons of water into the fragile topsoil. It seemed like a waste to me, but then again, I don't play golf.

I ordered a couple of Calistogas.

Irene Ergenweiler came striding up from the courts; she was carrying her racquets over her shoulder and she was walking with that fluid antelope-stride she had. She disappeared into the lodge and emerged moments later without her racquets and with her hair held together by a bright red ribbon.

Our waiter came bustling officiously up to the table with two Calistogas and a plate of large black pitted olives, which he deposited on the glass tabletop.

Irene came up to the table just as he was backing away. She took an olive and placed it in her mouth before sitting down, spitting the pit into her palm.

"So," she said decisively, "what did Plumbeck tell you?"

"He told me you blackmailed him into taking the hit on that business with Maison Jarr."

"Oh, he did, did he?" Irene fumed. "That little dickless wonder." She popped another olive in her mouth and chewed it vigorously, retaining the pit in her mouth.

"Not true?"

"Asher, *I* am the reason that Marvin Plumbeck is not sitting in some prison." She help up her hand dramatically. "I mean, *really.*"

I looked at her inquisitively. "Why don't you tell me what happened, Irene?"

Irene Ergenweiler stopped chewing her olive pit. "Why should I tell *you* what happened? I don't owe you any kind of explanation. You're not a person who cares for me. You're not my friend, Asher."

It was a short explosive bitter speech. I didn't say anything and Irene Ergenweiler didn't say anything. We both sat there without saying a word.

"He called me up in an absolute panic," she finally said.

"He called *you* up?"

"She was supposed to be all through with being a mistress. This *therapist* she was seeing somehow persuaded her she was *wasting* herself. Can you imagine, Asher? I mean, we are talking *bimbo* with a capital *B.* Wasting herself."

Irene snorted and shook her trim brown head to signify the absurdity of it all. She spat out her olive pit and popped another olive in her mouth.

"Anyway, I don't know exactly what happened—Asher, I don't *want* to know exactly what happened—but somehow Marvin talked her into spending one last night together and *of course* Marvin is Marvin and he must have laid out a line of coke for her and one thing led to another and she started to bleed."

Irene looked at me closely to see whether I was following her implicit story; she must have decided I wasn't.

"Don't look at me in that dopey way, Asher. It happens. Sometimes women bleed. Mostly it's no big deal, but Marvin was in an absolute panic. You know how Marvin gets."

"Why didn't he call nine-one-one?"

"I don't know. Maybe out of a sense that he'd have a hard time explaining just how some cute little number received such nasty, nasty lacerations. He's pretty good that way, our Marvin is. So anyway, I told him to get her into the tub, run some warm water. It's what they told *me* to do when I miscarried the twins. I said I'd get there as fast as I could."

The ice in our drinks had melted completely. A small flush of color had come over Irene's throat and face, showing up red against her brown skin.

"I know it all sounds a little callous, Asher, but really I thought it was just Marvin being a little too enthusiastic. Sometimes women can get too dry, and then if the man slips, that tissue back there is very delicate. I mean, it can tear a tiny bit and then you have a little blood. I thought what happened was that she was woozy from the coke and bleeding and Marvin just panicked. That's what I really thought."

"Not what happened?"

"I get there, she's in the tub, the tub is positively filled with blood, I mean *filled,* her face is this *ghastly* white. Marvin is absolutely no help at all. He is *standing* there like an idiot, wringing his hands, and all of a sudden I flash on what it's going to look like. I mean, Asher, there are still lines of coke on the table, the place positively *reeks* of sex, there is *blood* everywhere, and this, this *bimbo* is in the bathtub."

Irene withdrew another cigarette from her case and lit it voluptuously. It was her third cigarette in twenty minutes.

"Maybe I should have called the police," she said, "or called 911 or just opened the window and screamed. I'm not perfect, Asher. I did what I thought was best. I called up this therapist she was seeing. I mean, why not? It's almost the same thing as calling 911, isn't it?"

"Sure," I said. "No difference at all."

"Marvin got the number from her purse. The woman was actually very helpful."

"Probably told you that hemorrhaging is a sign of low self-esteem."

Irene looked at me with her cold glare. "She told us she'd take care of everything and to just get out of there."

"Is that what you did? Just get out of there."

"Yes," said Irene Ergenweiler defiantly. "That is just what we did. Do you have a problem with that?"

We Didn't Know

I DROVE BACK to the city that afternoon with the driver's side window wide open. I don't know what I thought: I thought maybe the cool, moist air coming in from the ocean would let me unhear what I had heard. At the entrance to the Golden Gate Bridge, a Day-Glowed and filthy Volkswagen bus rolled sedately in front of me, entering the freeway from the small ramp that led back into the Marin headlands. I swung around and pulled abreast of the bus. The driver looked to be in his fifties. He wore aviator sunglasses and had his hair swept back in a fluffy ponytail. He was pounding the steering wheel rhythmically, singing along with whatever was on the stereo. The woman by his side was sleeping, her head reclining backward over the seat, her throat exposed; for a moment, the sun filled the bus with radiance, the light winking off the windshield and the windows.

I got back to Greenwich Street as the day was gathering itself to a close. The peppy young mothers pushing baby carriages up the hill were busy being peppy. They stretched themselves out behind their carriages and pushed up the hill from their toes, cooing and gurgling to their wide-eyed adoring babies. A few of the house-proud retired parties at the top of the hill were out fussing with their shrubs and carefully dwarfed trees. A deliveryman from one of the upscale markets on the hill was unloading groceries from his van in front of the house next to mine, stacking carton after carton on the sidewalk.

I got myself upstairs, looked through my mail, and sat myself down at my desk. The bay looked cool in the clear afternoon light. "Look out there, Asher," one of my wives had said when she visited my apartment after the divorce. "The water has been there since before you were born. It's going to be there after you're dead, just moving back and forth under the Golden Gate Bridge. *It* doesn't know you're up here and it doesn't care."

It was a swell little speech.

After a while, I called Maxine Stuntvesal. I got her low fruity voice on her answering machine. I waited for the beep, but I didn't leave a message.

I called Stuntvesal again early the next morning. I thought she might answer her own telephone before taking on all her earnest fatties and bulimics. When I got her on the line and told her who I was she said, "I have *nothing* to say to you," and hung up the telephone in a big hurry.

I had no reason to think Capo Titus would be any more forthcoming, but I rang his home number in Mill Valley anyway.

"This is Aaron Asherfeld," I said. "I met you about a month ago at Maxine Stuntvesal's office."

"I know who you are," said Titus, with a wet grump that cleared his throat. "You're that fellow that barged into Maxine's office, made a lot of threats. Oh, I know who you are. What do you want?"

"I want to talk to you."

"Well, that's what you're doing. What do you want to talk about?"

"Same thing I wanted to talk about before. Alicia Tamaroff."

There was a guarded pause in Titus's breathing.

"What about her?"

"I thought you could tell me how she died."

Titus gasped. "She's dead? You're telling me that beautiful child is dead?"

"That's what I'm telling you."

And then Capo Titus began to sob into the telephone, great raspy old man's sobs.

We met later that day in the town square in Mill Valley, just in front of the old bus depot. Titus was there when I arrived; he was sitting on a bench underneath an enormous, stately Redwood. He was dressed in sandals and khaki shorts, which revealed his bony old knees, and a green khaki shirt, and he was wearing a gold chain whose pendant disappeared into his white chest hairs. He didn't bother to say hello.

"How do you know she's dead?" he asked when I sat next to him.

I told him what I had found and where I had found it. Titus listened calmly to what I had to say.

"She was a beautiful child," he said when I had finished. "I don't expect you to know what that means, Asherfeld."

"You're right," I said. "My type's too coarse for finer feelings. On the other hand, us coarse types don't have to worry a whole lot at night about being accessories to murder."

Titus shook himself and said: "That's a very ugly accusation, Asherfeld." He was preparing to convert his shock into anger. It's what everyone does.

"Or blackmail," I said. "As long as I'm making ugly accusations, I don't want to forget blackmail."

"What's that supposed to mean?"

"It means pay off or else, that's what it means."

"I know what the *word* means, Asherfeld."

"Then you know what the accusation means," I said.

"We had nothing to do with what happened," Titus said after a pause. "I want you to know that. Maxine and I had *nothing* to do with *whatever* happened to that child."

"Sure," I said. "You just didn't do a whole lot to stop it from happening."

Titus raised himself on his seat. "Asherfeld," he said. "Maxine is a therapist. She did what she thought was right."

"Tough moral choice," I said. "She gets a call, one of her patient's hemorrhaging somewhere, she *doesn't* call a doctor, *doesn't* call 911."

"The woman calling was hysterical, Asherfeld. Why won't you understand that? She *begged* Maxine not to involve the authorities."

"So what did she do?"

"Maxine? She did the logical thing. She called Alicia's brother, this Yuri fellow."

"That's it. You put in a call to good old Yuri, just wash your hands of the whole thing?"

"We didn't know anything bad was going to happen. We just didn't know."

"I don't believe you," I said flatly. "No one else is going to believe you either."

Titus stared out over the square. Two teenagers were throwing a Frisbee to one another with long fluid tosses. They were both shirtless.

"I'll tell you why you didn't call the police or call 911," I said. "You figured, bring in the authorities and there goes your sexual harassment meal ticket. So you call up good old Yuri. Now Yuri doesn't speak much English, so you must have spoken to his sister, Tatiana. You figure, the two of them'll go over there, hose Alicia down, problem solved."

Titus bit on his lower lip; he looked ready to weep.

"Only the problem isn't solved. The problem is dead. Not to worry. Yuri can still take care of things. But that still leaves you with a sexual harassment suit and no victim. No one to go on the tube and tell the world how terrible it was being put up in some body shop. Am I right? I mean, tell me if I've missed something here."

Titus shook his head softly.

"Then someone figures a blonde is a blonde, am I right? You have *Tatiana* go on the tube instead of Alicia, you don't even have to say *anything* to Irene Ergenweiler. An intelligent woman like that, she's bound to spot an impostor, draw all the right conclusions. It's kind of a new twist. Blackmail, the *victim* has to figure out they're *being* blackmailed."

We sat there in the golden Marin sunshine for a long time. Finally Titus said stiffly: "I want you to know we didn't see a penny of the money, Asherfeld, I want you to know that."

For a moment, I couldn't figure out what he was talking about.

And then I could. I rocked back on the chipped concrete bench and slapped my thigh and laughed out loud.

"They got you," I said. "The Russians *got* you. They put the bite on you and you paid them off."

Titus continued to sit there and stare into the sunshine.

At the Athenaeum

SEYBOLD KNESTERMAN'S SECRETARY told me that the great man was at his club, but when I asked that she tell him I wanted to see him there she hesitated. "I don't know, Mr. Asherfeld," she said, "is this something important?"

"Life and death, Frieda."

"If it's not Mr. Knesterman's, I don't know that he'll be very concerned."

"Attagirl," I said. "Spread around the milk of human kindness."

"I don't know why I should, Mr. Asherfeld. It's not something I'm paid to do."

I gave up trying to persuade Frieda to do anything and pulled on my blue windbreaker and headed off toward the Athenaeum on the top of Jackson. It's a hike up some of the most gorgeous real estate in San Francisco. There are old-fashioned apartment buildings on the hill, great looming stone structures, where the doormen have been standing in front of the building for more than half a century; and there are terrific old mansions on the shaded streets, great looming houses built before the 1906 earthquake when the city was swarming with thousands of skilled craftsmen—men who could work in wet plaster or turn California oak into curled door frames or cut Italian marble into precisely grooved parquet flooring. The Athenaeum is on the very top of Jackson. It faces the bay on one side and a beautiful park on the other. The park used to be the sort of place where dowagers wearing white gloves would walk their toy poodles. Now it's a trysting place for gays.

I hustled myself up the club's broad marble steps. At the front desk I asked the concierge to page Knesterman.

"Mr. Knesterman generally doesn't wish to be disturbed," he said. "Who shall I say . . . ?"

"Tell him it's Aaron Asherfeld. I'm his personal fitness trainer."

The concierge looked at me curiously. He was some sort of Russian aristocrat who had come to San Francisco from Paris and thought he had discovered heaven. He called himself Colonel Rudetsky.

"*You* are Mr. Knesterman's fitness trainer?"

"What," I said. "Is there an echo in here? That's what I said. I handle the man. I also do Sonny Bono when he's in town. I used to do Cher, but she couldn't stay off sugar, so I cut her out. I'm getting Knesterman ready for the Iron Man in Hawaii."

Colonel Rudetsky regarded me bleakly.

"You *are* talking about Seybold Knesterman," he said.

I nodded. "I know what you're going to say. He needs some work on his crawl. That's why I want to have him out doing wind sprints today. Did he get his high colonic yet, you know?"

Colonel Rudetsky said: "His high colonic?" in a way calculated to suggest disgust and amazement.

"Hey, not a problem," I said, "maybe you could do it for the man. We'll send out for a kit, I'll show you how to do an insertion in a jiffy."

Colonel Rudetsky edged away from the desk and addressed an intercom. "Boris," he said, "tell Mr. Knesterman his fitness trainer, Mr. Asherfeld, is here."

In a moment, Boris reported back: "Mr. Knesterman says to send him down to the pool."

I reached over to palpate Colonel Rudetsky on his biceps. "I got Mondays four-thirty A.M. open, Colonel. Fit you right in. Six weeks we'll have you doing ten K out in the park. Who knows, you could be registering again on the Peter Meter."

The colonel gave me a tight little grimace as I headed for the door downstairs. "For your information, Mr. Asherfeld," he said, "*no one* does high colonics at the Athenaeum."

I stopped by the door. "I know how it is, Colonel. That sort of thing, once you start who knows if you can ever stop."

I followed Boris's rolling shoulders down through the club's spotless halls. Downstairs, Knesterman was lying in a white deck chair beside the indoor Olympic-size pool, a white towel draped over the little mound of his potbelly. He looked up at me. "My fitness trainer? Really Asherfeld, couldn't this wait?"

I pulled one of the white deck chairs over to where Knesterman was lying, scraping its wooden feet on the marble floor; I perched myself on its side.

"I don't know if it can wait or not," I said. "It's not the sort of thing I want to discuss at your office. I think we both may have some unwanted exposure on this Plumbeck-Ergenweiler thing."

"Meaning what?" said Knesterman. He was a very good lawyer and he had managed to make himself seem alert and responsive without doing anything that I could see. I told him the story. He listened intently, interrupting whenever he was uncertain that he had gotten the point.

"And you say Irene Ergenweiler decided to settle this harassment thing simply because she was being pressured by this woman. . . ."

I nodded. "Stuntvesal."

"Why didn't she tell Plumbeck to pay her off? After all, according to what you've told me, Irene had already blackmailed Plumbeck once. I would think it gets easier the second time around."

"Could be, Knesterman. Trouble is, Plumbeck tapped out his liability insurance paying off the Feds on Maison Jarr. Irene must have known he simply didn't have any more money."

"Why do you say that?"

"Because Marvin and Eddie were partners. They held their insurance together."

"Yes, of course."

Knesterman reflected on what I had told him. Then he said: "So they destroyed themselves in this sordid business."

"More or less. They might free-lance. They can't set up a partnership without insurance."

"Cherchez la femme," said Knesterman. "That means *search for the woman,* you know."

"I know what it means, Knesterman."

"And you're convinced she's dead."

I told Knesterman about the tip I had gotten from Little Lulu and about finding Alicia's blouse.

Knesterman listened alertly. "Do you actually *know* what happened up there at 999 Green?" he asked.

"No, but I think I can piece it together."

Knesterman waited for me to go on, his intelligent long face impassive. I thought of the thousand stories he must have heard.

"It's not very dignified, Knesterman. I figure that the two of them show up, Yuri and Tatiana. They take one look at the situation and realize their meal ticket is lying there, bleeding out in a bathtub. They figure that Alicia's going to be nothing but trouble if they call the police."

"Why do you say that?"

"I think she really *was* sick and tired of being a kind of toy for men like Marvin and Eddie. She probably told Yuri, look, enough is enough. He shows up at nine-nine-nine Green and there is a problem on its way to becoming a solution."

"You're saying her *brother* did away with her, Asherfeld? That doesn't ring true."

"I don't know if he did away with her, Knesterman. She might have just conveniently bled out for all I know. But don't worry about the sentiment. He wasn't her brother at all."

"I'm not following you, Asherfeld. I thought you said you traced this Yuri fellow through his sister. You even showed her confirmation pictures around."

"Yuri had a sister all right," I said. "Only it wasn't Alicia at all. It was Tatiana. They looked enough alike so that people thought they recognized Alicia from Tatiana's picture. It's an easy mistake to make. I made it myself."

"And what are you saying set you right?"

"Alicia's about as Russian as I am, Knesterman. Consulate told me this Yuri had *one* sister. It had to be Tatiana. They were pimps, Knesterman. They ran women, the two of them. Alicia must have been their gold mine. They just didn't figure she'd go independent on them."

Knesterman said: "I see."

"With Alicia out of the way, they must have talked to Stuntvesal, realized they were sitting on something platinum with this sexual harassment thing. All they had to do was to substitute Tatiana for Alicia on the tube and either Ergenweiler or Plumbeck would settle."

"Very clever," said Knesterman. "At most they faced misdemeanor charges for impersonation in a civil suit."

"The clever part was that they managed to blackmail Irene Ergenweiler without ever threatening her with anything. They just figured she would spot Tatiana and put two and two together. And she did."

I had finished what I had to say. Knesterman sat there, his hands folded over his small round pot.

"You haven't discussed this with anyone, Asherfeld?" he asked.

"Of course not."

"Then don't discuss it with anyone in the future. You and I have no real exposure on this."

"That's pretty terrific, Knesterman. Beautiful young woman is dead and all the two of us can do is congratulate ourselves that we have no exposure?"

For the briefest part of a moment, Knesterman seemed pained. Then he said: "When you reach my age, Asherfeld, you'll discover that that is quite sufficient."

He rearranged the towel around his lap and hoisted himself to a sitting position.

"Now if you'll excuse me," he said. "I must take some steam."

Chess

I TOOK KNESTERMAN'S ADVICE. I didn't say anything to Plumbeck about what happened and I didn't say anything to Irene Ergenweiler either. They didn't call me and I didn't call them.

I thought I might track down Yuri and Tatiana. I wandered over to Centerfolds on one of those hot and strangely humid nights we sometimes get in San Francisco in late summer. The club bouncer may have given me a suspicious look, it was hard to tell. Tatiana was there all right. She looked at me and then she looked through me. I called Yuri's apartment a couple of times, and got a machine gabbling at me in Russian. I don't know what I would have said to either of them. I even thought of going to the police, but it's tough to pin a murder case on a blouse.

Alicia Tamaroff must have had parents somewhere who were worried about her, or a brother in Idaho who couldn't figure out what had happened to his swell little sister, but California is a big state and if someone was out ringing doorbells, I didn't know about it. People disappear every day. One day, they're sitting in their single-occupancy hotel rooms, eating Fritos or watching television, and the next day, poof, they're gone, and the room is empty, the empty Fritos bag simply lying on the floor. Perky young mothers go out into the night to buy a carton of milk and never come home. Solid young fathers who like to throw their children into the air and bang their fists into their palms when someone scores a touchdown on TV take off on road trips and fall in love with long distances. The city is covered with posters for children who get themselves vanished. It happens. For a few weeks, I saw Alicia's face at night when I lay down to sleep. Her golden hair would dissolve into a halo of fuzzy light; she would smile, her large square teeth glistening. She always seemed amused by the stir her beauty created.

The first week in September, a mortgage broker named Serena Wong asked me to check out some properties on the Peninsula. She was coordinating a complicated real-estate transaction and needed to make sure that the lot descriptions and the lots really matched up.

"You go B of A, pick up fiye foder," Wong said to me in her curious clipped English. She was a terrifically intelligent woman with an almost supernatural gift for figures. She kept her accounts in her head and never made a mistake.

It was slow, boring work that Wong wanted me to get done, but I had nothing better to do. I got myself showered and shaved. I could see the deep radiant blue of the morning sky from the top of my bathroom window. The foggy summer was just about over. Northern California doesn't get anything like a New England fall. A lot of people who come here from Massachusetts or New York State grump a lot about September and October and how it's absolutely terrific out there in the East to feel that stiffening wind and know that in three months there'll be snow on the ground and ice over the ponds. The season used to make one of my wives melancholy. "I need to feel that winter is coming, Asher," she said.

Me? I like the warm dry weather in fall and the still air and the way the sunshine spreads itself over the humped and folded hills.

I left my apartment and hustled myself down Greenwich in the golden morning light. The street was absolutely empty. The Chinese had begun moving up the slopes of Telegraph Hill, buying up the large houses and renting out apartments. Passing a little alleyway that gave out onto the street, I could hear the flap-flap sound of sheets drying on a clothesline in the gentle breeze. Chinese housewives still hang their wash out to dry in the open air.

Serena Wong kept an office in Burlingame, but she handled a lot of her paperwork through a property-management firm with headquarters in the Bank of America building. I needed to get her file folder and make sure the document set was complete.

It was too beautiful a day to take a taxicab and too beautiful a day even to think of getting on a Muni bus; I hiked up to Columbus and kept on going until I reached California.

The B of A building takes up a whole block of downtown San Francisco. It's easily the ugliest building outside of the former Soviet Union. In a city filled with light, the bank's architect had figured it would be a terrific idea to heave up a huge square black building. Someone in the city must have seen how awful the thing was going to be, so they made the bank put a plaza in front of the building. It's one of these empty formal spaces that you want to cross in a hurry.

I bought myself a cruller and an espresso from a cart on the corner of California and Pine and stood there for a moment, munching my pastry and sipping my espresso. A cable car came tootling sedately down the hill, the driver banging away on its bell, tourists in loud clothes hanging from the sides.

I finished up my pastry and tossed the rest of my espresso and crossed California against the light and started to cross Giannini Plaza on the diagonal. Up ahead of me, a couple exited the building's main revolving doors; what caught my eye was the woman's spray of golden hair. She paused to let the man swing through the doors and slipped her arm decorously through his. They walked directly toward me. I could see that she was a knockout. She was wearing a hot pink suit, with dark hose, and she walked with the kind of controlled wiggle that only sensationally beautiful women ever acquire.

When they were twenty yards or so from me, I felt my throat tighten. There was no mistaking her blonde gorgeousness, the way she had of completely commanding the space around her. It was Alicia Tamaroff. She was walking arm in arm with Yuri Vybotskaya.

I stood there and waited for the two of them to approach me. They had almost come abreast of where I was standing when Alicia recognized me. Her face lit up with a sunburst smile. "I know you," she said buoyantly.

"Aaron Asherfeld. We met in Marvin Plumbeck's office."

"That's *right,"* she said, as if I had settled a difficult problem for her. "Aaron Asherfeld, this is my brother Yuri."

"Pleasure to meet you, man," said Yuri Vybotskaya in lightly accented English. He had trimmed his hair and he was dressed in expensive well-cut clothes—silk shirt, black blazer, pleated slacks, and very shiny Gucci loafers. He didn't quite look like an American, but he no longer looked like a thug.

"I think we've met," I said.

"Could be," said Yuri.

"Yuri meets so many people," said Alicia, laughing, "and he is such a bubblehead."

Turning to Yuri, she seized his cheek playfully between her thumb and forefinger. "Aren't you a bubblehead?" she asked.

I looked at her, drinking in her fantastic blond beauty. The suit she was wearing was cut square; it seemed to swell with each breath that she took.

"A lot of people thought you were dead," I said.

Alicia laughed. She had a great unforced gusty laugh. "I can't help what other people think. Here I am, Aaron Asherfeld," she said. "Very much alive."

Yuri looked at his watch ostentatiously and said: "Got to go, babe." I must have looked stupefied. Alicia laughed again and then she reached over to place my head in her hands. It was the gesture she might have used with a child. She pulled herself close to me and ran her warm full lips over my ear. It took me a moment to disentangle what she said from the shock of her embrace.

"Goodbye, Aaron Asherfeld," she said. "Never play chess with two Russians. *Dosvidanya.*"

And then the two of them were walking away from me with brisk determined strides.

I stood there on the wind-whipped plaza and watched her shapely rear end move sinuously until she was just a pink blur on the far side of California Street.

One Last Thing

SOMETIME IN THE FALL, I got a call from a man named Puddingstone. He described himself as an information specialist, the CEO of an outfit called Systems International. He had an office somewhere south of Market and he wanted me to come down and hear out his latest ideas. I didn't have much else to do, and no one to do it with. I spent the morning walking around Telegraph Hill, looking down the crabbed little alleyways and admiring the Spanish-style houses high on the flanks of the Hill, with their high bougainvillea-covered walls and their fantastic verandahs. When I had had enough of looking at all that gorgeousness, I got in my car and swung myself around the long curve of the Embarcadero.

I parked in the same lot on Mission that I had parked before when I had gone to see Ray Chandler. The same Big Moose was sitting in the same wooden shack that he had been sitting in, listening to the same Spanish radio program.

When I crossed over to Fifth, I realized that Systems International was actually located in the same dingy building in which Raymond Chandler had kept his office for Maison Jarr. It didn't give me a real feeling of confidence in the venture.

As it turned out, Puddingstone *did* have a terrific idea. He was a short tubby little guy; he wore a jet black toupé and he had dandruff so ferocious the stuff was coming out of his eyebrows. He was looking to raise seventy-five thousand dollars in order to write software that would make fax machines intelligent.

"You go to your doctor, Asherfeld," he had said, "he wants to know whether it be a good idea prescribing calcium channel blockers, man of your age and so on, he fills out a questionnaire, faxes it over to Stanford Medical Center, the fax just sits there in some fax machine, complete waste of time."

"I can see how it's a problem," I said.

"You put *intelligent* software on his end, and *intelligent* software in the fax machine, the *machine* turns the fax over to the central computer, the machine *gets* the information, and the machine faxes it back to your doc."

"It's a wonderful idea," I said. "How's it beat the telephone?"

Puddingstone looked at me as if I had missed the whole point of the information age. "Asherfeld," he said, "you ever try reaching *your* doc on the telephone?"

I told Puddingstone he had a point; I told him I would try to steer some uncommitted money his way. We shook hands and wished one another luck.

When I left his office on the fifth floor, I decided on a whim to look in on Raymond Chandler. I knew that Maison Jarr had put itself into Chapter Eleven. The company had never recovered from Itchak Bupkiss and his column in *The Investor's Target.*

I walked down the two flights of stairs to Chandler's office, rapped on the metal door and let myself in. The pictures of Elizabeth Kneeblebone were gone and so was the office furniture. There were cartons stacked up against the wall. I could hear someone humming something from a Gilbert and Sullivan operetta in the back room.

I shouted: "Hey, Chandler, you there?"

The humming stopped and Chandler popped his head through the door. "Oh, hullo," he said. "You've come for the FedEx, have you?"

"No, Chandler, I haven't come for the FedEx. It's Aaron Asherfeld. We met in June when you were still running a company."

Chandler seemed to reflect for a moment and then he brightened: "Right-o," he said. "You're the chap couldn't wait to take a drink at eight in the morning. I suppose you'll be wanting to pop right down for a snort. Let me get my jacket. I'll be right there and keep you company."

We went downstairs to Thruggs—the same evil-smelling bar we had been to before.

The same slovenly waitress who had waited on us in June shambled over to our table. I ordered a beer and Chandler ordered a double gin and tonic.

"I'm drinking for two, love," he explained to the waitress.

The waitress cocked an eye at him but said nothing.

When the double gin and tonic arrived, Chandler took an enormous gulp and immediately brightened. I had seen men come alive after snorting coke. Chandler had the same reaction to alcohol.

"Must be pretty depressing, having the company collapse under you," I said.

Chandler tapped the yellow fingernail of his thumb with the nail of his index finger. "The fingernail dies after it's cut," he said. "The organism survives."

"That's very wonderful," I said.

"Very wonderful," Chandler agreed, finishing his drink with an enormous swallow. He cocked his hand and signaled the waitress for a second. He must have caught my look.

"I'm cutting back," he said brightly. "You're probably wondering why. I'm happy to tell you. There seems to be some unpleasantness in the area of my liver."

"Hard to imagine."

"Some men are given very large indefatigable livers. I am not one of them, I regret to say. My liver is positively lackadaisical. It's quite unfair."

"Chandler," I said, "there's something that I never did understand."

The waitress deposited another double gin and tonic in front of him; he took what by his standards must have been a chaste sip.

"I am all ears," he said.

"Only a handful of people knew about that due diligence business—me, Eddie Ergenweiler, Marvin Plumbeck, couple of attorneys. You have any idea who leaked the whole thing to Bupkiss at the *Target*?"

"Of course, silly," Chandler said. "I did."

I looked at him in stupefaction. "*You* leaked the story? Chandler, that story drove Maison Jarr's stock into the ground."

Chandler nodded happily and sipped again at his drink. He waved his hand in the air. "Elizabeth always says that every problem is an opportunity."

"That's terrific, Chandler, probably even sell a lot of pimple goop, but how do you make an opportunity out of financial catastrophe? You people are in Chapter Eleven, aren't you?"

"But that's just it, Asherfeld. That's how a problem becomes an opportunity."

"You're losing me, Chandler. This you've got to explain."

"Any time you know which way the price of a stock is going to move, Asherfeld, it's possible to make a good deal of money."

I sat there for a moment trying to take it all in. "You're telling me that this Kneeblebone deliberately sabotaged her own company so that she could sell her own stock short at twenty-four and buy it back for pennies? Chandler, that's inside trading. This gets out, the two of you go to jail."

"Dear boy," he said. "I was merely talking in hypotheticals. I'm sure that Elizabeth would never do anything improper. She is very, very firm that way."

"You guys must have cleared millions," I said. "I mean hypothetically."

"Millions," said Chandler imperturbably. "Hypothetically, of course."

Chandler finished his drink, tilting the glass upward to make sure that he didn't miss a delicate drop of the stuff. I could almost *see* the alcohol at work: it seemed to dilate the capillaries of his skin. We sat there in that evil smelling tavern for a few minutes more. Neither of us could think of a way of continuing the conversation. Finally, I told Chandler I was late for a meeting. I left him sitting there at Thruggs and walked into the sunshine.

I thought of telling Seybold Knesterman and Marvin Plumbeck and Irene Ergenweiler and Eddie Ergenweiler what had happened. I thought of telling them about Ray Chandler and how Chandler and Elizabeth Kneeblebone had played them for fools. I thought of telling them that Alicia Tamaroff hadn't become fish food after all.

"You can't go wrong with the truth, Asher," an attorney once told me as he was explaining his strategy for dealing with his infidelities.

I got to the parking lot on the corner of Mission and Fifth. The Big Moose hadn't left his wooden shack. I gave him my ticket and he punched it in the time clock.

"Seben dollars," he said woodenly.

"Let me ask you something," I said.

"Wha'? Wha'd you wanna ask me?"

"I want to ask you you think it's better to tell people the truth all the time or just sort of forget it."

Big Moose turned from his register. He looked at me closely. "Why you wanna know thees thing?"

I shrugged my shoulders. "It's something I have to decide."

"I tell you wha'd I think," he said, with a certain grave dignity. "Wha'd I think is I think nobody ever give you a prize you tell them the truth."

I swung the keys around my finger, letting the alarm beeper bang into my palm. The cracks on the side of the wooden shack seemed especially vivid in the bright thrilling harsh sunlight.

"You're probably right," I said.